THE
good girl

A NASHVILLE NEIGHBORHOOD BOOK

NIKKI SLOANE

ISBN 978-1-949409-15-4

For Nick

who made this book possible

ONE

Preston

My best friend Colin was a porn star. He'd been with his girl-friend for more than a year now, and they'd filmed all sorts of crazy stuff together, sometimes with different people too—or so I'd been told. I'd do nearly anything to support my friend and business partner, but I drew the line at watching him fuck.

It didn't bother me what they did. *Good for them*, I'd said when I'd found out.

Plus, his side hustle of creating adult content was what was helping get our business off the ground. The plan was we'd be partners, sharing the work, but he was the money backing us, and I'd promised myself to never forget that.

His adult work especially didn't bother me today, be-cause his girlfriend Madison was hot, and she must have in-vited a friend to join her at the group graduation party my dad was hosting.

The original plan had been a joint party for my dad's girlfriend Cassidy and me since we had both graduated from Vanderbilt, but Colin had graduated from Davidson Univer-sity the following week, too. His parents were dicks and had disowned him after they'd found out he was doing porn, so we'd agreed to include him.

My dad and I had done more for him than his parents

had the last few years. I was an only child, which meant he was as close to a brother as I could get. So, I was glad this joint party worked out.

It was good not having to split it with just Cassidy, too. Less chance for people to focus on the fact my dad's girlfriend was graduating at the same time as his son.

She wasn't just the same age as I was—she was also my ex.

God, that felt like a fucking lifetime ago. I tried not to think about it, not just because it was weird as hell she was with him, but mostly because I'd been a bit of a shithead back then. I liked to think I'd come a long way since then.

I stood on the back patio beside the hot tub, ignoring the rest of the partygoers who were scattered around the pool, and the *Congratulations* banner flapping in the breeze. My gaze sharpened on the hot brunette lingering beside Madison.

I'd clocked the girl right away when she arrived. She'd hesitated for a moment at the gate in the wrought iron fence that surrounded my back yard. There was a black gift bag with a graduation cap on it and gold tissue paper dangling from one of her hands, but she looked like she wasn't sure she was in the right place.

It was nice she'd brought a gift, but we grads had agreed no presents or cards for this party. It wasn't family here—just friends—and most of them were college kids who didn't need to waste money on dumb shit. I'd rather they saved their cash for the bars downtown. We'd planned to head to Broadway tonight, and every place on the busiest street in Nashville had overpriced drinks to gouge the tourists.

I'd seen the girl first, but Madison waved at her, and the

girl smiled brightly. Then she pushed through the gate and moved quickly to her friend, who was alone. Colin was probably still inside the house, stuck in an inescapable conversation with Steve. We were barely friends with him in high school. The dude had never been great, and he'd somehow gotten worse over the last four years.

I'd been forced into inviting him when one of our mutual friends had mentioned the party, and Steve had gone after me like a dog with a fucking bone. I knew I should go inside and rescue Colin from him, but I was much too interested in Madison's friend.

From where I was standing, I could only see the girl in profile, but that was more than enough for me to check her out. Her hair was a dark brown, curled in loose waves that went halfway down her back. Her green tank top wasn't low cut, but it was glued to her body, so it flaunted her small waist and nice-sized tits.

It wouldn't be June until next week, but it was already hot outside, and like everyone else, she wore shorts—except hers were so much better than all the other girls'. Hers were barely there, and I could see the bottom of her pockets peeking out from beneath the shredded hem of the denim cutoffs.

It meant every curve of her toned legs was on display before ending in black low-top Converse sneakers. The outfit on its own was innocent, but when this girl was poured into it?

Hot.

I studied her pretty face, and a tinge of familiarity washed through me.

Wait a minute. Colin filmed with a bunch of people

besides Madison, and while I didn't watch his stuff, I *did* consume a lot of porn. Had I seen some of this girl's work before? I scanned her with an evaluating eye, imagining what she'd look like if her tank top and sexy cutoffs suddenly vanished.

Well, then . . .

She'd be even *hotter*. Sweat dampened my back, making my cotton t-shirt stick awkwardly to it. I pictured her bare tits that were sized to perfect handfuls, and what the rest of her sexy body would look like naked.

My dick twitched.

Shit, I had to clear the visual from my mind immediately and took a sip of my beer to distract.

Had she sensed I was looking at her? The brunette's head turned in my direction, and her gaze slid over to me, locking onto my face. Her eyes widened and her lips parted, and even though I was standing on the other side of the pool, I'd swear I heard her sharp intake of breath.

Her eyes heated as they evaluated. Like me, the girl liked what she saw.

Normally, I would have smirked back, but my lips refused to move. Neither of us did; neither of us even blinked. The connection of our mutual stare grew intense and magnetic, to the point it was so deep it was almost uncomfortable. But I wasn't going to stop looking at her.

I was competitive, and I didn't want to come off as weak. She needed to break first.

There was a tightness in my chest I hadn't noticed until her gaze dropped and the tension inside me released. On the surface, I was glad she'd let me win, but it weirdly didn't feel like a victory. In fact, it bothered me I didn't have her attention anymore.

There was no game plan as I stalked toward her. I didn't bother coming up with a clever line or a good opening. All I did was let my feet carry me swiftly across the concrete surrounding the shallow end of the pool, shortening the space between us.

I flashed my best smile as I approached. "Hey, Madison. Who's your friend?"

Madison made a face, and I found her expression strange. She peered at me with confusion. "You two haven't met before?"

I swung my gaze to the new girl, who . . . maybe wasn't new to me?

Oh, crap. Had Madison done this introduction already and I'd forgotten? I wracked my brain, trying to recall the last time we went out as a big group. We'd gone to the bars once over spring break when our friend Troy was in town, but there was no way I hadn't noticed this girl then.

"I don't think so," I said.

The girl's mouth dropped open with surprise, and her eyes screamed a single word at me. *Really?*

Abruptly, she closed her mouth, straightened, and thrust her hand out, offering a handshake. I closed my hand around hers, finding it warm and soft, but her tone was dry.

"Hey, Preston. I'm Sydney Novak," she announced.

My other hand clenched so tightly on my plastic cup, the sides caved in, and beer flowed over my fist. The crunch of it drew both girls' attention, and when Sydney's focus returned to my face, amusement flooded her eyes.

"Well," I squeezed out a sheepish smile, "this is awkward."

And to make matters worse, I was still shaking her hand like a fucking idiot. I dropped my hold, switched my crinkled cup into my free hand, and shook the beer from my drenched fingers. I needed a moment to reconcile the girl in front of me with the one I'd known years ago.

How the *fuck* was this Colin's little sister?

"Sorry I didn't recognize you. It's been a long time," I said in my defense, "and you, uh, look different."

"Yeah," she said simply. Like it wasn't a big deal she'd grown up certifiably hot.

"When was the last time we saw each other?"

It felt like at least a decade. Sydney was four years younger than her brother, and they hadn't seemed all that close. It wasn't possible, really. Her parents had kicked Colin out when he was still in high school, and even though they'd reconciled for a while, he'd been off at college.

She'd lived under her oppressive parents' rule, too young to escape like he had.

Her face scrunched into a cute expression as she tried to remember. "I think the summer after you graduated from high school. You had a pool party, and that was when Colin was living here, so he brought me over."

"Oh, yeah."

That was four years ago, back when she was barely a sophomore in high school, and when I'd been totally in love with Cassidy. So, yeah. Definitely a lifetime ago.

I opened my mouth to ask how she was doing, but at

that moment, her brother appeared, and her attention shifted to him.

He held an unopened can of beer in each hand as he moved to stand beside his girlfriend. Colin looked happy to see his sister, and they embraced in a quick, awkward hug.

"Hey," he said. "Thanks for coming, Syd."

When Colin's parents had found out he was performing in adult film, they'd gone no-contact, but I was pleasantly surprised to know that wasn't the case for her.

"Of course." She stepped back from the hug and thrust the black gift bag she'd been carrying toward him. "Congrats on graduating."

He transferred a can to the other hand, holding the pair of beers with one so he could accept the present with the other. "Thanks, but you didn't need to get me anything."

She shrugged like she was embarrassed. "You don't have to open it now," she offered quickly. Then her gaze slid over to me. "Congrats to you, too, Preston."

I blinked, and time seemed to slow.

That strange, powerful connection we'd had from earlier was back, just as strong as it had been when the pool was separating us. If anything, it was more intense now that we were up close. My heart beat too fast, making me feel weird. Off balance.

Hopefully I didn't sound that way. "Thanks."

Colin and Madison were oblivious to the tension holding Sydney and me together. He passed one of the unopened beers to his girlfriend and then held the other out to his sister.

"You want one?"

Her gaze darted from the can to me, and hesitation filled her voice. "I'm not twenty-one."

Right. She was, what? Nineteen?

I waved a hand, brushing that off. "It's cool. My dad let us drink before we were legal, as long as we weren't stupid about it."

She took the beer, maybe only out of politeness, and when she popped the top, an enormous smile widened on her brother's face.

"What?" she demanded.

"This is a big moment for you," he teased. "Your first beer. I'm glad I got to be the one to give it to you."

She rolled her eyes and took a sip. "You know I've been to college, right?"

"Davidson?" I asked.

She licked her lips like she didn't love the taste of beer and shook her head. "Vanderbilt. Like you."

Of course. Because she was a good girl, had gotten into the prestigious university, and was worth the expensive tuition to her parents—unlike her brother, who'd they sent to a public school.

"I never saw you around," I said.

Her head tilted a half-degree, like this was a stupid thing to say, but she pressed out a polite smile. "It's a big school, and I don't think we hung out at the same places."

Because she'd probably been at the library studying while I'd been at the bars. I'd done the bare minimum to keep my grades decent. Plus, she was too young for the bars.

Still is, a voice reminded me.

Madison's focus went to her boyfriend. "I thought you got lost in there."

"Steve," he offered as his excuse, and apparently it was all she needed because she nodded with understanding.

"Steve . . . Hatfield?" Sydney asked. When it was clear this was who Colin was talking about, she lifted an eyebrow. "What's he doing here?"

"Lecturing me about how I wasn't setting up beer pong properly." He turned to glance at me, showing his disgust. "You should have heard the ridiculous rules he was making up."

I grinned. You could take the boy out of the frat, but you couldn't take the fraternity out of him. "I had to invite him, thanks to Patrick's loose lips. Believe me, I tried not to."

"I was going to ask Troy to play with you," Colin said, "but change of plans now that Syd's here. She can be my partner." He gave his girlfriend a regret-filled smile. "Sorry, Mads, but I want to win."

Madison pretended to look hurt and pressed her hand to her chest.

"Ouch." I chuckled. "Is she that bad?"

"No, she's not." His statement was a matter of fact. "But Sydney's going to crush you."

What? I eyed Sydney with a ton of skepticism. "Are you, like, a genius at beer pong or something?"

"No." She looked sheepish. "I've actually never played."

There wasn't a hint of concern from her brother, only curiosity. "Really?" When she nodded, he shrugged. "Doesn't matter. We're still going to win."

It was so ridiculous, I couldn't stop a laugh from escaping.

He thought this girl—who'd never played before—was going to beat me? My competitive side reared up, telling me this would be a cakewalk.

My voice dripped with confidence. "Yeah, we'll see about that."

TWO

Sydney

I was glad the beer was cold because that was all it had going for it. I hadn't acquired a taste for beer yet and wasn't sure if everyone secretly disliked it but had been gaslit into saying they did.

I needed the beer now because the way Preston had stared at me rattled me to my core.

All my friends in school had lusted over my brother and his friends. Troy Osbourne was usually who they wanted the most, but for me?

It had been *all* Preston Lowe.

Seeing him again made my feelings come rushing back. I'd had such a crush, it was embarrassing, and yet he hadn't even recognized me. Had no idea I'd existed. And I was genuinely annoyed with how he'd gotten hotter over the years.

His milk chocolate colored hair was short on the sides and full on the top, swept back to reveal his handsome face. It was stunning how much he'd changed. At some point over the years, he'd grown into a man—one who looked so good it threatened to turn me into mush.

My weak knees made it difficult to follow everyone as Colin led the way inside the Lowe house. Preston's dad was a doctor, and the large home had been built into the side of a hill. It allowed for a walk-out basement, and when I walked through the French doors, I took in the space.

There was a new-looking kitchenette to the side, and tile flooring gave way to carpet. The back half of the room had a wrap-around couch facing a big screen television, but in the middle, there was a long kitchen table. The chairs had been pulled to the side, and red Solo cups were arranged in a triangle on each end of the tabletop.

I'd seen people play before, so I understood the premise was to bounce ping pong balls into cups filled with beer, but that was about it.

"What are the rules?" I asked.

While Preston dug a package of ping pong balls out of a drawer in the kitchenette, Colin and Madison took turns explaining. I could toss the ball directly into a cup, or I could attempt to bounce it on the table first, but if I did that, it meant the other team was allowed to defend. I tried to focus on what they were saying, but it was so freaking hard not to be distracted.

Years of crushing on him weighed me down.

When Preston passed the balls out to each player, his fingers brushed mine, and it sent a spark zipping through my body. A cocky smirk tilted his lips. This had to be arrogance because he was sure he was going to win.

"Because I'm such a nice guy," his gaze captured mine, "I'll let the *virgin* go first."

Oh, my god! How the hell did he know that?

Hopefully, no one heard the sharp breath I sucked in, because as I blinked, I slowly realized he'd only meant the game and not that the virgin label applied to me in the standard way.

Even though it did.

I pushed the thought away, stepped up to the end of the table, and squared off my stance. He lined up opposite me at the other end, and I ignored how good he looked when he rested his hands on his hips. He worked out occasionally with my brother, and it showed. His toned biceps teased me from beneath his shirt sleeves.

I shouldn't have liked how cocky he was. I'd never found it sexy in any other guy.

Only him.

Everyone shifted their attention my way, waiting for me to take my first shot.

Aiming for a line drive into a cup without bouncing the ball on the table first was risky. I could miss, or come in too hot, and it could bounce right back out of the cup. But Preston couldn't block me if I attacked from the air.

I focused on the cup I wanted to hit, the single one at the front of the triangle, steadied my breathing, and flicked the ball forward. It sailed across the table and plunked down directly into the cup with a satisfying *plop*.

Colin was thrilled. "Nice."

Preston's stunned gaze lifted from the orange ball floating in the beer, rising until it met my eyes. For a split second, something flickered through his expression that looked a lot like annoyance. He didn't like how I'd sunk my first attempt.

But then he brightened and shook his head. "Lucky first shot."

It was Colin's turn next, and he decided to go with the bounce strategy . . .

But it backfired.

As it tapped its way across the tabletop, Madison swatted the ball away, knocking it to the carpet below.

With our shots done, all that was left was for Preston to drink. He fished the ping pong ball out of the front cup, set the ball aside, and as he brought the beer to his lips, he studied me.

The intense stare we'd shared across the pool was back, trapping me in my body. How did he do that? The way he stared at me was as if I was the only person he could see. He hadn't noticed me in years, and now he was making up for that lost time.

I swallowed thickly, breaking his gaze, and nervously tucked a lock of hair behind my ear. Even though I wasn't looking at him, I sensed his attention was fixed on me, and excitement buzzed through my system.

"You're up, Preston," Colin said.

The cup he'd drunk from was set on the counter nearby, and then Preston's relentless gaze came back to me. The corners of his mouth lifted in an evil smile as he readied to take his shot.

Like me, he went for the direct approach from above. He wound up, released the ball, and I tracked it as it flew toward our cups in seemingly slow motion. Down it dropped, splashing perfectly into one of them.

Damn.

I was disappointed to have to drink, but begrudgingly

impressed. His smirk was proud and victorious, and I didn't understand why I found it so sexy. Hadn't I left the crush back in high school?

Madison went next, and when the ball bounced high into the air, Colin easily slapped it away. It meant it was my turn to drink, and I peered at the cup with trepidation. I didn't like the taste of beer, and who knew how long this had been sitting out?

Please don't be warm.

I took the ball out of the cup and did the same thing Preston had done the last round—I watched him as I drank.

The beer didn't taste warm or quite as bad when I was preoccupied by the sight of him.

When I finished, I strolled the few steps to the counter, stacked the empty cup inside the one he'd placed there, and returned to my end of the table. Colin had rinsed off the ping pong balls in a cup filled with water and handed one to me.

I made my second shot easily.

Preston and Madison exchange a *what the fuck* look with each other, and then his annoyed gaze turned to me. He'd been stunned and maybe amused the first time, but this? It was less cute.

"Something you should know about Syd," my brother said, "is she's really good at stuff like this."

Preston's eyes narrowed. "Stuff like this?"

"Games," Colin clarified. "Things that use dumb skills. She wins every time."

"You mean she's lucky."

Preston's tone had been accusatory, but my brother's

was plain. "No, I mean she's good."

He took his shot, which bounced close but rimmed out. Preston snatched up the cup I'd landed my shot in, pulled out the ball, and slammed the drink. When he'd cleared away the cup, his gaze zeroed in on me.

"I hope you're thirsty, *good* girl." He put emphasis on the word, teasing me, and dear God, it sent a surge of electricity down my spine. He'd said it like being good was actually a bad thing, and the muscles low in my stomach clenched.

He wasn't wrong. I *was* a good girl, but sometimes, especially when I thought about him, all I wanted to be was bad.

He lined up to take his shot, only this time he wasn't successful. The ball pinged off two rims and flew away, landing on the ground and rolling across the carpet. The cocky expression he'd had froze, then drained away, and I had to press my lips together to hold back my smile.

"I wasn't looking." My brother pretended to be confused. "Did it go in?"

Preston sighed, and then he snorted. "That's what she said."

Madison's gaze flashed up to the ceiling for a second, the joke too stupid to acknowledge, before focusing on the game.

They put up a decent fight, but she and Preston were no match for Team Novak. On the third round, Colin finally landed a shot, and then we rolled full steam ahead and annihilated them. It was clear Preston didn't like losing, but as the game went along, his irritation faded. His curiosity about me seemed to outweigh it.

"We'll team up on the next round," he announced when

he finished the final cup of beer. "You and me together? We'd be unstoppable."

Oh, lord. Warmth crawled up my neck. Once again, he'd only meant the game, but my mind took the meaning elsewhere.

You and me together.

Had he ever thought about it? I wasn't that dorky fifteen-year-old anymore, and he'd broken up with Cassidy a long time ago.

I opened my mouth to agree to another round, but Colin shook his head. "No. She drove here."

I'd had less than one beer, but he had a point, and I struggled not to let my shoulders sag with disappointment. Now that I had Preston's attention, I didn't want to lose it, and teaming up with him sounded like fun.

Undeterred, he strolled toward me, taking up all the space around us. He held my gaze as he picked up one of the cups in front of me that was left over from the game. "You can crash here," he announced, took a sip of the beer, and then his tone thickened with heat. "There's plenty of room in my bed."

Holy shit.

My heart tripped and stumbled. He was flirting. Preston Lowe was flirting with *me.*

And he wasn't exactly being subtle either.

"What the fuck?" my brother snapped. His chest lifted with a deep breath, perhaps to puff it up, and the atmosphere in the room went taut. Colin glared at his friend, every inch of his face and posture announcing exactly how much Preston's comment had pissed him off.

Maybe it was because my brother hadn't been around much once I'd been old enough to date, but I found this reaction surprising. Our parents were strict, which had made him swing wildly the other direction—so I hadn't expected him to be protective of me. Or so controlling.

I didn't care what Colin did with his romantic life.

Shouldn't he feel the same way about me?

Preston laughed, lifted his hands in the air, and backed away from me with a sheepish grin. As if to say his flirting was harmless and he didn't mean it. He ripped his gaze away from mine and planted it on my brother.

"Chill, dude. I was just kidding."

I jammed my hands in the tiny pockets of my shorts to prevent me from balling them into fists. If that were true, it stung, and I reeled from the emotional whiplash. I'd been so excited about him flirting, and now I felt like a punchline.

Also, what the hell? Yes, Preston was my brother's best friend, but he'd never said his friends were off limits. My brother and I weren't close, and our friends didn't overlap.

So, why did he care if we flirted?

Or dated?

Colin's expression remained hard and fixed as he stared at Preston. "Seriously. That wasn't cool."

Preston shrugged and tilted back the cup he was holding, finishing the beer in a few quick gulps. "Sorry."

His gaze darted to mine, only for a single heartbeat and too short for anyone else to see—but it was a lifetime long.

It hinted he wasn't sorry at all, and a thrill shot through me, lighting up every inch of my body.

THREE

Sydney

I sat on the edge of a lounge chair beside the Lowes' pool, sharing my seat with Madison while we ate cupcakes, but all my attention was on Preston. Across the way, he relaxed at the patio table with his friends, chatting and smiling, and now seemed completely oblivious to me.

Meanwhile, his 'joke' echoed incessantly through my head. It made me dream of doing something wild and shocking—something like asking him if he wanted to go out. Not that I'd ever get the opportunity to do that, not to mention, the courage.

Plus, I didn't know if he was already seeing someone.

I hoped not. My gaze drifted away, only to land on Cassidy Shepard.

Years ago, I'd been so envious of her. She and Preston had been inseparable during their senior year of high school and so sweet, looking at them had given me a toothache.

How things had changed.

Today, she sat next to her boyfriend. Her *much older* boyfriend, whose arm casually rested behind her on the back of her chair. They looked carefree and comfortable together, but how could that be?

For three years, she'd dated Preston, and then suddenly

she was dating his freaking father instead. Dr. Lowe was at least twenty years older than her, and it continued to raise eyebrows in our small, tight-knit suburb.

Colin didn't talk about it, but I'd heard from a friend that Cassidy lived with Dr. Lowe now. It meant Preston had to share his home with his ex-girlfriend, the one who was dating his dad.

Yikes.

It couldn't have been easy for any of them.

My gaze drifted back to the patio table on the other side of the pool deck. Preston leaned back in his chair, his elbows on the armrests, and he casually sipped on his can of beer. The evening sun was fading, casting a warm hue over the back yard, and he looked so . . . inviting.

Like he was just waiting for a girl to crawl into his lap.

I swallowed a breath, bunched up my paper napkin, and rose from the chair. I'd handed over my gift, consumed a single beer, which included during the game, and eaten dinner plus a cupcake. It meant it was time to go. I'd shown up for my brother and told him how proud I was of him, graduating despite our parents cutting him off.

I didn't know if he'd ever have a relationship with them again, but I hoped that would never be the case with us.

I loved Colin, no matter what.

And while sometimes I didn't *love* what kind of work he was doing, I respected him for living his life free from our parents' control. He was an adult, who could make his own decisions and go after what he wanted without shame or worrying about other people's judgement.

It was easier to think about my brother like that, in vague terms, but sometimes, it wasn't possible. Thanks to Facebook, a lot of people knew about his career, and last week my friend Hailey drunkenly confessed she'd watched some of his videos.

I'd threatened her with death if she ever brought up the size of my brother's dick again, complimentary or not.

Gah. I blew out a breath, forcing the thought out with it, and strode toward the French doors, balling my cupcake wrapper and napkin together in my fist.

The trash can was just inside, and after I tossed my garbage, I turned to find a large figure blocking the doorway. Breath tightened in my lungs. Maybe I'd been wrong about him being oblivious to me a few moments ago because Preston's sudden appearance gave me the impression he'd followed me into the house.

"Hey. You sure you don't want to play another game?" His smile was infectious, and sexy, making me want to say yes—

But I couldn't.

I hadn't really told my parents where I was going tonight, and if I was gone much longer, they might use the location services on my phone. Good god, they'd lose their minds if they saw I was over at Preston's house.

Could he hear the hint of reluctance in my voice? "I think I'm going to head out."

"It's early," he scoffed. Then he glanced around the basement, making sure it was empty so no one, and especially Steve, would overhear. "We're meeting up at Murphy's as soon as the party's over."

I pressed my lips together. "I, uh, don't have a fake ID."

"Oh." He crossed his thick arms over his chest and leaned against the side of the doorframe, ignoring the fact he was letting bugs in. "Well . . . it was nice seeing you again, Sydney."

His brown eyes focused on my face, his attention sliding down from my eyes and onto my lips. He peered at them like he was considering what I might taste like. It made my heart skip faster, and the air around us went thin, leaving me breathless.

"Yeah, you too," I said in a rush.

Abruptly, he straightened as if a thought had just occurred to him. "You know what? Let me walk you to your car."

He lived in the nicest neighborhood in town, and my car was parked only a few houses down the street, so this was unnecessary, but if he was giving me the opportunity to be alone with him, even for a few short minutes, I wasn't going to say no.

I gave a bashful smile. "Sure."

He lingered beside me as I said goodbye to Colin and Madison, and my brother barely kept the unease from his expression, giving Preston all the side-eye possible. He didn't like his friend's proximity to me, which again, I found weird.

Wasn't Preston his best friend?

We went out through the gate and followed the stone path up the embankment around the house, and the sounds of the party faded into the distance. Or maybe I couldn't hear them anymore because a voice inside my head grew louder, drowning everything out.

Now's your chance, it chanted.

We were silent as we strolled down the driveway and into the quiet street, but my heart beat like a war drum. It was trying to pump me up, and blood rushed loudly in my ears.

Every step we took brought us closer to my mother's car I'd borrowed and closer to my window of opportunity closing.

I'd never asked a guy out before.

It was because I was shy to a fault, and if a guy didn't make a move, no matter how much I wanted him to, things never went anywhere. That couldn't happen tonight. I wasn't going to carry regret about not shooting my shot with him.

My racing heart climbed into my throat, but I was able to push the words past it. "Can I tell you a secret?"

Preston's leisurely pace slowed to a stop, and he turned to face me with interest lighting his eyes. "Sure."

Oh, god. There was no turning back now. My voice dropped to a whisper. "I had a crush on you when I was in high school."

He blinked back his surprise, and then a pleased smile curled across his lips. "You did?"

A single, subtle step was all it took for him to invade my space. I stared up, struggling to keep it together, and nodded quickly. He wasn't insanely tall or broad, but he was impressive nonetheless. He'd been on the swim team in high school, and in college he'd grown and filled out his frame.

Had he improved himself in other areas besides just his looks over the last four years? I longed to find out.

It was interesting how he examined me now. As if I were suddenly brand new. Or at least someone he now saw as a viable option. Heat smoldered in his eyes, and I stood utterly still as he lifted a hand and brushed his fingertips across my jawline.

His words were low and full of seduction. "What should we do about that?"

Thought vaporized into nothingness, and all the air left my body in a burst as he leaned in, bringing his mouth down on mine.

Holy shit.

It took me a full second to process what was happening. Preston was kissing me, in the middle of the street, where we'd be blocking traffic if there were any. But it was just us, all alone.

His lips were soft and warm and . . . persuasive.

Not that I needed much convincing. When his lips parted, urging me to do the same, I followed his lead and welcomed his tongue into my mouth. The slick glide of it made goosebumps flood down my arms, and electricity wash through my body, all the way to the tips of my fingers and toes.

The kiss started as just a gentle meeting of our mouths, but then his hands got involved. He threaded one into my hair and the other grasped my hip, pulling me against him. It held me in place so he could deepen the kiss, controlling the angle of my head so he could slip his tongue deeper into my mouth.

Everything was buzzing inside me, and my legs turned to jelly. So, wrapping my arms around him was as much about support as it was about desire. He was strong and solid, and smelled like coconut sunscreen and summer.

This kiss . . . it was rollercoaster. We'd crested the first big hill together, and now we were being pulled through the twists and turns at a speed that felt dangerous. Exhilarating.

Maybe out of control.

The intensity built as he shuffled us a few steps across the asphalt, and then suddenly the window of a parked car was hot against my back.

I hadn't a clue whose car he was pressing me against, and in that moment, I couldn't care less. Preston's kiss was shockingly hungry and wordlessly demanded I keep up with it. It made me chase my breath to the point I grew lightheaded.

He was a guy who knew how to kiss, and I instantly wondered what else he was good at. After Cassidy, he'd developed a bit of a reputation of sleeping around. I didn't judge him for that. He'd come off such a long-term relationship, maybe he'd felt the urge to make up for lost time.

I'd had my arms around his back, but I moved a hand around his body, gliding it up to rest on the center of his toned chest. Beneath my palm, his heart was racing nearly as fast as mine was, and warmth spread through me. It was nice to know I had this effect on him.

I curled the cotton of his t-shirt into my fist, needing something to grip as I endured his wild, reckless kiss. There was so much passion, if anyone saw us, they'd probably stop in their tracks and stare in amazement.

Perhaps he'd had a similar thought, because suddenly Preston was no longer kissing me. He'd broken it off and stepped back so abruptly, I swayed and leaned against the car to keep myself upright. I peered at him while being full of questions, only it was obvious he didn't have any answers.

He looked . . . baffled.

Like he hadn't expected our kiss to be that urgent, or desperate, and certainly not as hot as it had ended up being.

It'd caught him off-balance, and he took another step back, raking a hand through his hair. Maybe he'd done it to neaten his appearance, but it had the opposite effect. The strands were disheveled now, and it added another layer to his unsettled demeanor.

Why was he looking at me like that kiss scared the hell out of him?

Instinctively, I lifted a hand and touched my fingertips to my lips, like I wanted to feel if the warmth of him still lingered there. Proof of what had just happened.

"What was that?" I whispered through my fingers.

His shoulders rose and fell with his hurried breath. "Something I shouldn't have done."

Anxiety straightened my posture and my hand fell away from my mouth. "What? Why not?"

He blinked away the fog in his eyes, and then his gaze sharpened on me. It made me feel like I'd asked a stupid question. His tone turned serious, and he set his hands on his waist, giving me a stern look. "You're Colin's little sister."

"So?" That hadn't bothered him when he'd had his tongue in my mouth. "He wouldn't care if we wanted to date," I lied.

It was like I'd thrown a bucket of cold water on him— that was how hard he recoiled.

"*Date?*" The word came out with horror and was followed by a humorless laugh. "I don't date, Sydney. And even if I did," his face contorted, "I wouldn't do it with you."

Maybe he hadn't meant for his statement to be cruel, but

it slammed into me. His rejection, immediately on the heels of the greatest kiss of my life, was a fist to my heart.

I slumped back against the car, almost too wounded to speak, but I eked it out. "Because I'm his sister?"

His gaze drifted down my body, heavy with reluctance, and he let out a sigh before finally refocusing on my face. "No," he said. "Because you wouldn't be able to handle me. You're too much of a good girl."

My mouth dropped open.

I was competitive, and this rang as a challenge in my ears. But it also lit a fire in my belly, one that burned so hotly, smoke clogged my throat and choked down my words.

It meant that when he turned away and began his short trek back to the house, I simply watched him go, saying nothing at all.

FOUR

Preston

- ONE YEAR LATER -

It didn't take me long to figure out I'd made a mistake.

I'd met Charlotte earlier this week and asked her out almost immediately, but it was rapidly becoming clear we had nothing in common. When the hostess told us our table wasn't yet ready for dinner, we shuffled onto the side patio of the restaurant, and then struggled through awkward conversation for the next few minutes.

It was painful.

Her tone did nothing to hide her distaste. "So, you still live at home?"

"Yeah, but it's not like it sounds. My dad and his girlfriend are never there. He works all the time and she's in school to become a vet, so I have the place to myself most days." She looked like she needed more convincing I wasn't some gross guy who lived in his dad's basement. "I'll move out soon, but right now I'm saving money because I'm building up my business."

"Oh."

She said it like she didn't believe me. I swung my gaze away from her and tried to find something else to focus on.

The outdoor space and the restaurant beside it seemed nice. It was new and busy, a trendy grill and pub. I'd picked it because there was a banquet room attached that might be perfect for hosting cocktail events if the drinks here were good. And if this date was a bust, at least the evening wouldn't be a total loss.

Above, string lights stretched across the patio, hanging over two sets of cornhole games, which were in use by guests also waiting for tables. Charlotte and I watched as a bean bag sailed through the air and landed on the angled board, its momentum making it slide and drop down through the hole.

Three points for that guy.

He grinned proudly. "And . . . that's game."

The other man standing to the side of the board nodded, dropped the bean bags he was holding, and motioned toward the side door that I assumed led to the bar. "All right," he conceded. "Guess I'm buying. What do you want to drink?"

As they moved off, I glanced around. No one else in the small crowd seemed interested, and at least it'd give us something to do. I gestured to the available game. "You want to play?"

Charlotte made a face and waved the idea off. "No thanks. I'm terrible at it."

Great.

I'd asked her out before I'd known she was Ardy's daughter, and now I felt trapped. He was the owner of Warbler Entertainment, which was Troy's talent agency, and Colin and I needed them as a client.

The first official year of our company, Distinguished

Events, had gone okay, but not spectacular. Colin and I had coordinated bachelor and bachelorette parties, anniversaries, and even a few weddings, but we were barely turning a profit. Nearly everything we made was invested back in the business.

Nashville was a big town with a huge entertainment scene, and I was eager to tap into that. Bar mitzvahs and retirement parties kept us afloat and helped us build our network, but we needed a bigger event in our portfolio. Something too big to ignore, to really establish our name.

Troy's release party would be that event.

His newest album was dropping in two months, and Colin and I had pitched the event to Warbler. I liked to think we'd landed the job based on the strength of our proposal, and not our personal connection to Troy, but it didn't bother me if it'd given us an advantage.

I didn't care how Distinguished Events got its foot in the door—only that it happened.

And once Ardy had signed the contract, I'd walked out of the meeting riding a high, and asked the receptionist out without thinking it through. She was hot, my age, and seemed interested in me, and I'd been too excited to recognize she shared the same last name as Warbler's owner.

I stared at the cornhole boards that were decorated with Tennessee Titans helmets and held in a sigh. My competitive nature meant I wanted to play, but she'd already said she wasn't good at it, so beating her would be an empty victory anyway. I really liked playing against a worthy opponent.

I bet Sydney's good at it.

I clenched my teeth at the thought. It had been a fucking

year since I'd last seen her, and still—every time I played a game like darts, or pool, or even bowling, I found myself wondering about her.

Shit, I thought about her way more often than that. It wasn't just whenever I played a game. Her confession about her crush, and that kiss that had been fucking insane . . . It was so magnetic and unforgettable, I'd been infected with the idea of her ever since.

Part of me hated how good she'd been at kissing.

Mostly because we couldn't do it again. Like, ever.

Colin hadn't known I'd kissed her, but he'd seen us walk off together that night at our graduation party, and once I'd come back to the house, he'd cornered me and finally said out loud the rule that had remained unspoken between us for years.

Don't touch my sister.

Obviously, I didn't mention what had happened because there was no upside to doing that. If I told Colin his sister had given me the hottest kiss of my life, he'd probably punch me in the face, and I preferred that didn't happen.

I was a big fan of my face.

My gaze drifted over to Charlotte. She had her phone out and was scrolling through Instagram instead of talking to me. We were strangers, and she didn't seem the least bit interested in getting to know each other. Shit. Was I going to need to come up with an excuse to bail?

My phone vibrated with a text message, giving me hope until I read the screen.

"Good news," I forced out. "Our table's ready."

We met the hostess inside and followed her through the labyrinth of chairs and tables until she reached an empty spot near the back. The dining room was packed, overcrowded with furniture and guests, and I'd been so busy navigating the tight aisles, I hadn't paid attention to my surroundings. It wasn't until I put a hand on the back of my chair and glanced around that I noticed the problem.

"Son of a bitch," I said.

I'd meant to groan it in my head, but the words had burst from my lips, causing both women at the table right beside mine to look up. As soon as the older woman recognized me, her eyes narrowed into slits.

Mrs. Novak had never liked me, even before all the shit that went down with Colin, and honestly—the feeling was mutual.

But the girl across the table from her?

Well, I knew for a fact she had liked me once.

That seemed less likely now, given the shock and dismay that was painted across Sydney's face. She stared at me like I'd intruded and had no right to be here. Like I'd planned to ambush her by showing up tableside.

Except I felt the same way she did.

Of all the restaurants in town, of course she had picked this one. Now she'd be around to witness what could be one of my worst dates ever. Was the universe trying to punish me?

My grip tightened on the wooden rail of the chairback. I was angry she was here, sitting so close and looking so damn good. Fuck. I'd spent the last year wondering about her, unable to *stop* thinking about her and our fucking kiss, and it pissed me off how her crush had flipped and become mine.

And I got angry at Colin for telling me she was off-limits, and at Charlotte for the ridiculous reason that she was not Sydney.

But as I always did when I got angry, I pushed it down. I compacted it away and pretended it didn't exist. I plastered on a smile as I dragged out the chair I had originally intended to sit in and motioned for Charlotte to take a seat.

It would look like I was being a gentleman, but the truth was I wanted to sit on the other side of the table. That way, if my attention slipped to the right, it would go to Sydney. It would land on the good girl who I'd once said couldn't handle me, but now I was curious to know if that claim was true.

When I dropped down into my seat, she scowled and fixed her gaze forward. If she wanted to pretend I didn't exist—okay. I deserved that, and I'd do my best to try the same, even if it was fucking doubtful I'd be successful.

I picked up my food menu and scanned the text. "Do you want to split an app?"

"No, thanks." Charlotte didn't reach for the oversized sheet of paper that was laminated in thick plastic. "I'm not hungry."

I hesitated. "Are we not doing dinner?"

My question caught her off guard, which—it shouldn't have. I'd asked her if she would want to grab dinner with me some time and if I could have her number. And after we'd texted back and forth, we'd settled on meeting at this restaurant at seven o'clock. That seemed pretty obvious to me we would be eating, but she tilted her head in confusion.

"Maybe we should have drinks first and see how that goes."

Out of the corner of my eye, I saw a faint smile curl on Sydney's lips, and embarrassment sliced hotly down my spine.

I dropped the food menu, scooped up the cocktail list, and grinned. "You know what? That's a great idea."

Because that meant I could get out of this evening much faster than having a full meal with a date that wasn't going anywhere.

The restaurant was loud.

Not just the music playing through the speakers, but from the sounds of cutlery on plates and all the conversations going on around us. It made it difficult to overhear what Sydney was talking about with her mother. Although it seemed like her mom was doing most of it in a low voice, and Sydney was simply listening.

I picked up some keywords though, while I pretended to study the cocktail menu. They were talking about Vanderbilt next year, which made sense. It was late May, so she'd probably just finished her sophomore year.

But whatever her mother was saying, it caused unease in the younger woman. Her eyes grew wider, and her throat bobbed with a hard swallow.

It wasn't any of my business, but her reaction . . . I didn't like it. Different emotions played out on her face, and each left me more unsettled. Confusion was replaced with distrust, and then it morphed into something that looked a hell of a lot like panic.

Abruptly, she stiffened to sit upright in her chair.

"No." This word from her was loud and angry.

"I know you're upset, but be reasonable," her mom said, matching her daughter's volume. "If you still want to go when it's all done, that's fine. But get your degree first. Being a cook is a job, not a career, and you're too smart to have to work nights and weekends."

Charlotte was oblivious to the tension one table over. "I think I'm going to try the lavender lemon martini," she said in a bright voice. There wasn't a server at our table; she was talking to me like I wanted to know.

"Sounds great," I lied, shifting my focus back to the Novaks.

"Are you kidding?" Sydney's tone was a mixture of shock and betrayal. "We had a deal. I held up my end of the bargain."

Her mom's expression was skeptical. "Maybe we suggested you give it another year to see how you feel, but we didn't make any promises. There was no 'bargain.'" She straightened her shoulders and tipped her head down, using the same posture my mom used whenever she lectured me. "You might think you want this right now, but tomorrow that could change, and then what? We're talking about your future here."

Sydney opened her mouth to say something, but suddenly a thought sidelined her. She glared at her mother with accusatory eyes. "Is this why you insisted we go out tonight? You knew how I was going to react." She sucked in a sharp breath. "Oh, my god. Did you pick this place because you hoped I'd stay quiet?"

Mrs. Novak ignored her daughter's question. "I know you're disappointed, but your father and I just want what's best for you. Once you have your degree, if you still want to try culinary school, we'll be happy to help you. We just need to know you have an education to fall back on in case things don't work out."

Movement temporarily drew my attention back to the woman in front of me. Charlotte had crossed her arms and leaned on the table, staring at me expectantly like I'd missed something.

"Sorry," I said automatically.

"I asked what you were going to get to drink."

"Uh . . . haven't decided yet." I peered down at the narrow list of drinks but couldn't focus on any of the writing. Even without looking at her, Sydney held my attention. The friction that radiated from her toward her mother was like a bomb ready to explode.

And then I made the terrible mistake of lifting my gaze to glance at her.

Jesus. She looked . . . shattered.

Her world was collapsing inward, and it had a gravity I couldn't escape from. Her eyes turned blurry, clouded with disappointment and outrage, and her gaze reeled around wildly, searching for something.

When she discovered me, she latched on and blinked away some of the chaos, sharpening her focus. I had the weird sensation that staring at me was just barely keeping her afloat. I was a piece of wreckage that happened to drift by, and she had no better alternative to grab on to.

My heart thudded in my chest as her gaze intensified.

I'd spent the last year thinking she had infected me with

her kiss—but I'd been wrong. It had most likely happened during that powerful stare we'd given each other across the pool. It was the same one she was giving me now.

As if she didn't just want me to notice her, but to truly *see* her.

I didn't understand what exactly had happened between her and her mother, but it was clear something had broken Sydney's heart, and beneath the table, I balled my hand into a fist. Partly because I was angry on her behalf, and partly because of the way she continued to look at me.

It was fucking inescapable.

The longer her greedy eyes trapped mine, the deeper into them I wanted to go, until the restaurant and everyone inside it faded away.

Time slowed, suspending as we were gripped in the connection of our gazes. The hairs on my arms prickled with awareness, making my pulse climb. The sensation was disorienting but fascinating, and I wanted—

"Preston," a pointed voice said.

I tore my gaze from Sydney, finding a disgruntled-looking Charlotte with a male server standing beside her at the table. He'd taken her drink order and was ready for mine, but with the connection severed, it released Sydney. She pushed back from the table and jumped to her feet, darting away.

"Sydney," her mother cried, "come back here."

It didn't slow her down as she fled toward the exit.

"What are you doing?" Charlotte demanded abruptly.

It was because I had risen from my seat and taken a step toward the door. I hadn't realized I'd done it, and she and the server peered at me with confusion. Shit, what was I doing?

"I need a minute," I announced.

It didn't bother me how Charlotte lifted an eyebrow in annoyance, or the way Mrs. Novak's disapproving gaze followed me as I marched through the restaurant.

I pushed open the glass door, stepped outside while squinting against the bright evening sun, and scanned the people milling around who were waiting for tables.

Where was she?

"Sydney," I said as soon as I spotted her.

She stood beneath a tree in one of the islands of the parking lot and had her head tipped down as she studied the screen of her phone. But she lifted it upon hearing her name and seemed less than thrilled to see I was heading toward her.

The thought rolled loudly through her face. *My day just went from bad to worse.*

I had to ignore that. "Are you okay? What just happened?"

Her expression shuttered. "I don't want to talk about it." Her voice was raw, and she turned to the side, maybe not wanting me to see how hard she was trying to hold it together.

But when she moved, I caught a glimpse of the Uber app open on her screen. Had her mother driven them to dinner? Maybe she wanted to go home. Or maybe she wanted to go somewhere else entirely.

"You need a ride?" I asked. "I can drive you."

She blinked at my offer with distrust. Part of her wanted to say yes, but then she thought better of it. "What about your," she searched for the right word, "friend in there?"

Oh, right. "We came separately. I can text her

something came up."

I joined Sydney under the shade of the tree, probably standing too close, but she was distracted and didn't seem to mind.

"Where do you want to go?" I asked. "Home?" I came up with a better option. "Colin's place?"

She turned to give me her full attention, and—shit. She was overwhelmed. "I . . . don't know."

"That's okay." I shrugged. "Let's just drive around for a while, then."

She let out a tight breath, surprised by this idea. She glanced down at the phone in her hand as she considered it, then lifted her hesitant gaze back to me. "Are you sure that's okay?"

A voice inside me warned that this was definitely *not okay,* and was, in fact, a terrible idea. Last time we'd been alone together, I'd come away from it with a ridiculous crush. A longing I didn't want to have, but one that had grown much too strong to ignore.

What the fuck might happen this time?

So, I knew I shouldn't, but I couldn't stop myself.

"Yeah," I said confidently. "I'm sure."

FIVE

Sydney

Preston just, like, abandoned his date. He did text her as we walked to his car, but I pictured the woman sitting back at the table and imagined her mouth dropping open when she read his message.

It was hard to be mad at him, though. He'd left her for me.

We reached his car, and he pulled open the passenger door to a black Dodge Charger, gesturing for me to climb in. But I couldn't make my body cooperate.

My voice was flat. "I thought you didn't date."

"What?" He paused, thrown by my question.

Oh, my god, I was all over the place and my head was chaos. *This* was the most important thing to focus on right now?

"Last time I saw you, you told me you don't date, but the girl in there . . ."

His gaze shifted away. "Yeah, well, that was a while ago. Things have changed since then."

Had they?

He didn't seem that different from the last time I'd seen him. His hair was a little shorter, and maybe he looked a tiny bit more mature, but otherwise he was the same guy from before—the one who'd ruined kissing for me and then callously proclaimed I was too much of a good girl for him.

The sting of it had lingered over the last year, but to-day? God, it was extra sharp. At least the discomfort from thinking about it got me moving. I ducked into the passenger seat, let him close the door behind me, and watched as he quickly rounded the back of the car before slipping in behind the wheel.

We didn't say anything as we buckled our seat belts. Once he started the engine, the sound system came to life and the podcast he'd been listening to blared from the speakers. He turned it off quickly, but not before I caught the gist of it.

The woman had been talking about finding sales leads.

My mind was too jumbled to focus on that. All I wanted right now was to put some space between me and what my mom had said, and the tightness in my shoulders eased a little when he backed out of the parking space then headed for the highway.

With the sound system shut off, it meant we rode in to-tal silence. It should have been uncomfortable, but for some reason, it wasn't.

And as the seconds ticked by, I appreciated his patience. Preston didn't ask or pry. It was like he knew I needed some time to think about what I was going to do.

I turned to gaze out the window and watched the land-scape drift by. I'd gone out tonight thinking my future was written, and that was still true—more or less. But I was struggling to deal with the idea that I wasn't the one who got to write it.

I swallowed a breath and turned my attention back to

the man seated beside me.

He had a hand resting comfortably on the steering wheel and a focused look on his face as he watched the road. Had he dressed up for his date tonight? Put in effort to look good? Because he did. His short-sleeve button-down shirt was fitted across his chest, and he wore slacks instead of jeans.

He looked even more like a man, and less like the boy I'd once crushed over.

I'd gotten so mad at my mom that some of that anger spilled into other places. I didn't know the pretty girl he'd shown up with. She could have been a nice person, but it didn't matter. I was jealous.

So, I kind of hated her.

"How much of that conversation did you hear?" I asked it quietly and not accusatory.

He shifted subtly in his seat, and I got the sense he was relieved I finally wanted to talk. "Just the end, I guess." He sounded curious. "You want to go to culinary school?"

"Yeah." I tangled my fingers together and dropped them into my lap, trying to figure out how to explain. "I've known for forever I want to become a chef, but my parents don't want to hear it. They were convinced it was just a phase I'd grow out of. So, back when I was still in high school, we made a deal. I had to be good and give college the 'ol' college try.' If I still wanted to be a chef after two years, they promised to send me to culinary school."

His gaze darted to me for a moment. "Now they want to change it?"

I nodded. God, I wasn't just angry at them, but also at

myself. I hadn't seen my parents' betrayal coming, which was massively stupid on my part.

They'd done it before.

"She said two years wasn't enough," the words tasted bitter in my mouth, "that I barely got the college experience." I clenched my jaw. "She has no idea what she's talking about."

I'd gotten the *quintessential* college experience, both in and out of the classroom. I'd sat in lecture halls and listened to useless information I knew I'd never use, and I drank too much with friends at house parties. I'd shared a microscopic dorm room with a stranger who seemingly never left to go anywhere, and I'd walked all over campus, no matter the weather, to make it to class.

"You don't like Vanderbilt?" he asked.

"I like it fine, but it's not what I want. Honestly, it feels like it's just a waste of my time—and their money." I drew in a heavy breath. "I'm pretty sure they made that deal with no intention of honoring it. This new offer she's dangling? It's just as worthless. I could gut it out for another two years, cross into the endzone, and they'll just move the goalposts again."

"What happens if you say no?"

"If I don't get my degree?" My tone filled with sadness. "I don't know. Maybe they'll cut me out and do to me what they did to Colin. It's their house, their rules."

"Shit," he muttered.

"I know I should leave, but walking away . . . it isn't that simple for me."

When my parents had deemed my older brother a failure, they'd tightened their grip on me, determined not to have another child disappoint them. All their expectations had doubled, and I'd done my best not to buckle under the weight of it.

Now the urge to go and never look back was strong. In theory, nothing was keeping me under their control. I was a legal adult, who could get my own bank account and a place to live, and finally be free of my parents.

My brother had done it.

But . . .

"Colin had to burn every bridge with them to get away." I made a face. "Maybe not *every* bridge. I'm still a connection between them. But if I leave? That's it. That's the end. And while they've given up on each other," my voice turned small, "I'm not ready to."

I'd always hold out hope that someday our fractured family could heal.

When Preston didn't say anything, the silence grew taut. "You think that's stupid?"

Once again, he glanced over at me, only this time his expression was full of concern. "No, Sydney. I don't think that's stupid." His shoulders lifted in a half shrug. "You want to keep your family together. I get that." He paused, perhaps considering whether he should say more, and gave in. "Your folks are dicks, though."

The tiniest, sad smile cracked on my face. He wasn't wrong, and I understood why he felt that way. Once the Lowes had taken Colin in for the summer, they'd cemented their names on my parents' shit list.

I stared out through the windshield for a long moment

while considering the other issues keeping me from leaving.

"I don't have a car," I said, "or health insurance, or enough money to get my own place. Everything I've got is held on to by my parents, and only given out if I'm nice and," I struggled to find the perfect word, "obedient. Which I've always been. I followed their rules, made all these sacrifices because I thought if I was just good enough, for just long enough, eventually I'd get to do what I wanted."

That I'd get to *be* who I wanted to be.

I dropped my gaze to my fingers and felt the hot, angry sting of tears pricking at the corners of my eyes, but I refused to shed them.

"Shit," I spat out. "I've been this person they wanted me to be for so long, I don't know how to be anyone else, and for what? For a lie. For *nothing*." There was a tremble in my voice, but I had no idea if it was from emotion or rage, or a mixture of both. "Every sacrifice and compromise I've made over the last four years has been pointless, wasted."

That had been the thing that nearly sent me over the edge when I'd been seated across from my mother. It wasn't as much that I was mad about them changing the deal . . . it was the lost time I'd never get back.

"You know what really got me?" I asked, even though it was rhetorical. "She had the nerve to look disappointed, when I've done everything they've ever asked of me." I turned in my seat so I was facing him. "You said it, and you were right. All I've ever been is a *good girl*, and I'm so fucking tired. I don't want to be that person anymore."

He considered my statement for a long beat. "Then, don't."

Like it was just that simple.

"I don't know how to do that," I admitted.

"You don't know how to be bad?" This drew a short laugh from him. "I could show you."

His tone had been joking, but a dark part of me wanted this to be a legitimate offer. Oh, my god. My heart beat faster at the idea of him teaching me how to be bad. "Yeah? How?"

The easy smile on his lips froze. "What?"

"How would you show me?"

My question had weight, and it filled the empty space in the car, pushing out all the air. It made it impossible to breathe as he considered my question. His expression turned contemplative, and when a thought developed in his mind, it caused his hand to tighten on the steering wheel.

Like he both did and didn't like it.

Preston drew in a deep, preparing breath. "You could start dating a guy they don't approve of. Maybe someone they even hate."

When his head turned in my direction, he must have put everything he had into his evil smile. Every muscle inside me tensed. It announced he was more than willing to volunteer for this job, and holy god, was it sexy.

Thoughts flew around in my head like butterflies trapped in a jar. Had he seriously just offered to be my boyfriend? I opened my mouth to speak, but I had no idea what to say.

"It wouldn't be real, of course," he added. "We'd just make your parents think it was."

My soaring heart suddenly plummeted through my body, crashing in my stomach with a heavy thud.

"Only for show," I clarified, trying to keep the disappointment from my voice. "To piss them off."

"Right."

I pressed my lips together for a moment. "You'd do that?"

His easy smile was back. "Oh, yeah. For all the shit they put you and Colin through? I'm happy to help."

My pulse sped as I tried to muster the courage to ask for what I wanted. "And what if," I tried to look confident, even as I felt none of it, "it wasn't fake? What if we did it for real?"

His eyebrows tugged together, and the corners of his mouth turned down. "No way. You remember your brother happens to be my business partner, right? And he has been pretty fucking clear I'm not supposed to go near you."

His tone was strange, like he was mad about this rule Colin had put in place, and . . . I got it. I was mad too, because I certainly didn't need anyone else putting restrictions on my life. Him telling Preston to stay away from me was kind of bullshit.

"He said that?" I asked.

"Yeah. Last year, right after I kissed you."

My eyes went wide. "You told him we kissed?"

"What? No." He made a face. "He doesn't need to know about that."

"You kept it a secret." I wasn't surprised. In fact, I hadn't told Colin either.

He looked conflicted. "I thought it was better that way."

"Okay." I shifted to face forward in my seat, and my tone brightened. "Then I don't see why you'd have a hard time keeping anything else we want to do a secret."

Unease flitted through his expression. "That's a really bad idea."

It was, but try as he might, it was obvious he didn't totally hate the idea. Excitement sparked inside me.

"Isn't that the point, though?" I asked. "You said you could show me how to be bad."

The conversation with my mom had put me through the wringer, and for once it made it easy for me to be assertive. I spoke without worrying about the consequences.

"You could teach me," I said. "I mean, there's so much I haven't done yet." My voice fell to a hush, maybe making me sound provocative. "There are things I've wanted to do. Things that a good girl shouldn't."

He asked it like he couldn't help himself. "What kind of things?"

I bit my bottom lip. "Like, sex."

He held perfectly still. Perhaps he was trying not to react. "You telling me you're still a virgin?"

When I nodded, Preston let out a heavy breath, and he squeezed so hard on the steering wheel it made the leather creak. Then he abruptly swerved right and took an off-ramp. It had seemed like we had been heading toward Colin and Madison's place, but this was several exits too early, spitting us out in the middle of nowhere.

"Where are we going?"

"Someplace where I can focus on this conversation and not cause an accident," he muttered.

When we reached the top of the ramp, he glanced around, surveying our surroundings. He turned left and headed down a lonely, two-laned road that bisected newly planted farm fields.

Once the secret was out, it was like I couldn't hold any of the other ones in. "Whenever I thought about who I might lose my virginity to . . . I always pictured you."

"*Jesus,*" he groaned.

He glanced at me, and I could see the war raging inside his head. His gorgeous eyes were chaos, and his chest rose and fell like he was chasing his breath. Part of him liked hearing this, but the other part of him didn't.

Or maybe he just didn't like how much he enjoyed the idea.

"And you, like, ruined kissing for me," I blurted.

For a moment, he ignored me. Perhaps he only wanted to think about where we were going. But then he shifted in his seat as if a decision had been made.

"Is that so?" He sounded, of all things, irritated. But I couldn't tell what was causing it.

There was a break in the field up ahead. A thick group of trees sprouted up beside the road, and a gravel path disappeared between them. When he turned off the road and the car slipped under the shade of the large trees, loose stones crunched under the tires.

He pulled to a stop, put the car in park, and then turned to give me his full, undivided attention.

I didn't understand the expression on his handsome face. Why was he pissed at me? His gaze sliced down my body, then returned to meet my eyes. Heat was building inside his, and I couldn't move, couldn't blink.

"You should know," his voice was rough, "you ruined

kissing for me, too."

"That can't be true," I whispered.

I'd mistaken his heat for anger, but it was something *else*. The corner of his mouth quirked. "You calling me a liar?"

I was dumbfounded by his revelation. Had his last year been filled with lackluster kisses that left him craving someone else? Did he kiss people and secretly wish they were me, like I did with him?

My brain couldn't comprehend that.

He unbuckled his seatbelt and reached up to massage the back of his neck. "Fuck. I tried to forget it, but I remember every goddamn detail from that night, okay? I remember what you were wearing, and how you grabbed my shirt, and how you made that sexy-as-fuck moan when I put my tongue in your mouth." His hand fell away as his gaze drilled into me. "I wish I didn't remember, believe me. And I really wish I wasn't sitting here right now, wondering if you'd taste the same if I kissed you again."

I sucked in a sharp breath and thought drained from my mind. All that was left was an urgent clamoring for him to do it—and to do it right fucking now.

But he didn't.

Preston sat disappointingly still in his seat and frowned.

"If I did that," he said, "I'd be risking more than just my friendship with him. I could be blowing up our partnership and my company."

"But you *want* to kiss me." I said it like I could convince him.

He exhaled. "I want to do more than just fucking kiss

you. I want to," he struggled to find the right way to say it, "get to do all the things you want to do. To show you what you've been missing out on."

"You can," I said. "You could, like, teach me."

His gaze ran away from mine, and he turned his head to stare out the windshield. The muscle running over his jaw flexed, and as he wiped a hand over his mouth, I got the strange feeling he'd only done it to stop himself from saying what he wanted to.

Finally, he spoke, and his tone was quiet. Filled with regret. "I shouldn't."

Except his posture was tight, and his body language screamed how uncomfortable he was. How badly he wanted to say yes to me.

"Just a few lessons." I shifted, subtly leaning over the center console so I could be closer. "He doesn't have to know about it."

He peered at me, and the interior of the car was suddenly too small to contain the tension between us. Our intense stare was back, a string connecting us and pulling us together. There was a pressure valve inside me screaming toward release.

"Lying to your brother?" The leather of his seat squealed quietly as he moved, matching the way I'd leaned in, and his voice thickened with sin. "That's *bad*."

"Yeah?" I went breathless. "Well, maybe I'm a bad girl now."

"Hmm." His head dipped down so his lips were right at the shell of my ear. "We'll see about that."

SIX

Preston

Last time I'd kissed Sydney, she'd been unprepared, but this time she was ready. Even though I cupped her cheek, I didn't need to guide her. She turned into my kiss, meeting me eagerly. And she let out the same moan as last time when my tongue invaded her mouth.

I was curious to see if her amazing kiss had been a fluke. A one-time-only, perfect storm that couldn't be replicated. Or if it had only been good and I'd just built it up in my mind to become something spectacular.

Well . . . nope.

I was happy to discover it was just as good the second time around, if not better. At least now we didn't have to worry about anyone wandering by and catching us. She matched my intensity and kissed me like she'd been waiting a whole damn year for this moment.

The atmosphere in the car began to shift the longer we kissed. It swirled with sex and heat, feeding into the way our mouths attacked each other. I was greedy and maybe too dominating, but the lust for her? It caught me off guard and I couldn't seem to stop myself.

She didn't seem to mind, though, or the way we were awkwardly leaning over in our seats, like our bodies needed to be closer to each other. I wanted the center console gone from between us. More space to maneuver and get my hands on her—

Colin's warning was suddenly loud in my head.

Don't touch my sister.

After everything that had happened with Cassidy, he'd been the one to fill the best friend spot she'd vacated. He'd helped me deal with the fallout. He'd been the one to know when to call me out on the times I was being a prick.

I'd been the center of attention with both my parents growing up, and it meant I could be selfish. I was trying hard these days to be better. More thoughtful, and caring, and someone who could think about others first.

Shit, I wanted to be a good guy.

But a good guy wouldn't do this to his best friend, would he? He'd stop kissing his friend's sister, tell her he wasn't interested in taking her virginity, and then drive her wherever she wanted to go. A good guy wouldn't be wondering if there was a minimum number of 'lessons' he could give her that wouldn't be *that* bad.

How many times could I fuck Sydney that Colin would tolerate if he found out? Was there a chance that number was greater than zero?

Fucking doubtful. So, of course, I shifted to find ways to justify it. If I didn't help her, she'd find someone else who would, and . . . shit, I didn't want that. That guy could be an asshole who wouldn't know how to do it right. He wouldn't have the kind of connection to her that I did. That meant there was no way he'd treat her as good as I would.

It was a warped, fucked-up way of looking at it, but maybe I could be a good guy after all. I'd be saving her from the experience of a terrible first time.

I abruptly broke off the kiss. "How many lessons?"

"What?" Her eyes were hazy, and her full lips were damp, and if I focused on them too long, I began to imagine what they'd look like wrapped around my dick.

"How many lessons do you want?"

"Uh . . ." She looked at me like I'd just demanded she do complex math. "Are you asking me how many lessons it'll take for you to teach me how to be bad?" Her eyebrows tugged together as she considered it. "Wouldn't you know better than me?"

Fuck, she had a point. "Two?"

"*Two?*" She didn't like my lowball offer. "No, I think it's got to be at least ten."

"You want me to fuck you ten times?"

She inhaled sharply and her eyes widened. "I thought . . ."

My question had flustered the virgin, and she looked so innocent and sexy, I groaned inside my head. It shouldn't turn me on, but it really fucking did.

She swallowed hard enough I heard the click of her throat, and then she lifted her chin to try to look unaffected. "I didn't know we were talking about sex. I thought the lessons would, like, be about other things too."

"Other things," I repeated. I both wanted her to clarify, and to see how much I could make her blush.

"I don't know." But she did. "Like, fooling around."

I reached over and set my palm on the bare skin of her

thigh, just above her knee, and a smile curled on my lips when her gaze dropped to it. Her skin was warm and smooth. While I liked the feel of this simple touch, I loved the way her breathing went uneven.

"Like, hand jobs?" I began to slide my hand up her thigh at a painstakingly slow pace while her attention was glued to it. "Like, me finger fucking you?"

She flinched, and a sound of panicked excitement escaped her, but she pressed her lips together to try to contain it. I tilted my head and leaned in to set my mouth against the pulse point in her neck.

"Like, me going down on you?" I goaded in a low voice. "You sucking my cock?"

My fingers inched beneath one of the legs of her shorts. The air conditioning was blowing in the car, but I was sweating, and my shirt clung uncomfortably to my back.

"Yes," she whispered. "Things like that."

Her voice was tight, choked with desire, but it was also tinged with something else. Shame? I didn't like that idea. I was sure her parents had done a number on her and convinced her sex was bad. I was excited to show her how wrong they were.

I sucked on her neck, and when she shivered, it caused my dick to flex against the zipper of my pants. I was already half-hard and desperate to have the obstruction between us gone.

"Let's get in the back seat," I said, brushing my lips over her skin, "and I'll give you your first lesson."

All the air seemed to leave her body in a long sweep. It

sounded like relief, but when I drew back, her expression was nervous, and she didn't reach for the door handle. In fact, she didn't move at all. Something was making her hesitate, and it took me a second to figure it out.

I gave her a reassuring smile. "You don't want to lose your virginity in the back seat of my car, but don't worry. I wasn't planning on asking for that."

She blinked her eyes, took a deep breath as if building up courage, and reached for the door handle.

I left the car running, turned up the fans on the air conditioning, and slid my seat as far forward as it would go, but still beat her into the back seat. It meant I got to watch her climb in, shut the door behind her, and then look lost on what to do next.

She wasn't exactly skittish, but she was anxious. Her bashful gaze darted to me and then dropped to her hands resting on her legs, like she wasn't sure what to do with them, or how to get back to where we'd been before the interruption.

But I had that covered.

"Come here," I urged. "Sit in my lap."

Her expression hung. She was a little scared and a lot excited to do it, and maybe she worried how she was going to execute the maneuver in the cramped back seat. I had moved my seat forward, and that had helped, but there still wasn't a lot of space.

She slowly turned toward me, making the leather seats creak beneath her, and I figured I might as well help her. I put my hands on her waist and guided her, getting her to lift one leg over mine so she could plant a knee on either side of my hips. Her head nearly hit the ceiling, but she lowered in until she was straddling me.

"What are we doing?" Her tone was soft.

It wasn't clear if she was asking about my lesson plan, what we were doing right this second, or if she meant in general. "Practicing," I said. "We need to get comfortable with each other like this."

She set her hands on my chest, looking awkward but trying not to. "Like what?"

"You know. Fucking around. Being more than friends."

"Were we ever friends?" Her voice went plain. "You didn't even recognize me at your graduation party."

"That's not my fault. I hadn't seen you in years, and you showed up looking way too hot to be Colin's little sister."

She liked the compliment, even if she didn't want to, but she had a point. We hadn't hung out when we'd been in high school, and once I'd gone to college, I saw even less of her. I only knew *of* her, really, instead of who she was.

"You're right." My focus drifted away from her for a moment, and I stared at the darkening clouds on the horizon. "We weren't friends, but that's a good thing."

Her tone was dubious. "How's that?"

"I'm better than I was back then." She could interpret my statement however she wanted, whether I was talking about how good I'd become at sex, or my personality.

It was true in both cases.

Cassidy and I had lost our virginity to each other, and the truth was I hadn't a fucking clue what I was doing back then. Of course, at the time, I was sure I did. Worse, I believed I was *amazing* at it.

Naturally talented.

Fucking gifted.

Like me, Cassidy hadn't known what she was doing either. She had nothing to compare me to, no way to know how much I sucked—which meant I didn't get negative feedback from her. Really, I didn't get any feedback at all.

No, that came from my other ex-girlfriend, Iris.

We'd dated my sophomore year at Vanderbilt and been together six months when she'd left her phone in my room by accident. My name in a text message rolled across her screen, catching my attention.

Apparently, she'd told her friends in a group chat about my less than spectacular performance, and I'd become a running joke to all of them.

The damage to my ego was intense, and fatal for our relationship.

After the messy breakup, I'd gone to visit Colin at his fraternity, we both got wasted, and I confessed all the hurtful things Iris had said about me. It was fucking embarrassing, but—shit. I needed help. I loved sex and wanted to keep having it, plus I was competitive.

If I was going to do something, it was important I be the best at it.

Colin had given me all the pointers he had, explaining I'd get better if I studied. He didn't mean porn either. I needed real-life experience, to get hands-on with as many partners as possible, and be 'open to their honest evaluation,' he'd said.

If you needed ten thousand hours to be considered an expert, then I had to start honing my craft as soon as possible. And I'd done that over the last three years. Surprisingly, I'd gotten addicted to, like . . . learning.

Sex when we were both having a good time? It was on a whole different level from anything I'd had before. So, I was confident I no longer sucked. In fact, the last few girls I'd been with had told me, unprompted, how much I *didn't* suck.

The first few raindrops splattered against the roof of the car, then built into a steady drum.

My hands were still on Sydney's waist, and I subtly tightened my grip as I stared up at her. She was all wide-eyed and innocent looking, with a flush across her cheeks, and her chest moved rapidly with her uneven breath.

As if being this close to me was dangerous and thrilling.

The dark, bad part of me wanted to ruin sex with other guys for her, for it to be all downhill after me. Was that possible? The thought made me pull her closer, urging her to rock her hips and feel the sensation of my dick between her legs, even with clothes in our way.

"Ride me." I hadn't meant for it to sound like a demand, but like a dutiful student, she followed my order.

Oh, *fuck*.

One hesitant move of her hips wiped everything from my mind. She swiveled again, dragging the center seam of her shorts along my zipper—and my rapidly hardening dick— and the sensation felt so much better than I expected. The grind of her body against mine . . . fuck. Each move she made was a torturous, pleasure-filled stroke.

Thunder rumbled in the distance and the curtains of rain closed around the car. It meant it was just us. No one who drove by would see the way the car rocked as Sydney dry-humped me, or how desire began to twist through her face.

I wasn't the only one who liked how it felt. I'd bet she liked it a hell of a lot more, judging by her hooded eyes and ragged breath.

Blood rushed loudly in my ears when she clasped her hands on the sides of my face and gripped me tightly. Was she worried I'd turn my head and break the connection of her intense gaze?

No. Not a chance.

Every inch of this girl seemed to be filled with lust.

"Yes," I said in a low voice. I slid a hand down and gripped a handful of her ass, guiding her to rock faster. "That's a good girl."

The phrase had spilled from my mouth without thought, and she jolted, but I didn't get the sense it was a turn-off. I'd only caught her by surprise, and it caused her to pick up the pace.

I was rock hard now, which was unreal. We were fully clothed, but the back-and-forth glide of her body had me moving in time with her, nudging and rubbing and grinding right where my dick wanted to drive into her.

A whimper of pleasure leaked from her mouth, and at the sound, I lurched forward. My mouth crashed into hers, and I jammed my tongue inside, wanting to fuck her right now in all the ways that weren't actually sex.

There was a powerful craving building in me, sharp and

disorienting. I wanted her, and maybe more than I'd ever wanted someone in my life. I needed my fingers inside her, my mouth on her tits, my tongue teasing her little clit. I was anxious to make her come in a bunch of different ways—not just from my dick.

And I wanted to know what her orgasms sounded like. If she'd quiver as she hit her climax, or if I could get her to scream.

As she kept up her urgent pace, my mouth and hands ventured to new places. My lips ghosted kisses against the side of her neck, my hands stroked down her bare thighs, and I cracked a smile when I felt goosebumps lift on her skin.

God, I fucking loved this position. It gave her control and gave me easy access to her tits. I inched a hand under the hem of her shirt and moved it up until my palm was on the warm skin of her stomach. It was clear what I intended to do, but she didn't slow the rhythm of her hips. Maybe she was too greedy or focused on how good it felt.

My gaze slid up to her face, only to discover her eyes were shut.

"Look at me," I commanded.

Her eyes fluttered open and were hazy.

I skated my fingertips in a line up her stomach, carrying her shirt up on my forearm. "If I go too fast," my tone was heavy and seductive, "or I do something you don't like, you tell me."

She nodded quickly, far more focused on what we were doing than my words. My fingers ceased moving when they reached the center of her chest and the edge of fabric covering her tits. I lingered there, waiting for her to acknowledge how serious I was.

"Okay," she whispered. "Same for you."

"What?"

"You have to tell me if I move too fast or do something you don't like."

I held in a laugh, but just barely. "Not possible. I like everything."

My fingers resumed moving, sliding across the bare skin just at the edge of her bra, teasing her until neither of us seemed to be able to stand it any longer. Finally, I trailed my touch down over the satin fabric and closed my hand around her breast, gently gripping her. She arched her back in response and made a sexy sound of contentment.

It was so hot, I wanted to see all of it. "Take off your shirt."

She froze with my hand still cupped around her breast. "Someone might see."

Not a chance. The rain was thick and gray, plus we were secluded in the trees. Even she hadn't sounded that concerned, so I shot her a smile that announced this was a challenge. "What if they do? Would you like that?" I fumbled my hand from one breast to the other, moving beneath the fabric of her shirt. "What if you were really *bad* and got naked?"

Excitement flashed through her eyes like a surge of electricity, but I only caught a glimpse of it because she grabbed the bottom of her shirt and tugged it up. The shirt was pulled all the way off and dropped in a heap on the seat beside us, and my gaze traced over the black bra she wore. It was simple, yet sexy as hell, and—*Jesus*. I wasn't prepared for how good she looked, especially with my hand on her.

And it made my irritation at Colin flare up.

How dare he have a sister this fucking hot? It wasn't my fault I wanted her so badly, and it was criminal she was supposed to be off limits.

My hand on her might have been tame, but it felt anything *but* tame. The way she ground herself on me was hypnotic. I was drunk and greedy for more, so my fingers curled around the cup of her bra and jerked it aside.

It exposed her pointed nipple to me. The soft pink gave way to pale skin surrounding it that probably hadn't ever seen the sun.

Virgin skin.

Was it wrong to think every inch of her was like that? Untouched. Waiting to be explored.

Shit, I couldn't fucking wait.

She gasped when I dipped my head, latched my mouth around her nipple, and sucked. It made her squirm in my lap, and that only increased the ache in my body. The heat she caused was insane.

Sydney's breathing was ragged, but as I swiped my tongue over her sensitive skin, she let out a desperate moan. It didn't contain a word, but I heard her plea anyway.

More, she begged.

My hands moved on instinct. I slipped my fingers behind her, searching for the clasp, and as soon as I found it, I got to work. It wasn't that challenging to undo her bra, and once it was released, I tossed it on top of the shirt resting on the seat beside us.

The sight of her topless made my dick fucking throb. It strained against my pants, pushing harder against the center of her legs. The sensation was both pleasurable and torturous.

Her tits were so goddamn great.

They were perfect handfuls, which I took advantage of, filling my palms with their weight. When her mouth landed on mine, I zeroed in on one of her nipples and gave it a pinch. Not hard—just enough to make it feel good.

God, the way this girl rode me—it was straight fire. Her fingers tangled in my hair while my tongue clashed with hers, and my heart pounded so fast, sweat beaded at my temples. Outside, the cool rain beat down on my car, but inside?

It was sweltering.

She may have been a virgin, but she knew what she was doing when it came to kissing. I was supposed to be coaching her, to teach her all about sex, but it was clear she was going to show me some things, too.

I dragged my mouth down her neck, letting my hot breath bounce off her skin as I worked my way back to her tits. I was all over her, licking and nipping at her breasts, and her quiet gasps and sighs flooded the back seat.

Tension was building inside us.

It made her undulate faster, and I sucked in a breath through tight teeth. The way she was grinding felt so good, it was kind of worrying. I was twenty-four years old, not fifteen, and coming in my pants wasn't an option. Certainly not from dry-humping, and definitely not with Colin's little sister.

If he knew what we were doing right now, how she was topless and breathless from riding my lap, he'd fucking kill me. It was so wrong.

Bad.

But that was what she wanted to be, right?

A dark thought wormed its way into my brain, seizing control. It had me grabbing one of her wrists and pulling it behind her back, making her arch and shove her tits further in my face.

"You're such a good girl, Sydney," I teased, my mouth going from one nipple to the other. "Fuck. Grind that virgin pussy on me."

Her breath left her in a loud exhale. Had my words given her an unexpected punch of pleasure? Her moans swelled and her hips moved ruthlessly. She was humping me like a needy, desperate creature, panting from the exertion. And she didn't seem to be in control of her body anymore—only the urge to find satisfaction was driving her.

It might have been the sexiest thing I'd ever seen.

No, scratch that.

When she let out a deep groan and abruptly began to shudder uncontrollably—*that* was the sexiest thing ever. The back-and-forth jerk of her hips slowed to a stop, and her head lolled forward so she could drop her forehead down onto my shoulder.

Everything went quiet except for her as she struggled to find air, and the patter of rain falling against the windows.

"Did you just come?" I whispered.

I released her wrist and she melted into me, her warm breasts flattening to my bare chest. I could feel how fast her heart was beating and the quiver that shook her legs. It made me pulse, intensifying the ache in my pants.

Her head didn't move. She continued to rest it on my shoulder, but I got the sense it wasn't fatigue holding her there. Was she . . . embarrassed?

Sydney's voice was so quiet and rushed, it was hard to understand. "That's a first."

I went still and my chest tightened. "Your first orgasm?"

Shit, it was wrong how much I wanted that to be true. I was greedy and selfish, wanting all her firsts.

She pulled back and straightened, but her eyes wouldn't meet mine. Her gaze latched on to my chest, focusing there like she was too shy to look anywhere else. "No," she said. "Just my first time," she hesitated, "in front of someone else."

Well, fuck me.

This answer was even better than the one I'd hoped for.

SEVEN

Sydney

Sparks continued to ricochet through my body even as my orgasm faded, and I stared at Preston's chest, unable to look him in the eye. I'd never lost control like that in front of someone else. The sounds I'd made, the way I'd acted . . . It was impossible not to be embarrassed.

"Okay," he said, "that's seriously hot."

I couldn't interpret his tone. Was he making fun of me? I crossed my arms over my chest to cover my nakedness, and my gaze flew to his face. But it seemed he'd meant it genuinely, judging by his thrilled smile.

I had no idea what I looked like to him. My face had to be flushed because it was a million degrees inside his car, and I couldn't catch my breath. I'd had plenty of orgasms before, but they'd been late at night and in the safety of my own bed.

Where I didn't care how I sounded or what I looked like.

I didn't know how to feel about having an audience, especially one who'd undoubtedly seen this before with plenty of other partners. What if he compared me to them? What if I'd done it wrong, or I'd made a weird face, or—

Preston's hands closed around the arms I'd banded tightly across my chest, and he gently eased them apart, not stopping until he had our fingers laced together in each hand.

It was so comfortable, so intimate.

His warm, evaluating gaze slid across my body. "You okay? You look nervous."

I swallowed thickly. "Nope, I'm fine."

Except my voice was tight and my shoulders were tense, signaling I was lying, and he didn't like that. He used his hold on me to pull me close. I'd expected him to kiss me, but instead he tilted his head and fitted his face into the crook of my neck.

"What's going on?"

His gentle, hushed question was so unexpected, it nearly broke me. He wasn't exactly known for being thoughtful or considerate, so to see this side of him was stunning.

"I don't know," I whispered. But I *did* know. "I'm embarrassed," I admitted.

"Why?" His lips were just below my ear, and his hot breath tickled the loose hairs there. It made me shiver, but in a good way, and I was sure he knew he was the cause. "You're so fucking sexy."

I closed my eyes, enjoying what he'd said. Maybe he fed this line to all the girls he'd been with, but—shit—I wanted to believe it.

He unlaced our fingers, freeing his hands up so they could glide over my bare back. "I'll have to get you to do that again."

"What?"

"Make you come. I don't mind doing it over and over again until you're comfortable."

He sounded so matter of fact about it.

I let out a short laugh that was mixed with disbelief. "It's just that easy for you, huh?"

Because it hadn't been for anyone else.

Only him.

"Apparently, it is." His tone turned seductive. "And we've barely gotten started, Sydney."

He had a point. Things had gotten hot and heavy between us, but weirdly we also hadn't done much. Sure, I was topless, and he was hard between my legs, but most of our clothes were on and neither of our hands had strayed below the belt.

Plus, he'd said we weren't having sex today.

His lips glanced across my skin, planting a series of kisses that threatened to make me weaker than I was already. My unfocused gaze turned to stare out the back windshield and I watched the rain as it fell, enjoying the sensation of his mouth while pleasure continued to buzz through my system.

But as good as it felt, I wanted to distract him from trying to get me to orgasm again so soon. It was his turn for that, wasn't it?

When I attempted to slither out of his hold, for a moment he looked concerned and maybe a little disappointed I was disrupting his plans, but he said nothing. He was quiet as I pushed my shirt and bra onto the floor, climbed off, and sat beside him. Lust clouded his eyes when I set a hand on his chest and began to drag it downward.

A provocative smile bowed on his lips, and he asked it even when he already knew the answer. "What are you doing?"

My fingers glided down his stomach, inching toward his

crotch and landing on his fly. "I want to touch you."

He nudged my hand out of the way, quickly undoing the button and dropping his zipper. "Is that all?"

"I don't know." Heat coursed through my veins, making me feel bold. "Maybe . . . I'll put it in my mouth too."

"Fuck." He let out a heavy breath, but his tone turned wicked. "You probably shouldn't, though. A good girl like you? What would your parents think?"

My breath caught as I stared at him. His teasing question did something to me, and it intensified when he pulled open his pants and pushed both them and his underwear down off his hips.

All the moisture in my body began to flow toward the center of my legs.

My gaze worked its way over his bare thighs, moving on to his large, hard dick, and up his body before settling on his face. It was sexy seeing him like this, and it grew stronger still when he worked to undo the line of buttons on his shirt, throwing it open to show off his notched abs and toned chest.

Good god.

How was a girl supposed to look at him and *not* think about sex?

He lifted an arm and cast it across the top of the back seat, inviting me to look and touch and study him however I wanted. When a proud smirk tilted his lips, he became so scorching hot, it was downright lethal.

There was also a playful challenge in his eyes, and since I was competitive, I couldn't ignore it. He'd teased that I shouldn't go down on him because I was a good girl, but it was obvious how much he *didn't* want me to be good right now.

Some unknown force took control and loaded my voice with sin. "You're right," I said. "I shouldn't. Colin wouldn't like it either."

He jolted, and for a tense second, I was sure I'd made a mistake. Crossed a line I shouldn't have. I gripped air tightly in my lungs.

Preston's eyes became magnets, sucking me in, and an electric charge crackled in the tension between us. It was so taut, I couldn't move. I didn't want to break the spell. He blinked oh-so-slowly, like maybe he didn't want to disrupt the spell either.

"No, he wouldn't," he said finally. "But you're not going to let that stop you, are you?"

I shook my head quickly, agreeing.

His chest rose with an enormous breath when my fingers tentatively curled around him, and he let out that same heavy breath as I stroked down the length, going from tip to base. His skin was warm and velvety soft, in contrast to the firmness beneath.

It was wild I was here right now, doing this. I'd spent years lusting after him, never believing it'd be anything more than fantasy. I was nearly giddy, and my excitement destroyed any sense in my brain.

"You've got a really nice dick," I said.

Holy shit! I froze and pressed my lips together, wishing they were glued shut. Where the hell had that come from?

My out of the blue comment fucking thrilled him, and Preston's *nice dick* jerked in my hand. "Thanks. It's not as nice as your tits, though."

And to reinforce his statement, his gaze drifted long-ingly over my bare breasts. It would have made my heart beat faster if that had been possible, but it wasn't. I was already at max speed, struggling to keep up.

I'd been naked with a few guys before, but this was so different. Even with the rain, it was still daylight outside, and light filled the interior of the car, leaving few shadows to hide in.

Plus, I'd never had a guy look at me the way he did now. As if I were so sexy, it was taking everything in him not to change his mind and ask me if I wanted to go all the way.

I resumed the slow glide of my fist over his dick and watched with fascination as his eyes hooded and he slumped back against the seat. He was enjoying the hand job I was giving him, but his hips moved, urging me to go faster.

When I picked up the pace, satisfaction dripped off his expression and his chest lifted in a hurried rhythm. It was so freaking erotic that I had to pinch my thighs together against the ache deep inside me.

Watching him was fun, but giving a hand job wasn't my favorite activity. I never knew how hard to squeeze, or how fast to go, or if his face was actually filled with a grimace in-stead of pleasure.

But blow jobs?

Those were a lot easier to get right.

I gave him a final stroke, adjusted my position beside him, and leaned over his lap, preparing to take him in my mouth.

"Does the good girl know how to suck cock?"

His dirty question lit a fire in me, burning away inhibitions. "I may be a virgin, but don't worry. I've sucked plenty of dicks before yours."

Something that looked suspiciously like jealousy flitted through his eyes. "Pro tip," his smile was pained, "maybe don't talk about other dicks when you're about to suck mine."

I froze.

Oh, shit. Had I offended him?

He ringed a hand around the base and held his cock out from his body, before quirking his lips in a half-smile. "I want you to focus on this one right now." His tone was commanding. "Mine, and *only* mine."

In response, a muscle low in belly tightened. I nodded, lowered in, and parted my lips over the head of his dick. Down I slid, taking him as far as I could.

A long, low sound of satisfaction rolled out of him, and it encouraged me to tighten my mouth and suck until my cheeks hollowed out. I tried not to think about anything, like how he was my brother's best friend or how many times I'd imagined myself with him in the back seat of his car.

One of Preston's hands was abruptly warm on the center of my back, but he didn't put any force behind it. He wasn't trying to guide me—his palm simply rested there. It was as if he wanted an extra connection with me through this gentle touch.

When I swirled my tongue around his tip, he pulsed.

God, it was *so* sexy.

And it was sexier still when he groaned appreciatively.

Up and down I bobbed, and he didn't sit still for long.

His hips began to buck, forcing the head of his dick to hit the back of my throat. The sensation was almost overwhelming, but his fingertips moved, tracing lines sensually up and down my spine, and I focused on that instead.

"Goddamn," he murmured, "that feels good."

Pleasure skittered across my skin.

My whole life, I'd been trained to please other people. To obey and be good. It had been drilled into me so hard, a small part of me worried that was the main reason I'd gravitated toward the culinary world. I hungered for praise.

His thrusts had started subtle, but there was purpose and urgency in them now. His breathing was ragged, louder than the rain outside, and I closed my eyes to listen better. Needy sighs crept in, and beneath me, the muscles of his thighs tightened.

His tone was wicked. "You like sucking that dick, don't you?"

I moaned instantly in agreement, surprising myself. But it was the truth. I liked *everything* about this.

"I'm going to come in that pretty little mouth of yours," he said. "And you're going to swallow every last drop, aren't you?"

Oh, my god.

His filthy mouth was shocking and exhilarating. Was it possible to have a full body blush? Because that was how I felt. Hot, and jittery, and like I was doing something I wasn't supposed to, but it was too much fun to stop.

My jaw began to ache from how wide I had it held open, but I didn't slow down. I kept up with his demanding pace, even as saliva pooled in the crevices of my mouth and began to drip down his shaft.

"Fuck, get ready," he warned.

His thighs tensed into stone, and the hard muscle filling my mouth flexed at the same instant he let loose a deep groan. His labored breathing went erratic as he came, and the explosion of pleasure inside him must have been epic, because he shook violently. Pulse after pulse filled my mouth with hot, thick liquid, and I slowed to a stop, swallowing as quickly as I could.

His voice was breathless. "Good girl."

I shuddered in satisfaction at his praise, and while he continued to recover, I drew back and looked at him. Never in a million years did I think I'd see him like this. Even as his breathing was slowing, his chest rose and fell rapidly, and his eyes studied me like I'd ambushed him, and he didn't trust what he was seeing either.

Lightning flashed across the sky, followed by a sharp crack of thunder, making me flinch.

As my body began to cool, I became acutely aware I was still topless, and although I doubted it would happen, there was a chance someone could see. I reached for my bra and struggled into it, but he made no effort to pull up his pants.

Preston just sat there with his damp dick resting across his thigh, watching me.

"I guess the lesson's over," he said.

Confusion made me move slower as I tugged on my shirt. Was it not over? He didn't seem like the kind of guy who wanted to snuggle after fooling around, but at the same time, I didn't know him all that well.

"Uh—" I started.

"We didn't decide how many lessons." He grabbed the sides of his undone pants and jerked them up. It was mesmerizing watching the tendons in his forearms flex as he zipped up his fly and did the button. "The last thing you said was ten, but that's . . . too many. I think three more should do it."

Was he serious? "Three more isn't going to be enough." I lifted my chin and tried to sound firm. "Six."

"No." He was far more successful at sounding resolute. "If we're doing this, we're keeping it to a minimum."

His posture announced he wasn't going to negotiate. This was his one and only offer, and it made me wonder why. Was it that we'd be hiding it from Colin, or was there more to it, like he worried about catching feelings?

"Fine," I said, not masking my disappointment. "Three more lessons."

He looked relieved. "Okay."

My phone buzzed, shattering the moment, and dread lined the pit of my stomach. Without looking at the screen, I knew exactly who was calling me right now. I sensed Preston did, too, judging by the irritation that clung to the edges of his eyes.

I flashed an apologetic look, straightened, and dug out my phone.

As soon as I clicked the button to answer the call, my mother started speaking. She didn't wait for a greeting. "What's going on?" she demanded. "It looks like you're stuck on the side of the road."

My mother was loud enough for him to hear her side of the conversation, and he arched an eyebrow.

"I'm fine," I said.

There was rustling on her end, followed by an electronic chime and a door slamming shut. "I'm getting in the car. I'll be there in fifteen minutes."

My spine went straight with alarm. "No, you don't need to do that."

"Well, what's happened? Did your Uber driver abandon you in the middle of nowhere while it's raining?"

"No." I swallowed a lump. "Preston offered to drive me to Colin's." It wasn't technically a lie, but it rolled awkwardly off my tongue. "We stopped to talk."

There was utter silence on her end, and I could picture the horror on her face. Did she believe that talking was all we'd done? I'd never given her a reason not to trust me, but maybe all bets were off once Preston was involved.

The uncomfortable quiet stretched, causing me to scramble to placate her.

"I'm heading home now," I blurted.

"All right." Her tone was cool. "I'll be here if you want to finish the discussion we were having before you walked out on me."

I clenched my teeth so hard, my jaw ached. "What discussion? You made it clear the decision has already been made. Let's not bother pretending I get a say in it."

"You're being rude, Sydney." She sounded shocked, like she didn't know it was possible, and ugliness rose inside me.

Get ready, I thought.

She wasn't used to any pushback from me, but I was going to show her everything I was capable of.

EIGHT

Preston

I pulled into the Novaks' driveway, parked, and considered that for once, it wouldn't be stressful to ring the doorbell and wait for the girl to appear. If anything, picking up my 'date' would be fun today.

Even though Colin was my best friend, I'd only been over to his place a handful of times before, and that had stopped completely after our senior prom. His parents had never said I wasn't welcome at their house, but the giant stick up their ass ensured we never had much fun hanging out at his place.

The house was nice, but they didn't have a pool like I did, and for years my dad was so chill, my friends and I could do whatever we wanted. So everyone, including me, preferred my place.

I shut off my engine, got out, and strolled up the path to the front porch. The early June sun was high in the sky and relentlessly bright, making me squint behind my sunglasses. I climbed the two brick steps, pressed the doorbell, and swiped a hand through my hair.

The mechanical chime summoned someone with heavy footsteps, and when the door swung open, it revealed Mr. Novak.

Perfect.

Hopefully, my smile looked friendly and not smug.

My arrival caught him off guard, and as soon as he recognized me, his gaze narrowed. "Colin doesn't live here anymore."

He didn't even bother to say hello, didn't want me darkening his door.

"I know," I said. "I'm not here for Colin." My smile widened as I hooked my thumbs through the belt loops of my shorts. "I'm here for Sydney."

His chin pulled back, and the muscles of his jaw tightened. Oh, yeah. He fucking hated hearing that.

His tone went rough. "What do you want with my daughter?"

I took a breath to stop myself from saying something stupid, like telling him *exactly* what I wanted with his daughter. The time I'd spent with her in my back seat had been so hot, I only allowed myself to think about it when I was alone.

No need to embarrass myself in public.

I didn't get a chance to answer her father's question because Sydney appeared from deeper in the house and came bounding toward us like a ray of fucking sunshine. She wore a royal blue dress with tiny white dots scattered over it, and the top was held up by tiny straps tied in bows on her shoulders.

It'd been two days since we'd seen each other, and my body instantly whined it had been way too long. She wasn't wearing a bra, and I didn't miss the way her tits bounced as she strutted forward.

Fuck me. I was *dying* to give her my next lesson.

"Hey." Her voice was warm. "You ready?"

Her friendly greeting was partly a performance, but it made my heart beat faster anyway. She was so sexy, and yet somehow she didn't have a fucking clue.

Mr. Novak cleared his throat, but he might as well have told me to stop leering.

I smiled and jerked my head toward my car parked in the driveway. "Yeah. Come on."

Displeasure rolled off her dad in waves, but she pretended to be oblivious. Her sandals flopped against the soles of her feet as she joined me on the porch and started down the front steps.

"Where are you going?" His tone was sharp, strict.

She glanced back at him, and then at me as if she wanted my support. Didn't she know she had it? This had been my idea, and we both wanted to piss her parents off. I nodded subtly.

"We're going to play miniature golf," she said.

After the rain had stopped and I'd driven her home, I'd gotten her number, and yesterday I'd suggested we go mini golfing for our 'date.' Our schedules had worked out. She was off tonight at the restaurant where she worked, and I didn't have any events or client meetings this evening.

"Will Colin be there?"

Some of the sunshine she'd had faded from her expression. "Why are you asking? You have a message you want me to pass along?"

Her dad shifted uncomfortably on his feet. "No. I was"— his suspicious gaze flicked to me—"just curious."

"No," she said. "Colin won't be there."

"Just the two of you, then?" He barely hid his horror.

She laughed lightly. "It's not like that. We're just *friends.*" Her tone was cavalier, but the gleam in her eyes, paired with a dark smile announced this was a lie. "Right, Preston?"

"You got it."

I felt Mr. Novak's hard gaze on us the whole way as we walked to my Charger, and for added effect, I opened her door for her. I acted like I was a gentleman, but I was sure he thought I was anything but a good guy.

And he was right.

The miniature golf place I'd booked was one of those indoor, high-tech ones, with neon lights and glow in the dark paint. I'd never been before, but it was fun inside. It was themed like a fairytale forest, complete with oversized mushrooms and gnomes, which for the most part weren't totally creepy.

It was cute when Sydney got her first hole in one, but it was a lot less entertaining when she sank another one on the fifth hole. Her pink ball glowed under the blacklights as it rolled up and over the astroturf bridge and then down the slope toward the pin.

She let out a satisfied sound when it pinged off the mini flagpole and fell into the cup.

"Okay, seriously." I'd never been so impressed and annoyed at the same time. "How the fuck?"

She bent and retrieved her ball, and when she straightened, she flashed a sheepish smile. Like she was embarrassed by how good she was. The person who should be embarrassed was me.

I fucking *hated* losing.

"Do you play a lot of golf?" It was less of a question from me and more of an accusation.

She shrugged. "Not really."

My grip tightened on my putter. "Then, why are you so good at this?"

Why are you better than me, was what I really wanted to ask.

Her eyebrows tugged together as she struggled to put it into words. "I don't know. It's kind of always been like this. I think about what I need to do to succeed. Every time I throw a dart, or make a shot in pool, or putt . . . I evaluate what I could do to make the next attempt even better."

Was she kidding? That wasn't magic, or even special. "Everyone does that."

At least, I did.

"Well, I visualize," she said. "I try really hard, and I want it really bad, and that usually makes it happen for me." Her expression shifted to a bashful one. "But it doesn't work for everything. Like, serious sports? Forget it. I'm terrible. If we were playing regular golf right now, you'd have no problem beating me. But the games anyone can play—those are the ones where I kick ass."

Well, she wasn't kicking my ass just yet. I was only a few strokes behind, but if this continued? I was going to lose. I needed something to throw her off her game.

Sydney stood off to the side of the fairway, watching me as I dropped my lime green ball onto the artificial turf and took my shot. Except I misjudged the amount of force to use, meaning my ball carried too much speed over the hill and gained even more as it rolled down. It blew right past the hole, ricocheting off the stone outline at the back of the fairway, and miraculously rolled back toward the pin.

"Lucky," she commented when my ball dropped into the hole.

"No, I'm just that good."

Like I'd planned it that way, even though it was total bullshit. I bent and retrieved my ball, then set my gaze on her. "Hey, question for you. How the hell are you still a virgin?"

She jolted and glanced around to see if anyone had overheard me, but no one had. I'd been careful. I didn't want to embarrass her, or for her to think she should feel shame about this. All I hoped to do was fluster her. To give myself a tiny chance at not losing.

Plus, this question had been eating at me ever since she'd confessed it. I couldn't figure out how it was possible. Her parents weren't that religious, and she didn't seem to be either, so surely that wasn't the reason. But her folks had a weird hold over her. It was possible they'd locked her up in some sort of metaphorical chastity belt.

"What?" she whispered.

"You're gorgeous," I said, stating a simple fact. "Plus, you suck cock like a champ." Her eyes widened and she froze, but I kept going. "Are you waiting for marriage?"

She blinked her stunned eyes, looking off-kilter. "No."

I knew it was none of my business, but I couldn't stop myself. "Then, why?"

She held her putter with both hands, and they tightened on the grip. It took her a lifetime to find the words. "Maybe I haven't found the right guy yet."

I pushed out a breath, recalling what she'd said in the car—how she'd always imagined I'd be the one to take her virginity. And maybe that was true, but that didn't explain the past twelve months. I'd pushed her away after our fucking incredible kiss last year, instead of hooking up with her.

Only a fool would continue to wait for me after that.

I hadn't waited for her.

No, you just thought about her all the damn time.

I shot her a look and tilted my head. "You need to get better at lying if you're going to be bad."

Alarm spiked in her expression. *Busted.*

I got that she was shy, but she didn't seem to be painfully so. At least, no more than some of the other girls I'd been with, so that probably wasn't the reason either. It had to be something else.

It only took two steps to bring me right in front of her and my voice went quiet. "Are you, like, not interested in sex?"

A strangled noise escaped from her throat, and she matched my low tone. "No, I'm very interested in . . . that."

Her focus slid down my body, and *fuck.* My pulse climbed.

When the pools of her eyes heated, it was clear she was thinking the same thing I was at that moment. She pictured us naked, her legs wrapped around my waist as I pushed my dick inside her for the first time. Maybe she'd make that same noise of surprise I'd just heard from her.

But she blinked away the desire and her guard came up, creating a wall between us. I didn't like it, and that overrode the voice in my head telling me not to push her. "Tell me."

My tone wasn't demanding, but it didn't matter. The second it was out, I winced, knowing I'd made a mistake.

Her single word was cold and definitive. "No."

I was irritated with myself. She'd tell me if and when she wanted to, and I needed to get that. I shouldn't care what her reasons were—only that she'd come to *me* for help when she could have gone to anyone else. Plus, my insistence might be making her feel like I thought there was something wrong with her, when . . . shit, no. That wasn't what I thought at all.

The longer I was around her, the more obsessed I became.

But I was honestly confused on why she was so hell-bent on hooking up with me. Sure, I was good-looking, but I wasn't the only hot guy on the planet. Why bother with me when she could have someone less complicated?

At the very least, she could have someone who wasn't best friends with Colin.

When we'd stepped onto the golf course, it hadn't been busy, but there was a couple behind us now who was finishing the previous hole. I felt their impatient stares at the same time she must have because Sydney abruptly moved.

She stalked to the next hole, dropped her ball to the astroturf, and swung without even setting her feet. So, it wasn't all that surprising when her ball plinked off the rock in the center of the green and rolled to a stop in a corner that didn't have a clear path to the hole. It was a terrible, rushed shot. She didn't seem to care, though. She marched to the side, moving out of the way for me to tee off.

Unease made my shoulders tight, but I tried to ignore it. I drew in a breath, lined up, and took my shot.

I didn't get another hole-in-one, but I came really close. I tapped my ball in, retrieved it, and waited with my mouth shut as I watched her finish the round—

Which was a disaster.

My plan had been to fluster her, and it had worked a little too well.

Sydney no longer cared about the game, and when she missed her next two shots, I began to feel bad. I liked winning, but this felt . . . wrong. Empty.

She finally knocked the ball in, and we shuffled on to the next hole. I struggled to find a way to make it right and get rid of the weird vibe between us. I needed her to focus on something else so I could bring back the sunny girl she'd been earlier.

"You've always wanted to be a chef?" I asked.

For a moment, it looked like she was going to ignore my question, but then she sighed, and her attention turned my way. "Yeah."

I made sure it sounded light. Conversational. "Why?"

She dropped her ball and swung her putter, making the ball careen carelessly across the fairway. "I don't know. I guess it's a little like this can be. How you get better every time you do it, and so I'm always trying to improve and one-up myself. To make the dish better each time I make it."

She was competing with herself, and that? I totally related. "I do that, too. Every event I host, I want it to be better than the last."

"How'd you get into event planning?"

"My mom has her own company in North Carolina, and I used to help out when I lived with her. I kind of hated it back then, but now . . ." I shrugged. "It sounds weird, but I like managing all the moving parts and bringing them together to make something great. Even if it's stressful or chaotic leading up to it. If the result makes my clients happy, then I'm happy."

She looked pleasantly surprised. "I get it. That's how I feel when I finish a dish. When I have all these elements with different timing, and I execute it just right and get them on the plate together—it's like a rush."

I understood completely. I got that same swell of pride she was talking about whenever I pulled off an event that I knew was going to exceed expectations. Plus, it was awesome seeing all my work fall into place to create the finished product.

It shouldn't have been surprising we had shit in common. We were both into creative, customer-driven fields, and yet it caught me off guard anyway. It made me wonder where else we might be similar.

Wait, no.

I was already more interested in her than I wanted to be. It'd be easier to give her a few lessons, get this lingering desire out of my system, and move on if I didn't get too invested.

So, I swung my gaze to the hole and focused on that. I had the option of taking the long way around the mushroom obstacle, or I could aim for the tunnel running through it and get a straight shot to the hole.

Sydney whistled appreciatively when I threaded the needle and my ball dropped into the cup.

I grinned as I retrieved it, and because I was so excited about getting another hole-in-one, I forgot not to be a cocky asshole. "Maybe take your time on your next shot," I half-joked, "unless you want to fall farther behind me."

There was no change in her expression, but she gave me one long, slow blink. And then her gaze shifted away like she was considering something.

The idea took shape and her tone suddenly went friendly. Maybe overly excited. "Let's make a bet."

"Yeah?" Intrigue pulled one of my eyebrows up. "I'm listening."

"If I win the game," her smile was wicked, "you have to give me another lesson."

I chuckled. *This* was the best she could come up with? Sure, I didn't want her to get too attached to me, but one more lesson wasn't that bad. It certainly wasn't the end of the world, and besides—with my newest hole-in-one, I was several strokes ahead. "And what do I get when I win?"

Her shoulders lifted with a deep breath. "I'll tell you why I'm still a"—she glanced around—"virgin."

Shit, even if I wasn't competitive, there was no way I was going to turn down this offer. I grinned. "All right. You're on."

The corner of her mouth lifted in a sexy smirk.

It should have been a warning, but I didn't heed it. I was too dumb to think that maybe this had been a ploy. A hustle.

I spent the rest of the game doing my best to keep her off guard. I'd stand too close to her or make comments when she had a long putt to make—but it was useless.

She fed off my attempts.

Every gleeful smile she gave me when she gained a stroke on me filled my head with static. When I invaded her personal space, rather than get flustered, she leaned into me. It made it so I would smell whatever fruity product she'd used in her hair, and I didn't like how appealing it was.

It was irritating that the better she got at her golf game, the worse mine became. Nerves, for the first time in my fucking life, became an issue. I missed an easy putt, using too much force and sending it wide of the hole, which made my next attempt that much harder.

The air conditioning was pumping, making my sweat cold when we made it to the final round. Shit, I was down by two strokes.

"Take your time," she said as I lined up on the tee. Maybe she only meant it to be helpful, but it felt patronizing, like she knew I was about to lose. It pissed me off. She'd probably argue I deserved to lose because I'd underestimated her. Plus, I'd been so confident I had the game in the bag.

What if this was my only chance to know why this sexy girl hadn't let anyone have her the way she wanted me to have her?

I tried to block it out and focus, and I did what she said she did—I pictured the outcome I wanted.

The fairway led to a big ramp that would send my ball up onto a board with a bullseye painted on it. If I hit the spot in the center, my ball would go down a tube, come out the other side, and roll directly into the hole.

But anything outside of the center? It would drain down the board into one of the other tubes, and who the fuck knew where it would be spat out? I needed a hole-in-one, plus a miracle.

So, I blew out a breath and swung my club.

My ball took off, launching up the ramp, and made a loud thud as it hit just above the bullseye's center. It chattered down the board before being caught by one of the other tubes and disappeared down it.

"Son of a bitch," I groaned.

We watched as my green ball shot out the other side, bounced off the rock edging and came to a stop a good six feet from the hole. Worse, there was a hump in my path to the hole, and I'd been misjudging how to play them all afternoon.

Of course she got her ball into the center tube, scoring her yet another hole-in-one. She pushed a section of her dark brown hair back over her shoulder and delivered a fucking epic smile. Victory banners waved in her eyes.

"I think maybe," her voice was teasing, "you wanted me to win."

I forced out a smile, but it was only to mask the unease her statement caused. Was that true? I'd played so poorly, it was sort of comforting to think I might have done it on purpose. Like, subconsciously. An extra lesson with her wasn't a hardship. But I wasn't thrilled with losing.

I meant it to be a demand, but it rang out like a plea. "We'll play again."

"Yeah, I don't think so." She spun her putter in her grip. "I figure you can give me the lesson after dinner."

"Dinner?" My heart thudded.

We hadn't made any plans other than the golf game, and this fake date already felt enough like a real one. Adding in dinner was a bad idea, and I didn't want her to get the wrong idea. Our arrangement needed to stay 'friends with benefits,' with no feelings involved. That was the only way to make sure she didn't get hurt when this thing came to an end.

"I'm making you dinner at my place," she said. "I got it all prepped earlier today." Whatever face I was making, it caused her to tilt her head and look at me like I was being silly. "It's just a way to say thank you," she cast a hand between us, "for helping. Plus, you get that I like cooking for other people, right? My parents don't seem to care anymore, so . . . it'll be nice to have someone else."

She tried to mask her disappointment with her parents, but it was impossible to ignore. What the fuck was wrong with them? I pictured them walking into the kitchen and discovering me and her at the table, enjoying the meal she'd just cooked. Her folks would lose their goddamn minds.

Also, I was a shitty cook and had no plans for dinner. I should be thrilled she wanted to volunteer. "What are you making?"

She said it like it was as easy and common as a grilled cheese sandwich. "Lobster ravioli in garlic cream sauce."

Holy shit.

I hadn't realized I was hungry before, and now my mouth watered. That sounded awesome, but also like a ton of work.

She wanted to do that . . . for me?

"Is that okay?" She paused. "Oh, crap. Are you allergic to shellfish? I should have asked if you have any allergies."

"I don't," I said. "And, yeah. That sounds good."

Relief washed through her expression. "Okay. Great."

We both glanced at the exit, and then turned back to look at each other expectantly.

"Should we go, then?" I asked.

I didn't know how much time it'd take her, and I didn't see a point in finishing the final round. I'd lost, and now I was eager to see just how good this good girl could be when she was in her wheelhouse.

She nodded, so I returned my ball and club to the stand beside the cashier, and she followed suit. We didn't say a word to each other as we pushed through the glass doors, out into the bright afternoon sun.

Maybe she thought I was trying not to be a sore loser, but that wasn't it. The silence between us was weirdly comfortable. Like we'd been friends for a long time, even though we hadn't been.

I was only a few steps away from my car when she spoke.

"Preston." I turned to discover her with her hand outstretched. She was offering me a handshake. "Good game."

When I had her soft, warm hand closed in mine, something . . . happened. I wasn't one to believe in sparks, but a weird energy surged through me. It was as if I'd been wanting the connection to her all day and now relief flooded down my body.

I knew I should let go of her, but I couldn't.

Instead, I used my hold to haul her close, bringing us chest to chest, and surprise darted through her big, pretty eyes. The urge to kiss her came on sharp and aggressive, but somehow I held it back. I'd lost to her and didn't want to give up any more ground. I needed to gain some control back.

"Just so we're clear," my voice was low, "I'm the one who says when the lessons happen. I'm the teacher, and you? You're going to be my perfect little student, aren't you?"

Her breath caught, sex thickened in her eyes, and her hand tried to clench inside mine. Fuck if it wasn't the hottest thing ever.

"Yes," she whispered.

A devious smile peeled back my lips. "Good girl."

NINE

Sydney

After I'd agreed to be Preston's 'perfect student,' I'd been so sure he was going to kiss me . . . but it didn't happen. Instead, he dropped my hand, turned on his heel, and strode to the driver's side of his car. Disappointment sagged my shoulders. It left me with no options, so I walked to the other side, pulled open the door, and climbed in.

He had just finished buckling his seatbelt when I was finally ready to talk about it. "Do you want to know why I'm still a virgin?"

His hand froze, hovering over the button to start the engine, and his expression clouded over. He turned to look at me like he was sure this was a trap. It made sense for him to be skeptical, but the real reason I hadn't told him before was because I needed us to be alone.

"I'm a virgin," I said, "because I'm stupid."

This was the last thing he expected me to say. "What?"

Warmth heated my face, but I was determined to do this. "When I was younger, I made this rule for myself." I fidgeted with the part of the seatbelt strap that was stretched across my lap. "I don't know why. Maybe I did it because I wanted to please my parents. They're really anti-sex, but *especially* premarital sex."

They'd probably never understand the full effect their lectures and shaming had on my brother and me. Colin had rebelled immediately, sleeping with as many people as he could.

But me?

I was obedient. I had followed them without question and done my best to respect their wishes.

"So, I made a pact with myself," I said. "I'd be a good girl in high school. If I was still a virgin when I graduated, then I wouldn't feel guilty about giving it up after that. I'd be an adult, after all."

Preston blinked and his voice turned quiet. "That's not stupid."

"Well, I did it. I got my diploma," I placed my hand dramatically on my chest and lifted my chin, affecting a holier-than-thou attitude, "with my virtue intact."

He didn't react, and maybe he didn't know how to.

I sighed and dropped the charade. "So, when I got to college, I thought, 'I'm ready.' A few weeks into the semester, I went to a house party with my roommate."

The muscles in his shoulder tensed, and a worried look filled his deep eyes. Did he sense where the story was headed?

"I met this guy named Mason who seemed cool, and after a few beers, I agreed to go upstairs with him." The warmth on my face graduated to fire. I understood I hadn't done anything wrong, but—still. It was embarrassing that I hadn't been smarter. That I hadn't realized at the time how I'd put myself in such a vulnerable position. "I wasn't wanting to have sex." I lifted my shoulder in a shy shrug. "I thought we'd just fool around. But things . . . I don't know. He moved fast, and he went super high-pressure when I told him I didn't want to go any farther."

Preston didn't like the sound of that. His jaw tightened and his throat bobbed like he'd had to swallow back the words he wanted to say.

It made me speak faster, wanting to get through it.

"I was tipsy, and I didn't know him." All the strength left my voice. "I didn't want my first time to be like that."

"No," he agreed.

"But Mason was impatient, and it got to the point where— for just a moment—I wasn't sure I was going to make it out of the room until he got what he wanted." I struggled to say it. "And that . . . scared me."

The anger in his face shifted and was replaced with something new. It looked a hell of a lot like concern, and it was surprising to see, because he struck me as the type of guy who didn't think that much about other people.

At least, not unless they were important to him.

Did that mean I was important to him?

"You don't have to look at me like that," I said softly. "It all worked out, and it was a while ago. I'm fine."

He didn't believe that at all. "Did you tell Colin?"

I made a face. "No. Why would I? I don't need my brother to protect me, and more importantly, nothing happened." I adjusted myself in the seat, wishing I could shake off the uncomfortableness lingering in my body. "But after that, I'm more careful, and," I considered the right word, "selective. That's why I want it to be you. You're not some stranger—you're safe. I know what I'm getting with you."

He looked dubious. "Is that so?"

"Yeah." It was meant to sound teasing, but there was truth buried in it. "I'm not afraid of you." He searched my face like he didn't believe me, and I felt compelled to show him. "And I can prove it."

His lips parted. Maybe he was going to ask me how I planned to do that, but I didn't give him the chance. I had a momentary surge of courage and went with it, leaning over the center console and reached up to pull his face to mine.

My kiss surprised us both.

I hadn't meant it to be a big deal. My thought was it'd be short and sweet, just something to prove I was willing to initiate. But the second our lips touched, my plan flash boiled away in the heat of our connection.

As soon as he finished recovering from his surprise, Preston took control. He set a hand on my shoulder, and his palm smoothed up the curve of my neck, not stopping until he had my face cradled in his hand.

Oh, my god, the way he kissed me. All the times I'd imagined it over the years, I hadn't come close to doing it justice. His tongue filled my mouth, and the stroke of it against mine sent sparks skittering down my spine.

It created new, bold thoughts inside me. What if I took my seatbelt off and tried to climb into his lap? Or if I took his hand and guided it between my legs to where I was suddenly aching for him to touch me?

Blood thundered through my veins and my heart raced as I worked up the courage to try it, but just as I was ready to pull the trigger, his hand moved. It glided down my throat, inched along my chest, and then closed around one of my breasts.

I inhaled sharply.

Like last time we'd been in his car, it was daylight, but otherwise it was totally different. We weren't secluded now—we were in a semi-full parking lot where anyone could walk by and see us making out. They could look in and see the way his thumb brushed over my pebbled nipple through the fabric at the top of my dress.

The word was searingly hot as it sliced through my mind. *Bad.*

Except it didn't feel bad. Not at all, plus I didn't give a damn who saw. If anything, I kind of hoped somebody was watching. They'd glance inside Preston's car and maybe they'd think I was one of the words my parents had said I'd become if I wasn't careful.

Tramp.

Slut.

Whore.

Shit, it was crazy how much I wanted those words to be true now. A lifetime of denying myself, of believing there was something wrong with me for being interested in sex . . . I was wild in my newfound freedom.

And I couldn't get enough of the wrongness. Of being a bad girl. Preston was only giving me a taste when I wanted the whole damn entrée. So, I moaned my approval against his lips and arched into his touch. I wanted his hand under my shirt, or up my skirt, or his fingers inside me—

Abruptly, he pulled back, and his posture stiffened. "Wait."

It was like he'd walked me to the edge of a cliff and suddenly backed away. My eyes flew open, and I found his expression strange. It was filled with regret.

"What's wrong?"

His gaze shifted away from me. "I'm sorry."

I was totally lost. "For what?"

Rather than answer, he smoothed his palms down his thighs and then started the car. The air conditioning blew out hot air for a moment, before cooling down and giving us some relief in the uncomfortably stuffy interior.

Oh, no.

I recognized what this was. The last guy I'd told this story to had reacted the same way. He'd been so worried about not pressuring me that he'd swung too far the other way. He'd needed constant consent and encouragement to try anything, and because I was kind of shy, it'd only made things harder and more awkward.

I was sure Preston wouldn't have that issue. Not only because he wasn't the most considerate person, but because we'd already done stuff together. Hadn't I shown him I was more than okay with fooling around? Yes, that night at the house party had made me cautious, but it hadn't scared me off from sex forever.

I repeated my question, but my tone was sharper this time. "What's wrong?"

"Nothing." His handsome face twisted down into a frown. "Fuck. You just told me that guy moved too fast, and now I'm doing the exact same thing."

A short laugh burst from my lips. "Um, no. You aren't moving too fast." It just came out. "If anything, you're not moving fast enough." He looked skeptical. "Seriously, Preston." I tried not to squirm in my seat. "I was thinking about taking your hand and putting it between my legs."

His shoulders lifted with a deep breath. "Yeah?" The atmosphere in the car thickened, filling with smoke and seduction. "Is that all?"

He peered at me like he already knew the answer, and his intense gaze made me swallow thickly.

"I . . . want your fingers inside me."

I couldn't believe I said it out loud, and my disbelief grew when he all but giggled with delight. "Right now?" He made a production out of glancing around. "Where anyone could see?"

I bit down on my bottom lip and nodded.

Electricity warmed his eyes. He fucking *loved* this answer. "We could get caught." His voice dripped with sex. "Maybe that's what you want? Someone to watch while I finger-fuck your virgin pussy?"

"Oh, my god," I gasped. His dirty words and the visual it created were a punch of desire. My body wouldn't allow any other answer. "Yes."

"*Bad girl.*" Although he said it like it was the highest of praise. "That wouldn't be moving too fast for you?"

"No. I mean, how could it be? The goal is to have sex. And like I said, I know I'm safe with you."

My statement was a cool breeze washing over him. His

sexy expression drained away and turned serious. Instead of touching me, he set his hands on the steering wheel and turned his attention forward. "I'm glad you feel that way, because you are. But while I'm safe for you," tension curled his fingers tighter around the wheel, "you aren't for me."

"What?"

"This thing between us, it has to be about the lessons, and nothing more. Just sex." He glanced at me. "I can't date you."

Was he telling me, or himself?

"Because you don't date." Except I'd seen him out on one, hadn't I?

"No, because Colin would never allow it. Remember?"

I pressed my lips together as I considered his statement. I understood he was taking on a huge risk and life would certainly be easier for him if he steered clear of me.

And yet . . . he didn't.

Was it possible he felt the same inescapable pull toward me as I felt toward him? God, I hoped so.

"But you *do* date," I said quietly. "You were out one when you were seated next to me and my mom."

"Yeah."

That was the only response he was going to give me? My heart beat too fast for my thoughts to keep up with it. "Are you going to see her again?"

He grimaced. "No."

"What about other people?" I dreaded what his answer might be. "Will you be seeing them," I tried to sound casual, "while you're giving me lessons?"

He turned his head slowly to face me, and his

expression was unreadable. "No." He paused. "And it'll be the same for you."

I was more than fine with that, but . . . "If we're hanging out and fooling around, and we're exclusive to each other, that kind of sounds like we're dating."

"No," he grumbled. "We're not."

I stifled the urge to smile and lifted my hands in mock surrender. "Okay."

He was uncomfortable with the label, and there was no reason to have it, anyway, since no one—outside of my parents—was supposed to think we were together. So, it was best to drop it.

But a sarcastic voice filled my head, drowning everything else out.

Every time we'd been together, he'd given me blistering, all-consuming kisses, but—sure. He could continue to claim we were just friends. It wasn't like sleeping together was going to change anything.

Right?

TEN

Sydney

Preston sat at one of the stools at the bar in my parents' kitchen, watching me as I dropped a half a stick of butter into a large sauté pan. When I'd told him I needed twenty minutes to bring the dish together, he'd pulled his phone out like he was going to give it all his attention and leave me to work in silence.

But he hadn't.

His iPhone sat on the counter, completely forgotten from the moment I put on an apron. It was an old one from my first job as a line cook. The black apron had lasted much longer than the restaurant—the little upstart Italian place, *Vesuvio's,* had shuttered its doors just six months after opening.

"I learned so much at that place," I told him. "It's just a shame a lot of it was what *not* to do."

As I waited for the deep pot of water on one burner to come to a boil, I gathered the rest of my ingredients for the sauce. Cream, parmesan, garlic, chicken stock, and a lemon for acidity. I felt Preston's gaze on me as I moved with efficiency. Salt was tossed into the pot of water, and then I retrieved a cutting board and knife from my section of the kitchen.

His focus went from one side of the counter to the other.

Was he wondering why there were two knife blocks? Two different containers of utensils like spatulas and spoons?

I gave him a sheepish smile. "I'm kind of protective of my stuff. Especially my knives." Because my parents didn't cook much, and when they did—they were careless. "I don't know when the last time was they had theirs sharpened." Not to mention, mine were much higher quality.

Practically all the money I made went into building my collection of tools and specialty items. For Christmas, I'd gotten the pasta machine I'd asked for, and since we were running low on cabinet space, I'd had to bring it down from my bedroom this morning to roll out the dough for the raviolis.

I smashed the cloves of garlic under the thick blade of my knife, peeling away the skin, and got to mincing them. As the sharp edge of the blade rocked back and forth, making quick cuts, his focus dropped to it.

Or maybe he was looking at my hands. Did he notice the two scars dotting my fingers? I'd burned and nicked myself more than a few times over the last three years while doing prep work, but only two had been gnarly enough to leave scars. I wasn't ashamed of them—I wore them with pride. Every decent chef had them, along with desensitized hands from grabbing hot pans.

I'd earned my hands of steel after working many nights as the expediter at the window. The heavy plates waited under powerful heat lamps to keep the dishes warm, and sometimes they sat too long, baking the ceramic to well above one-hundred-fifty degrees.

He seemed fascinated as I worked, and it caused an

excited flutter inside me.

Cooking was the only area of my life where I wasn't shy. The head chef at *Vesuvio's* had seen to that. He hadn't wanted to hire me, but no one else had applied, so he made me pay for it every time I stepped on his line. He'd screamed and shouted and told me there was no fucking room for timid people in his kitchen, least of all a girl who was a high school senior.

It was fun getting to be confident in front of Preston, and it made me wonder. Was that how he'd feel when he gave me his lesson tonight? I was anxious to find out.

There was a tray in the fridge, covered by a damp towel, and beneath it were the raviolis I'd spent several hours crafting this morning. I'd had to make the dough, cook and portion the filling, and then seal each pillow closed while trying not to trap air in the pocket between the two sheets of pasta. I'd crimped the edges, then laid the raviolis out on the baking sheet so they'd be ready to go.

I took off the towel, dumped the pasta into the water, and turned my attention to the sauce.

I didn't use a recipe or any measurements because I'd made this dish many times before, plus I had a good sense of ratios. After adding the garlic to the bubbling butter, I estimated how much stock, cream, and parmesan to add. I seasoned, but when I used a spoon to taste the sauce, it wasn't quite there, so I added a touch more salt.

"Do you want some wine?" I used a mesh skimmer to fish the floating raviolis out of the pot and add them to the sauté pan, because they needed to finish in the sauce.

When he didn't answer, I glanced over and saw his confusion.

He was wondering how I, not yet twenty-one and with strict parents, had access to wine.

I quirked a smile. "My dad bought it for me. I told him I needed it for the recipe."

Now it was his turn to smile. It was just a little white lie I'd told my parents, but he approved, and wanted to participate in this rebellious act.

I jerked the pan to coat the pasta and nodded toward the fridge. "It's in there. Glasses are in the cabinet next to the sink."

He got up from his seat, retrieved the bottle of Pinot Grigio from inside the door, and then pulled down two wine glasses.

"Corkscrew?" he asked.

"Over here." I tugged open a drawer and plucked one out, holding it up for him to take.

We made a good team, him opening the bottle and pouring glasses while I halved the lemon and squeezed it over the ravioli, then pulled the garlic bread from the oven. He handed me the plates when I asked for them, I divided up the ravioli and bread, and then we carried our dinner and wine glasses to the kitchen table.

I was confident in my dish, but it didn't matter. My heart was still lodged in my throat as I watched Preston take his first bite.

His eyes widened as he stared at me. "Holy fuck, that's good." He went in for a second bite as if he needed confirmation the first one wasn't a fluke—which it wasn't. He sounded awestruck. "Jesus."

It made my knees weak to see his reaction and hear his praise. And he wasn't just saying it to be nice. This was genuine.

I used the side of my fork to cut a piece of pasta, and then swirled the bite in the sauce. The pasta was nice and tender, and while the sauce was rich, it wasn't too heavy.

"Seriously," he added between bites. "Any time you want to cook for me, feel free. You can be my personal chef."

I chuckled. "You couldn't afford me."

His eyes gleamed. "I could pay you with sex."

My breath caught. "You saying you'll give me more lessons?"

For a single heartbeat, he considered it, but then a smile spread across his face, and he shook his head. "I was just kidding." He took a sip of his wine, set the glass down, and his expression turned serious. "Also, I don't have a clue how much a personal chef makes."

"It depends on the job. One of the guys I worked with last summer took a job as some celebrity's chef. He said it was like a hundred thousand a year, but it was also six days a week."

"You ever consider doing it?"

"Yeah, I'd love to, someday. It's kind of my dream job, but no one is going to hire me without culinary training."

An odd, pleasant sensation flitted through me. No one outside of the restaurant ever asked me what I wanted to do. It was nice Preston seemed genuinely interested.

"Some chefs look down on it, you know," I added. "They

say private chefs can't hack it on the line or they aren't team players, but I don't think that's true at all. You're still on a team, it's just your coworkers are your clients instead of other chefs."

He nodded. "I get what you mean. My events are always better when the client participates in the planning and trusts me to get it done."

"That's the other thing that I like about going the private route, the menu planning. The variety. I wouldn't be cooking parts of the same twenty dishes every night."

He took another bite of his dinner. "Again, I get it." His tone was warm as he pointed to himself. "Big fan of planning right here."

We were quiet for a moment, simply enjoying each other's company.

"Can I ask you something?" A voice inside my head warned me not to do it, but I ignored it. "The girl you went on the date with. She was really pretty. How come you don't want to see her again?"

If there'd been a whiff of jealousy in my question, he hadn't noticed. He picked up his glass and took a sip while he considered how to answer. "I didn't know her when I asked her out, so I didn't realize we had nothing in common. There was no," he searched for the word, "spark, which sounds dumb, but it was true. I figured that out too late. Colin and I had just landed Troy's agency as a new account, and that girl? She's the owner's daughter."

The sting was immediate. "You asked her out?"

He looked, of all things, embarrassed. "Okay, yeah.

I told you I don't date, but that was a while ago. Things have changed."

Let it go, Sydney.

But I couldn't. "How so?"

Thankfully, my tone sounded more curious than anything else, and it made Preston shrug. "Back then, I didn't want anything serious. Now that school's over, things are different. All my friends have already found, like, their person. Colin, and Troy, and Cassidy—"

His expression abruptly went blank.

Her name had rolled off his tongue with ease, and it seemed he'd surprised himself. It certainly surprised me that he still considered her a friend after everything.

Or maybe his stunned look was caused by something else. Was he coming to terms with the idea that Cassidy's *person . . .* was his dad?

His gaze dropped to his plate, and he pushed the silverware around, straightening the place setting while trying to hide his discomfort.

"I remember what that was like." His voice wasn't as normal. "Having someone you want all the time." He made a face, displeased with himself. "I don't just mean sex, either. Someone you want to *be* around all the time."

When his focus lifted back to me, everything went still.

"I miss that," he said. "Sometimes it feels like I might not ever get to feel that way again." He frowned, and irritation edged his brown eyes. "It doesn't help that the girl I've spent the last year thinking about is off-limits."

His statement sent a shock wave through my body, and

even he wasn't immune to the effects of his truth bomb. It was obvious he hadn't meant to say it out loud, and panic streaked through his expression.

The silence stretched between us until it was taut, and as fragile as a souffle. Could he hear my heart as it thundered in my chest?

I barely whispered the question. "You spent the last year thinking about me?"

Abruptly, he moved. He stabbed his fork into the plate, picked up the last bite of a ravioli, and eyed it with suspicion. "What'd you put in this? Truth serum?"

"Preston." When he lifted his gaze, my words tumbled out in a rush. "I thought about you all the time, too."

He didn't look happy to hear it, though. "Don't tell me that. I don't want to know."

"Why not?"

His intense stare was back, drilling down into me. "You know why."

I opened my mouth to try to convince him, but just then a figure appeared in the kitchen doorway, silencing the conversation.

My father's expression was pure dismay as he stared back at us, and it grew to anger as his gaze swept over the table, noting the meal I'd prepared, and the two wine glasses.

Anxiety and excitement mixed inside me.

How would he react? If he told Preston to leave, what excuse would he give? As far as he could tell, we weren't doing anything but having dinner. One that maybe looked romantic, although I'd told Preston it wasn't. Plus, a half a glass of wine for me wasn't a big deal, and Preston was twenty-four. He hadn't done anything to warrant my father kicking him out.

But he hovered in the doorway with narrow eyes, looking like he was considering doing just that.

If he did, there'd be hell to pay.

I'd reached my breaking point with them controlling me, and it seemed like my father sensed that. Changing the deal we'd struck about culinary school was one thing, but if he tried to tell me who I was and wasn't allowed to hang out with, he knew that'd be pushing me too far. The final straw.

So, he said nothing. He marched to the fridge, pulled out a can of soda, and then couldn't seem to get out of the kitchen quick enough.

As soon as he was gone, a thrilled look overtook Preston's face. He'd enjoyed making my dad uncomfortable almost as much as I had.

"If he doesn't like me in his kitchen," his tone was full of corruption, "imagine how much he'll hate it when you take me upstairs to your bedroom."

Oh, my god. Heat pooled inside my body at his devilish smile. He was going to give me my next lesson *here*? It was so wrong and bad.

Fuck, I couldn't wait to do it.

When we'd finished our dinner, I attempted to clear the table, but Preston launched to his feet. "The rule at my house is whoever makes the food doesn't have to do the dishes."

While I appreciated the gesture, I convinced him it'd be faster if we did it together, so we half-assed our way through them, and then he followed me up the stairs. I was sure my dad knew I was headed to my bedroom, and that I wasn't going alone, either.

The stairs creaked under our feet as we ascended them.

Anxiety made my breath go shallow when we entered my room. Not because I was nervous about what was going to happen. It was because Preston Lowe was in my bedroom.

It felt so private. Intimate. He was seeing the place where my crush for him had grown. The location of so many of my fantasies. And the bed where I slept every night, where I sometimes got off while thinking about him.

I was so distracted by my thoughts I didn't notice what he was doing until my bedroom door clicked shut.

No, a loud, angry voice boomed in my head, making me jolt.

It had sounded exactly like my father, and the memory came flooding back. I was in eighth grade when Colin had a girl over for the first time. They'd gone into his bedroom, and when my father had discovered the door shut, he'd yelled the word so forcefully, my mother and I had come running to see what was wrong.

I grabbed the doorknob, twisted, and pulled. "No, it has to stay open."

His lips parted, and for a moment, he looked too stunned to speak. Then irritation lifted his eyebrows. "Seriously? That's fucking ridiculous." He asked it even when he knew the answer. "Aren't you twenty years old?"

"Yes." I gave him the same reasoning I'd given to anyone else I'd brought up here. "But it's their house. I have to follow their rules."

His gaze swept over the space, taking in the room that was just large enough to contain a full-sized bed, an end table and dresser, and a closet that was so packed with clothes, I hadn't been able to shut the sliding door for years.

I'd tried to tidy up my bedroom before he came over, but even with the bed made and the never-ending laundry from work put away, it still looked messy. His focus went back to the door that stood wide open.

"Maybe we should go back to my place," he offered.

I sucked in a breath. On the one hand, I wanted to be alone with him, where no one would interrupt us. But on the other . . . "Are you worried about us getting caught?"

My question caught him off guard. "Aren't you?"

"Yeah, but," my voice was hushed, "is it weird if I find the idea kind of exciting?"

Messing around with any boy in my room was dangerous, but with him? It would be flirting with disaster. When my parents caught Colin having sex, they'd kicked him out of the house.

So, the stakes were high, and yet I longed to do it. I wanted it almost as badly as I wanted Preston, and nervous, eager energy fluttered inside me.

I'd told him I thought the danger was exciting, and his grin was slow and sexy. "Oh, you do?"

The heat radiating from him was so strong, all I could

do was nod.

He surveyed the room with fresh eyes and seemed to change his mind about leaving when his focus zeroed in on the full-length mirror by the closet. It was a cheap one I'd bought for my dorm room that came home with me each summer. So, it wasn't mounted to anything right now. Instead, it leaned against the corner of the open closet door, giving us an angle of the far side of the bed.

He strolled toward it, only to slow when his attention snagged on the pinboard hanging above the dresser. What was he looking at? One side of the board was dry-erase, and I'd scribbled some menu ideas on it. The other side had random items pinned in a haphazard fashion. A 'save the date' card for my cousin's wedding. An old pamphlet I'd gotten from the Culinary Institute of America. A picture of me with Colin last year at his graduation ceremony—

Shit.

Was Preston remembering how we were going behind my brother's back? I needed to keep him from thinking about it.

"You want to watch a movie?" I asked quickly. "I've got Netflix on my laptop."

"No." His tone was cryptic as he resumed moving. He rounded the end of the bed, and sat on the pale gray bedspread, facing the mirror so I could see his expression. Like his tone, it was unreadable. "Come here."

The intense stare he gave me was no less powerful when it was reflected through the mirror. It made the air in the room go thin, and my blood heat. I swallowed thickly and put one foot in front of the other, bringing myself to stand in front of him.

It wasn't hard to read his expression now.

Desire teemed in his eyes, and he stretched out a hand, grazing it over my legs as he played with the ruffle at the hem of my skirt.

"I meant to tell you," smoke filled his voice, "how hot you look in this dress." His hand slipped under the edge of the fabric, and the backs of his fingers ghosted across the bare skin of my thighs. "You knew what you were doing when you put it on, didn't you? You wanted to look like a cocktease."

My lips fell open, but only so I could draw in a sharp breath. I had worn the sundress because I thought it was cute and I'd hoped he'd like it, but this reaction . . .

God, it was so much better.

"I can practically see your tits through it." He wasn't scolding me—he was thrilled I'd opted not to wear a bra. He was damn near drooling as he stared up at me. "It makes me want to touch them."

The softest sigh escaped my lips, but he heard it loud and clear. His fingers slipped between my knees and glided up the inside of my thigh at a painfully slow pace. I got the impression his teasing touch was payback for how my dress had teased him.

It was instinctive the way my gaze flicked to the open bedroom door, checking to see if anyone was there. It was un-necessary because I'd hear anyone coming up the stairs, but—

Better safe than sorry.

His palm inched up, nearly to my underwear, only to stroke back down disappointingly toward my knee. It made me shudder with anticipation and longing, and perhaps the tiniest bit of frustration. I was impatient, ready to do more, and although he'd barely touched me, I was already on fucking fire.

Up he stroked a second time, his fingers tracing a line across my sensitized skin. In response, my knees wobbled. It made it so hard to stand.

His smile only reached his eyes. "You want to sit down?"

I'd expected him to pull me down into his lap so I was straddling him like we'd done in his back seat, but instead he shifted back on the bed and widened his legs, making room for me.

"Turn around," he said. "Put your back to me."

I hated being controlled, and yet I liked it a lot when he told me what to do. It just felt easier. Natural. *Right*. Plus, I wasn't as worried about doing something dumb or awkward.

I turned and sat in the space he'd created, and when my gaze went forward, I found his in the mirror. My heart stopped at the sight of us. I understood why he was apprehensive about us dating, but couldn't he see how good we looked together?

My eyelids went heavy as he leaned in and set his damp, warm mouth on my shoulder, just beside the thin strap that was looped into a bow there. While his gentle kisses marched across my skin, his hands grasped my waist.

"How bad," he said in a hush, "does the good girl want to be tonight?"

There was no other answer. The word poun
in my brain.

"*Bad*," I breathed.

ELEVEN

Sydney

Preston made a sound of satisfaction, and it caused a sharp ache deep between my legs. I softened back into him on the side of the bed, wanting to become dough that he could twist and pull and shape into whatever form he desired.

The tip of his nose traced a line up my neck. It was sensual, and I was wholly unprepared for how seductive he could be. I stared at us in the mirror, curling an arm back behind his head while his hands drifted lower toward my lap.

"You still want my fingers inside you?"

His question doused me in lava, and I gasped. "Yes."

He peered at my reflection, and the carnal look that lurked in his eyes . . . shit, it was so hot. He looked at me like I was an expertly prepared dish he was ready to devour.

"You'll have to be quiet," he reminded.

I nodded quickly in understanding, and my gaze locked on to the mirror, focusing on the way his hands rested on my thighs. His fingers were splayed out, and he began to curl them in, making the skirt of my dress creep up.

He said it so quietly, I wondered if I'd imagined it. Had he somehow spoken only inside my head? "Open your legs for me."

I didn't know how I did it. Everything in me was anxious

and excited, and my body was no longer communicating with my brain, but my knees parted. My legs slid open wide enough that my thighs were touching the insides of his, and my skirt rode up even farther.

When a hint of my panties was exposed, that seemed to be the signal Preston needed. His right hand abandoned my skirt and went to my center to cup me, letting the heat of his palm soak through the whisper-thin fabric covering my most intimate part.

My underwear was pale pink satin, and when he stroked his fingertips over it, the pleasure was so acute, I tried to pinch my knees together. He wasn't deterred, though. He did it again, and *again*, and I bucked in response, my legs jerking erratically back open,

"Oh," I groaned, "*fuck.*"

I wasn't in control of my body, but I didn't care. His mouth was at the pulse point in my neck, and I tightened my grip on the hair at the back of his head. I was powerless in my enjoyment as his touch stroked up over the front of my panties and when his fingers inched beneath the waist, breath hung in my lungs.

Finally.

His skilled fingertips found my clit and strummed it, moving beneath the pink satin, and satisfaction bolted through my center. I clenched my free hand on his knee, enduring the stroke of his fingers that was so pleasurable, I wondered if I'd turn into liquid.

"You know what I'd do if Mommy and Daddy weren't downstairs right now?" His voice was hypnotic as it invaded my mind. "I'd untie the knots holding up your dress and peel it down. I'd get you fucking naked so fast."

His fingers rubbed faster, drawing a moan from me, and I saw the visual of it so perfectly, it felt like I was experiencing it. In my head, I felt the knots at my shoulder tug free and the fabric glide down to expose my breasts to him.

"And then," he murmured against the shell of my ear, "I'd put my tongue inside you and make you come on my face."

He slid a finger deep inside me, causing my lips to round into a silent '*oh.*' I arched at the intrusion, enjoying the sensation. I felt possessed. Claimed by him in a way I'd wanted for so long. My breathing was ragged and my head foggy with lust, so all I could do was stare at the erotic scene playing out before us in the mirror.

He affected a disappointed tone. "But I can't do any of that. Just imagine what would happen if your parents walked in right now and caught me with my head between their little girl's legs, my lips buried in her virgin pussy."

"Oh, my god," I moaned, and I wasn't quiet either.

It was all too wrong, and too fucking sexy for me not to think about.

I pictured him on his knees at the side of the bed, my thighs perched on his shoulders as his tongue lashed at me. And I heard my parents' voices over my shoulder yelling *how dare you do this in my house.*

They shouted what a bad girl I'd become.

"Shh," Preston teased, although maybe he was halfway serious. I'd been kind of loud.

A cocky smile glanced across his lips, hinting at his

thoughts, and then his hand that had been resting on my thigh moved. It rose and landed on my collarbone before sliding down inside the top of my dress. As he palmed my breasts, his other hand worked below my waist.

Shit, his fingers. They alternated between rubbing my clit and plunging inside me, and my overwhelmed mind had no idea which sensation I liked more. They were both so good.

Without thought, I turned my head toward him. Looking at him in the mirror was nice, but seeing him up close and without the glass between us? That was even better, and the urge to kiss him was so crushing, I had no choice but to surrender to it.

My eyes fluttered close as his mouth captured mine, and he seemed happy to drink up my little whimpers of pleasure. My chest heaved and my heart pounded in my ears, and need built inside my center like the temperature rising in a pressure cooker.

His greedy hands seemed to be everywhere, touching me in ways and places no one had done before. I was so lost in him and his kiss, I hadn't realized how loud my moans had become until it was too late.

He drew back and scrutinized me with narrow eyes. "Are you going to be good and stay quiet for me?" He didn't pause long enough for me to answer. "Here. I'll help you."

The finger buried inside me retreated. It was so he could grab at one side of my underwear and give it a tug down over my hip. My gaze snapped forward, watching in the mirror as he repeated the action on the other side, trying to work the pink satin down.

"Off," he commanded. "And then give them to me."

I swallowed so hard, I was sure he heard it. My hands shook as I did as told, but not because I was afraid. It was because I was so turned on, I was vibrating.

I'd barely pulled my panties over my ankles before he leaned forward and snatched them from my grasp. He balled them up tightly in his fist, and I sensed what was coming even before he said it out loud.

"Open your mouth."

Holy shit.

My jaw dropped open with shock, but it was exactly what he'd asked for, and I stopped breathing as my wadded-up underwear was pushed past my lips. The satin fabric filled my mouth, and for added effect, his palm sealed over my lips, suppressing any sound I might make.

My gaze was fixed on the image of us. My eyes were wide and unblinking, while he resumed what he'd been doing before with his hand between my now bare lower body. Only this time he used two fingers, pumping them in and out of me at a steady, deliberate pace. The stretch of them heightened my pleasure, as did the visual of his palm covering my mouth, holding in my damp panties and my desperate moans.

Adding to it all, one strap of my dress fell off my shoulder, and the weight of the bow tying the straps together was just heavy enough to make the top of my dress peel down. It snagged on my pebbled nipple for a moment before breaking free and exposing my breast. My gaze bounced from it, to his hand on my mouth, and then to the fingers moving between my thighs.

It was so fucking *erotic*.

Too hot to look at for more than a few seconds, and heat blazed in my cheeks. I'd never seen myself like that, and I had to fight the urge to tell myself I wasn't allowed to look that . . . sexual.

That *dirty*.

If one of my parents were to walk in right now, there'd be no coming back from this. And yet—I couldn't find the strength to care. All I could focus on was the way Preston caused pleasure to flood down my limbs. How he seemed to know exactly what I craved and how to give it to me.

"Have you ever touched yourself while thinking about me?" he asked.

The fire inside me burned infinitely hotter. I pressed my lips together beneath his palm and nodded.

He couldn't have looked more pleased if he'd tried. "I bet you did it right here in this bed, too." He said it like it was a simple request. "Show me."

My body stiffened and I choked off a sound of surprise. My shocked eyes stared at the mirror, wordlessly asking if he was serious.

"I want to see," he said. "Show me how you do it."

My heart tripped and stumbled. What he was asking was so personal. It was more intimate than anything else I'd ever done. Maybe even more than sex—although I wouldn't know for sure until I experienced that.

"A bad girl would do it," he urged.

It was my total undoing.

I let go of his hair, and as my hand slowly drifted down

my body, my gaze dropped to the bottom of the mirror. I was unable to look at him as my fingers wandered lower, reaching beneath the skirt bunched at my waist.

"*Fuck*," he swore the second my fingertips found the button of flesh just above the spot where his two middle fingers were driving into me. "Good girl. That's so fucking sexy."

His praise sent a wave of satisfaction washing over me, lighting my body up. My spine arched in response, and I had no choice but to set my other hand on the bed behind us for support.

I stirred my fingers faster, and with each tiny circuit, I was able to shed some of my shyness and lift my gaze to meet the reflection of his.

"You, Sydney,"—his breathing was hurried—"are the *hottest* goddamn thing I've ever seen."

His words poured more fire all over me, and my skin heated to a million degrees. His touch, paired with mine, felt so good, I wondered if it should be illegal.

As the tempo of his fingers increased, I rubbed faster to match. I gasped, panting for air through my nose, and the tension inside me was so intense, it was crushing. My noisy moans dripped through his fingers.

"You're still so loud." His tone was teasing. "Maybe you want to get caught."

Oh, my god. Was that true?

No, it couldn't be. The idea turned me on, but that was all it was. It carried serious, life-changing consequences I wasn't ready for. So, I made more of an effort to be quiet. To be the good girl he'd told me to be.

I could feel his erection at my back. The hard bulge pressed against the base of my spine, and I wanted him to experience at least a fraction of the pleasure he was giving me, so I reached behind myself and wedged my free hand between our bodies.

He seemed to know my intention and shifted to prevent my touch. "No," he whispered. "You focus on those fingers inside you—and being quiet when I make you come."

I shuddered and the muscles inside me clenched instinctively, which only made the sensation better. It was all too much. Not just the physical satisfaction, but the visual too. I'd been too shy to glance at us in the mirror at first, and now there was nowhere else to look.

I watched how his fingers, wet with my arousal, pumped in and out of me at a hurried pace. I saw the way my legs were spread wide, and how my fingers rubbed my clit, giving me sparks of bliss, all while he had his palm clamped over my mouth and his face right beside mine. His gaze was locked onto me, delivering a look so intense, how could I not shatter beneath it?

The panties trapped inside my mouth were soaked from my saliva, and as I came, I gnashed my teeth on them, squeezing until my jaw ached. The pleasure detonated and sent shockwaves of ecstasy radiating outward. It made me boneless, and I became a quivering mess in his hands.

My long, deep moan tried to escape from beneath his hand, but he wouldn't let it. His grip tightened, pressing harder on my lips and reminding me of the danger of being too loud.

My climax was much longer and more intense than anything else I'd ever had on this bed, and as it began to drain away, I wondered if he'd ruin orgasms for me. What if the ones I gave myself were never as satisfying as the ones he gave me? He was already two-for-two in that department, and I didn't want to get addicted.

My heart was still pounding, and my breath came and went in short bursts, but he seemed to sense the fireworks were over. His fingers retreated from my body, and as his hand fell away from my mouth, he pulled the panties out and dropped them to the carpet in a crumpled, damp-stained heap.

Even though I was weak with aftershocks from my orgasm, I somehow found the strength to turn my body toward him. I closed my knees and hitched them up over his legs so I was sideways to him, making it much easier for me to kiss him.

He welcomed it, too. All the passion we had with our previous kisses was there, but this one was decidedly more sexual. When his tongue slid against mine, I felt it *everywhere*. Heat pulsed in my center, reviving the ache he'd temporarily satisfied.

He felt that same ache.

The front of his shorts was tented, and I set a hand on his erection, smoothing my palm down the bulge. It made him groan and kiss me harder.

But it was awkward trying to touch him in this position, and after I fumbled my way through several strokes like that, I decided to move. I slid down off him and the edge of the bed, until I was on my knees in front of him. As I peered up at him and settled into my new position, I tugged the strap of my dress back up onto my shoulder, covering myself.

His chest rose with a deep breath as he studied me. It was like he was weighing the pros and cons of what I was getting ready to do, and he looked so incredibly conflicted. He didn't have much to lose. My parents disliked him, and so if they caught us in a compromising situation, the worst they could do was throw him out.

Maybe they'd call his dad and tell him, but that was doubtful, and Dr. Lowe probably wouldn't care anyway. His son was an adult. Plus, Dr. Lowe was dating Preston's ex, so it was unlikely he'd punish his son for anything these days.

No, I was the one who had everything to lose tonight.

If my parents caught us, I wouldn't just get kicked out. I'd get cut off, meaning I'd lose out on a place to live, my future, and probably any chance of my parents reconciling with my brother.

And yet, I couldn't stop myself from making the wrong decision. My hands walked up his thighs.

I'd held back everything I'd wanted to do for too long. I'd been good and walled it off, but time added weight and stress fractures, and then my parents' betrayal caused catastrophic failure. Now all my desires and the bad things I'd wanted for years came tumbling out, and I was powerless to control them or myself.

I curled my fingers around the waist of Preston's shorts, trying to work the button free.

"You weren't fucking around about wanting to be bad,"

he said in a low, dark voice.

He pushed my hands away, but it was only so he could move. He climbed down off the bed, joining me on the floor, except he shifted toward the end of the bed, making it so he wasn't in front of the mirror. He sat on the carpet, leaned back against the side of the box spring and mattress, and undid his fly.

When he pushed the shorts and underwear down over his hips, his dick bounced free. It was thick and impossibly hard, and blood rushed to my face. I wasn't seeing him naked for the first time, and yet it felt that way. Maybe because we were in my bedroom and the door was open, and danger swirled around us.

He reached for my waist and pulled me toward his lap. Sex glittered in his gorgeous eyes as he issued his command. "Come here."

Holy shit.

TWELVE

Preston

I had hold of Sydney's waist, but when I urged her to climb on top of me, she froze with shock. Trepidation seemed to fill every inch of her body.

Shit.

I hadn't meant I wanted her to jump on my dick right now, but I got why she'd thought that.

"Not sex," I clarified. "Just some more practice."

She was dubious as she repeated the word. "Practice."

"Yeah. Like we did in my back seat." Except this time, there wouldn't be any clothes in our way. "I want you to get comfortable with the feeling of *this*," I stroked a fist over my cock, "between your legs. Not inside you, just rubbing against you."

Her gaze followed the slow glide of my hand as it moved back and forth, and the longer she looked, the more interested she became. I'd watched her touch herself, and it had been so fucking hot, it only seemed fair to return the favor.

While she considered my request, it dawned on me how fucking risky it'd be if she said yes. Not just because her parents were downstairs and her bedroom door was open, either, which was fucking insane. It was risky because letting her rub her pussy on my bare cock meant we'd only be a heartbeat away from sex.

One wrong move by either of us, and I might accidentally slide inside her.

And without a condom on.

I'd made a fuck-ton of mistakes when it came to women, but this was the one area where I never screwed up. My parents didn't give me details on how I'd been conceived, thankfully, and as soon as I was old enough to understand, it was apparent I wasn't planned.

They'd never married, and I didn't know if they had dated for long or if I was the product of a one-night stand. But they were both honest about how in college, they had been young and stupid and hadn't used protection.

So, it had been drilled into me that I should be more responsible than they had been. I *always* used condoms. I wasn't ready to be a father any more than my dad had been.

The thought vaporized away as Sydney grabbed the hem of her dress, hitched a leg over my lap, and positioned herself over me. I steadied her with both of my hands on her hips, but she wobbled—

Wait, no. She was fucking trembling.

She paused as she hovered over me on her knees, the skirt of her dress held up and pinned to her stomach under one of her hands. It meant I could see the tiny landing strip she had maintained just above her slit, and her pussy was only an inch away from my dick.

This hesitation . . . did it mean she didn't trust me? I hated the idea. And I hated that fucking guy in her past, the one who'd pushed and scared her.

My heart dropped into my stomach. Was that what I was doing now?

"We don't have to if you don't—" I started.

But she shook her head. "No, I *want* to." She didn't just sound genuine, she was adamant. "I just, uh, need a second."

"Sure," I said instantly.

I should have told her to take all the time she wanted. I was perfectly happy to enjoy the view. But she exhaled slowly and eased herself down, settling on top of my lap and trapping my cock between our bodies.

All thought ceased when her damp skin made contact with me.

"*Fuck*," we swore together.

How the hell did that feel so good? She hadn't even moved yet. It had to be the danger of her open door heightening the sensation. I let go of her waist so I could lift a hand and brush a lock of her hair back out of her face. It'd fallen in the way, and I didn't like that.

I needed to see everything she felt reflected in her expressive face, with nothing between the connection of our bodies or our gazes.

The irises of her eyes were a blue-gray, and the color seemed to darken when she made the first tentative rock of her hips. Or maybe that was just my vision blurring from how incredible the slick glide of her pussy was.

Her hands gripped the sides of my face as she leaned in, and our mouths crashed together. Jesus Christ, the way she undulated her hip was going to kill me. My heart fell out of rhythm, and then sped faster.

Her soft moan mingled with mine, and worry crawled over me. She'd struggled to stay quiet when I was focused on her. How loud would we be if we got off together? Could my mouth pressed to hers be enough to suppress the fire building inside us?

Maybe this had been a bad idea because I wanted her so fucking much, it was painful. The heat of her body wrapped around me made it hard to focus on anything else. My mouth drifted down from hers, ending up on her collarbone as her chest heaved with her labored breath. And my hands were on her bare ass beneath her skirt, guiding her to ride my erection faster.

If someone were to walk in right now, at first glance, we probably wouldn't look *that* bad. Yes, my shorts were undone and pushed down, but the skirt of her dress was covering that. They wouldn't know how dangerously close to sex we were or that she wasn't wearing any underwear.

Unless they, like, saw her panties on the floor beside us.

I took my hand off her, grabbed the sexy pink underwear, and tossed it under the bed so it'd be out of view. And then I was back under her skirt, gripping a handful of her perfect little ass.

When my sensitive tip brushed against her clit, she whimpered, and I liked knowing that the way she was rubbing herself on me gave us both satisfaction. She was sliding her hips back and forth, and beneath her, I moved in shallow thrusts. Her rapid breath was punctuated by little gasps and moans.

Was she getting close?

I was greedy, wanting to watch her come again. I loved seeing her eyes pinch shut and her face twist with ecstasy, and I *really* loved knowing I was the only person on this earth who'd gotten to see it.

As hot as it was fucking around with her parents just downstairs, my body was kind of over it. It begged me to shift and nudge and encourage her to line us up so I could push inside her.

No.

The voice inside my head was loud and pissed at me for even thinking about it for one hot second.

I didn't want her first time to be like this—some fast, quiet fuck. She deserved more than that, and I'd promised to show her a good time. Plus, I'd grown to love planning things, and I had plenty of ideas of how I thought our first time together should go.

I'd already drafted my next lesson plan in my head.

Could I do it tonight? If I asked her again to go back to my place, would all of the evening count as the same lesson? Because I only had so many, and I wanted to use them wisely.

When my lips found hers again, I plotted my next move. Maybe if I—

There was a creak off in the distance from somewhere deep inside the house, and Sydney's body went rigid. It only lasted for a microsecond, and then she was spurred into action. She bolted off my lap and her hands flew to the undone sides of my shorts, trying to jerk them up.

The alarm in her face said it all. *Someone's coming.*

I took over, pulling everything up to my waist and my

hurried hands worked to zip my fly closed over my hard-on. When she saw I had the task of getting dressed handled, she shifted gears and scrambled for one of the decorative pillows on her bed.

If I wasn't so concerned about getting us covered, I might have admired how great we worked together as a team. As she tossed the pillow into my lap, I jerked out my phone, and unlocked the screen at lightning speed. I swiped to the You-Tube icon, and as soon as I had the app launched, I smashed a finger on the first video to appear in my feed.

Footsteps padded into the room, and her father's voice teemed with suspicion. "What are you doing?"

"Nothing." Sydney turned to glance over her shoulder at him, and her guilty voice announced this was a lie. "Preston was just showing me a video on his phone."

It was at this moment we realized what was playing on-screen. It was a video comparing waxing your chest versus shaving it.

Well, fuck.

I didn't need to see his expression to know he wasn't buying what we were selling. But I stopped the video and slowly turned my shoulders so I could give him my attention.

His eyes were piercing and full of animosity as he glared back at me. He disliked everything about this situation. How I was in her room, and why we were weirdly sitting on the floor behind her bed, and that she'd lied about what we were doing.

But he didn't have any proof that we'd done something wrong.

We'd followed his rules. The door had been left obnoxiously wide open.

"I think it's time for Preston to head home." It wasn't a request from him. This was a decree.

"What? Why?" Confusion drove her focus to the clock on the nightstand. "It's early. My curfew isn't for another ninety minutes."

Curfew?

Sweet Jesus. The poor girl.

Mr. Novak shifted on his feet and put a hand on his waist. "I need him to move his car so I can back out of the garage."

As far as lies went, it was plausible—but this reason was also bullshit.

When we'd returned from mini-golf, I'd made sure to keep my Charger to one side of their wide, long driveway, and I'd also parked more than a car's length away from the garage. There was plenty of room to back out.

Unless the asshole didn't know how to drive.

"Where are you going?" She sounded just as skeptical as I felt.

"The store."

Hmm. So descriptive and believable.

"For what?" she demanded.

His story was likely as true as when she'd said we were just watching videos, but I couldn't exactly call her dad out on it.

But I could make him uncomfortable.

Thank fuck I'd worn this pair of shorts tonight. The canvas was thick and heavy, meaning my flagging erection would be pretty easy to hide. I set the pillow aside, and as I stood, I dug my car keys out of my pocket and used that as an excuse to adjust myself while my back was facing him.

"It's okay." I turned toward the door and the man lurking there and forced casualness into my voice. "I'm ready to call it a night, anyway."

"You are?" She sounded surprised and disappointed, and I got that. I would have rather stayed where we were, too, but now her cockblocking dad was here, and I was sure he'd find other reasons to come upstairs and interrupt us if I stayed.

And finding out she had a curfew? Well, that ruled out her coming over to my place tonight because I didn't want to rush things. I couldn't do that if I was worried about getting the good girl home in time.

I leveled my gaze at Mr. Novak. "I don't want to overstay my welcome."

He stared right back at me dead in the eye. "Great. I'll walk you out."

I nodded and offered my hand to help Sydney up from the floor, but she stared at it like the conversation had moved too fast for her.

"Thanks for dinner," I said. "It was awesome."

She seemed conflicted. She was pleased I'd enjoyed her food, but she was unhappy I was leaving, and she sighed before finally accepting my offered hand.

"You're welcome." As soon as I had her pulled to her feet, a smile ghosted across her lips. "Thanks for letting me win at golf."

Her comment landed a direct hit, and I chuckled.

If the roles had been reversed, I would have said the same thing to her, and fuck me. It made me hot for her all over again. And it also made a devious idea pop into my head. I didn't just want to make Mr. Novak uncomfortable . . .

I wanted to go for the jugular.

My hand tightened on hers, holding her in place as I leaned in and planted a kiss square on her lips. She was too stunned to move, and it was unclear who was more surprised by what I'd done—her or her dad.

When I pulled back, her eyes were hazy and unfocused, and it sort of looked like my kiss had left her drunk. I shouldn't have liked that idea, but warmth rolled through my chest.

"Talk to you later," I said.

Her voice was uneven, still adrift. "Yeah."

Mr. Novak was silent as he marched down the steps, but he wordlessly demanded I follow him. His swift feet carried him toward the front door, and I had to move at a fast clip to keep up.

Shit, this guy couldn't wait to be rid of me. He jerked the door open and then set the full force of his disapproving glare on me.

"Just friends, huh?" he said bitterly.

I nodded, and since he threw our lie in my face, I did the same to him right before ducking outside. "Have fun at the *store*."

I'd barely hit the first porch step when I heard the door shut behind me, and a grin burned across my lips. Once I was seated behind the wheel of my Charger, I thumbed out a text message to Sydney.

Preston: Sorry for bailing. I'll make it up to you at our next lesson. Until then, I have an assignment for you.

Her response came quickly.

Sydney: You're giving me homework?

Preston: Yes. You should think about me whenever you jerk off.

I pictured her seated on the side of her bed, staring at the phone in her hand while a blush flashed across her cheeks. Had she put her pink panties back on yet, or was she still bare under her dress? I dropped a hand between my legs and squeezed against the ache in my dick.

Sydney: Will you be doing the same?

Was she kidding?

Preston: You better fucking believe it.

Sydney: Okay. I'll do your homework.

Preston: Good girl.

Last month, Distinguished Events had acquired enough random shit that we'd had to rent a small storage unit. Up until then, I'd had all the boxes stacked to one side of the spare room my dad was letting me use as an office. But it had gotten out of hand after the Wilkerson wedding.

They'd been indecisive and had money to burn, which

was a dangerous combination. It was why my company now owned three hundred gold charging plates. The bride had been obsessed with them, so she'd ponied up the cash, had us take delivery, and the week before the wedding she declared they didn't fit her vision.

I tried to return them, but the company refused since the window had closed months ago, and the bride didn't seem to care.

"You can keep them," she'd said.

They were brand new, nice, and relatively generic. I wasn't sure if I'd find a use for them with a future client, or if I should try to sell them—but one thing was certain. I was out of space to store them at my house.

I was unloading the last box from the trunk of my car when my phone buzzed with a message.

> **Sydney:** I'm free tonight. The restaurant is closed on Mondays.

I'd texted her today when I arrived at the storage unit and asked about her schedule. It'd been three days since our 'date,' and I was more than ready to give her my next lesson.

I probably would have caved and asked to see her sooner, but my weekend had been dominated by the wedding. Plus, Friday and Saturday nights were the busiest for her, too.

Over this summer while she lived with her parents, those nights were the only ones when she didn't have a curfew, and it was because she usually wasn't done cleaning up her station at the restaurant until after eleven.

I knew all the details about her parents' terrible curfews

because I'd been talking to her every day. It had started with a simple flirty text from me the morning after our date, asking how she had done with her homework. I hadn't meant it to turn into anything more, or some big conversation—but it had. She was easy to talk to.

And she wasn't my girlfriend.

It meant I could say whatever I wanted and not worry about impressing her or if I might come off self-centered. I could just be me. The whole thing was relaxed. Low pressure. Surprisingly effortless.

But if we were getting together tonight, I'd need to put forth some serious effort. My bedroom was a fucking disaster.

I dropped the box on top of the others in the corner of the unit and fired off a text.

Preston: Tonight works for me. Pick you up at 7?

Sydney: See you then!

I began drafting my plan of attack. The first order of business when I got home would be laundry. It'd been an embarrassingly long time since I'd washed my sheets, and if everything went the way I hoped it would tonight, we'd definitely be using my bed.

The image leapt into my mind. Sydney, naked and tangled in my sheets. Her hair was spread out on my pillow and her face was sweaty and flushed because I'd just fucked her brains out—

"Preston."

I turned to find Colin standing beneath the rolled-up door, backlit by the bright sun outside. He tilted his head as he peered at me, looking like he'd been trying to get my attention for a while.

"Hey, man." He grinned. "I know I'm late, but you don't have to ignore me."

"Sorry. I didn't hear you."

Because I was too busy thinking about fucking your little sister.

I knew he was coming to help with the boxes, but I wasn't prepared to see him. Guilt sat heavy on my shoulders and chest, making me feel like a piece of shit. He'd been there for me, the closest thing I'd ever had to a brother, and this was how I repaid him? Doing the one thing he asked me not to?

It was betrayal.

And yet I felt powerless to stop it. I wanted Sydney too much to turn back now.

Fuck. I was a terrible friend.

Colin strolled inside the storage unit and jerked his head toward the stack of new boxes. "You finish already? You should have waited. I would have helped."

"It's fine. There weren't that many." My gaze shifted away, landing on the clear plastic container where we stored stuff for bachelorette parties. It was full of pink and white feather boas and more dick-themed items than I could have ever imagined.

"Madison came home for lunch," he added, "and I got . . . distracted."

"Hope you got some good content," I teased.

"You know, sometimes we fuck just because we want to, right?" he said lightly. "There doesn't need to be a camera rolling."

I shrugged. "Okay."

He'd been shooting porn for two years, and I was fine with that, but every once in a while, I remembered how wild it was. Strangers paid to watch my friend and his girlfriend do *everything*, including other people.

I had mad respect for them because I couldn't do it. Even if I had that much confidence in my body, and my game, to put it all out there, I couldn't picture myself having a strong enough relationship where I was sure my partner would come back after being with someone else.

I was far too competitive to share.

But the voyeur aspect? Yeah. That wouldn't bother me at all. It was kind of hot.

"I'm not saying we didn't record it, though." Colin flashed me a guilty smile. "Sorry I didn't get here sooner." He glanced around the space before refocusing on me. "What else needs to get done?"

"We need to talk about Troy's launch party. Did you see the email from Warbler?"

The biggest thing we needed to discuss was changes to the VIP section, now that they'd confirmed Stella would be attending as a special guest. She was a massive star, and had been the one to help launch Troy's career, but her attendance came with challenges. We'd need more space for her people in the VIP area, which meant we'd have to adjust the layout with the furniture rental company.

"Yeah," he said. "I have some ideas about that."

There was a coffee shop nearby, and we spent the next

ninety minutes there with our laptops, dividing and con-
quering our punch list for the event. We'd found our rhythm
as co-owners over the last year. He was the negotiator, the
marketer, and the money, whereas I managed the planning
and design.

Once we'd tackled all the things we wanted to discuss, I
began to pack up my things.

Colin eyed me with interest. "You in a hurry?"

Yeah, I need to clean my room so I can bang your sister.

I swallowed hard. "Uh, not really, but I—"

"You remember Mads' friend Jen? She was at the
barbeque."

Last month, Colin and Madison had hosted a Memorial
Day thing with all their friends.

"Vaguely," I lied because I hadn't remembered being interested in anyone that day. It was probably because I'd been
too hung up on Sydney. "Why?"

"She asked me if you're single."

I slowed to a stop with my laptop only halfway inside
its protective sleeve and stared at him. Hopefully, the dread
I felt wasn't displayed on my face, and I forced indifference
into the word. "Yeah?"

"Mads was wondering if the four of us could hang out
some time." He'd tried to sound nonchalant, but he'd failed.

I finished putting my laptop away and narrowed my
eyes. "Like a double date?"

Colin lifted a hand in a gesture that said *you got me.* "I
think you'd like her. She's . . . fun."

What the fuck did that mean? He'd said it like it was

some sort of code word and gave me a knowing look.

Oh, shit. In the past he'd introduced some of his coworkers to me as *friends*.

My tone was heavy with annoyance. "I'm not cool going out with someone you guys have worked with."

Colin made a face. "What? No. I was trying to tell you she's," he searched for the right phrase, "not picky with guys." He chuckled. "Mads knows her from before. They were sorority sisters."

"Not picky?" I repeated, momentarily offended.

He had the audacity to look at me like I needed to get real. "I could say the same thing about you."

In the past, he would have been right. I wasn't the most selective when it came to getting laid. But now?

Well, now I was *highly* selective. As in, there was only one girl I wanted.

"Think I'm gonna pass," I said dryly.

It was like I'd just told him I didn't like sex. His expression hung with confusion. "Why? She's cute enough to give her one date."

It wasn't warm in the coffee shop, but I began to sweat anyway. "I'm not interested in dating right now."

He looked dumbfounded. "Didn't you ask out the receptionist at Warbler right after we closed with them?"

"That was a mistake," I grumbled. Except if I hadn't gone on that lackluster date with Charlotte, I wouldn't have run into Sydney.

So, *was* it a mistake?

He laughed. "No shit. I tried to warn you."

"You did." I put my laptop sleeve into my bag and drained the last of my drink while trying to come up with a new excuse. "I'm going to hit pause on dating," I said, "and focus on me right now."

His expression filled with disbelief. "You're going to . . ." Abruptly, he shook his head and his tone turned sarcastic. "Okay. I'm sure that'll be a huge change for you."

THIRTEEN

Sydney

I'd put on more eye shadow than my mother thought was appropriate. Ever since they'd reneged on our deal, I'd looked for ways to test my parents. To push their boundaries. My clothes and makeup were excellent pressure points, so tonight I loaded my brush with the darkest gray shadow in my palette and went to town.

I was sitting on the couch in the front room, waiting for Preston, when my mom spotted me, and she made her displeasure known with a raised eyebrow.

Her tone verged on patronizing. "You look nice. Going somewhere?"

"To a movie with a friend."

It was stunning how easily it rolled off my tongue, but she inhaled sharply, making me wonder if my lie hadn't been as convincing as I'd thought. Her gaze scrutinized every inch of my body, examining my teal sleeveless top and black shorts. My outfit was too nice for a simple movie night hang.

"Is this friend named Preston?" She asked it when she already knew the answer.

"So what if it is?"

The sound she made was a mixture of irritation and disappointment. "You know I don't care for that boy."

"Why?"

My question caught her off-guard, and she paused, unsure how to respond.

I'd always suspected my parents' dislike stemmed from how Preston and his dad had undercut their attempt to punish my brother. When they'd kicked him out with only a month left of high school, they'd expected him to struggle and come groveling back.

Instead, he'd landed at one of the nicest houses in our small suburb, with an in-ground pool, and no curfew. Freedom to do whatever he wanted with whoever he wanted. God, my parents had *hated* that. I'd had to convince them to let Colin come home, and if he hadn't needed support for college, I probably would have needed to convince him, too.

I was curious what answer my mom would give me. If she'd tell me the truth.

Her shoulders straightened. "His father's dating a girl half his age. The same one who used to be his son's girlfriend. It's," she contemplated the right word, "unseemly."

I blinked. "And how is that Preston's fault?"

She was so stunned I'd pushed back, she literally retreated. She took a step back and her mouth dropped open. "I don't know what's gotten into you recently, but this new attitude of yours? It sucks." Her expression hardened. "Do I have him to thank for that?"

I rolled my eyes, and a split second later, a text message popped up on my phone.

Preston: I'm here.

My heart stumbled over itself with excitement.

Sydney: Coming out.

I rose from the couch, but only made it a few steps toward the door.

"I don't think you should see him anymore," she said. "He was a bad influence on your brother, and now he's doing the same thing to you."

She seriously thought Preston had corrupted Colin, like he'd turned my brother against them, when it had been their iron grip that had done it. A dark part inside me wanted to give her a sneering smile and tell her she had no idea just how much I planned to let Preston corrupt me.

But instead, I pushed a lock of hair back over my shoulder and gave her a firm look. "You control enough of my life. You don't get to tell me who I'm allowed to be friends with."

I didn't wait for her to respond. I marched to the front door, yanked it open, and walked through it. When I pulled it closed behind me, its loud thud echoed a period at the end of a statement.

"Hi, friend," I said to Preston when I got into the passenger seat.

He shot me a confused, amused look. "Hey there."

As I buckled my seatbelt, I felt his gaze wander suggestively over my bare legs, and my pulse jumped. Blood rushed to heat my face. I loved the way he made me feel, and I tried to imprint this as a memory I'd hold on to, because by my count, we only had three lessons left.

We had to make them count.

"Ready?" he asked.

He'd only meant if I was ready to go, but I swallowed a breath, feeling like his question went deeper. I peered up at his handsome face, feeling more confident than ever. "Ready."

He put the car in gear, backed out of the driveway, and once we'd started down the street, his hand came off the steering wheel. He didn't rest it casually in his lap, though. The warmth of his palm slid onto the top of my thigh, resting just above my knee.

I gasped and my gaze darted to him, but his expression was plain. He didn't even bother to take his eyes off the road. "What?" he challenged. "I felt like touching you. It's not a big deal."

I smashed my lips together to hold back my incredulous grin. This gesture was so intimate and affectionate, it threatened to make me lightheaded.

"You're right," I said breathlessly. "It's not."

So, I set my hand on top of his, daring him to pull away. But he didn't.

We rode the rest of the way like that, his hand on me and mine casing his.

A tinge of sadness washed over me when we reached his house, because it meant this strange and wonderful handholding was coming to an end, but I reminded myself that a hell of a lot more was on the menu for tonight.

The three-car garage at his house was empty until he pulled his car in.

"Nobody's home?" I asked.

"Nope. My dad's working, and Cassidy's out with friends."

He shut off the car, and his attention dropped to the hands on my leg. "It's just us tonight."

Dear lord. All the moisture in my body began to migrate south, making my mouth dry. "Oh."

"Come on." A seductive smile stretched across his lips as he undid his seatbelt. "I've got something for you. It's in my bedroom."

I filled my voice with suspicion. "Is it your penis?"

My question surprised him so much, it punched a laugh from his chest. "No, but it can be, if you want."

"What is it?"

"Guess you'll have to come see."

His eyes glimmered with sex and mischief before he pulled his hand out from beneath mine and reached for his car door.

I was sort of glad he'd said something because I was more focused on my curiosity, rather than my nerves as we came into the house and descended the steps into the basement. He moved fast, maybe in an attempt to keep me from stopping and looking at the pictures lining the staircase on either side.

There weren't any embarrassing ones, nor were any of them from before he was in high school, but that sort of made sense. He hadn't moved in with his dad until he was sixteen. But had he not been a part of his father's life before then?

I was curious, but that seemed too invasive of a question to ask, so I focused elsewhere. There were graduation pictures, both high school and college, plus a few family trips. One even included Cassidy in the mix, and I couldn't help but wonder how that worked.

Bad enough to have your ex dating your father, but to be a third wheel to them? *Yikes.*

It'd been a year since I'd been in the Lowes' basement, but it hadn't changed much. The only difference was the table where we'd played beer pong was now empty and surrounded by chairs.

"You want something to drink?" He went to the fridge and pulled it open, but it wasn't to show me the selection. It was so he could pull out a can of Coke for himself.

"Sure. I'll have one of those." I nodded to the can he was holding.

"You want something to go in it?" He motioned to the bottles of hard liquor on the inside of the fridge door. "Like rum?"

"I'm not twenty-one," I said automatically.

The second it was out, I wished I could take it back.

A lazy grin dawned on his face. "Right. I forgot for a second that you're a good girl."

I didn't miss the challenge he'd lobbed at me. I shifted my stance, striving to look confident. "You know what? Rum would be great."

He laughed as he pulled a bottle with a white label from the shelf. Plastic cups were retrieved from the upper cabinet and then filled with ice, followed by the tiniest pour known to man of rum into each one.

"Let's not go crazy," I teased. "Those drinks are almost as much of a virgin as I am."

He chuckled, popped the top on the can, and distributed the soda between the cups. "Yeah, they're weak, but you can have as much as you want . . . after the lesson."

I knew what he was doing. He didn't want either of us hammered, or even tipsy, judging by the miniscule amount of alcohol he'd doled out. Was he worried he might take advantage of me? It wasn't possible. I wanted him even when I was stone-cold sober.

He put away the rum, picked up the cups, and then offered one to me. "Cheers."

I took the drink, and although my heart beat faster, my voice sounded steady. "To lesson number three."

His eyes glinted, announcing he approved of my toast. Our plastic cups were tapped together, and we each took a sip, and when it was done, I turned my focus toward the dark doorway that I suspected was the entrance to his bedroom.

"This thing you have for me—that's *not* your penis," I gestured to the door with my hand holding the cup, "is it in there?"

His expression was unreadable. "It is."

Was he waiting on me? When he didn't move, I took a breath and strolled forward without an invitation.

Because we were heading into summer, it was still light outside. Some of it seeped through the high window on the far wall, but it was filtered through a set of closed blinds. It meant the long, narrow bedroom wasn't completely dark—but it was close.

It took my eyes a moment to adjust before I could make everything out.

There was a beige couch against the wall that looked older, but it was still in decent shape, and opposite it sat a queen-sized bed with mismatched nightstands on either side. The bed was made with a silver bedspread and black pillows decorating it. Decidedly more manly and grown-up than the pale pink one in my room.

That was where he slept.

It's where he jerked off the other night while thinking about you.

I knew this because he'd casually dropped that information in a text he'd sent me yesterday, and I had to hold in a shudder of pleasure now as I stared at the appealing, yet intimidating bed.

My gaze drifted over to the dresser situated under the window. There wasn't much on it. A few picture frames, a jar of spare coins, and some . . . candles? That was surprising, as was how clean the room seemed to be. There weren't dirty clothes on the floor, or crumpled receipts littering the dresser, or the useless clutter that always seemed to accumulate when you were busy.

Everything was put away, in its place.

Weren't boys supposed to be messy?

Colin's room had always been a disaster, and even though he lived with Madison now, it hadn't improved that much the few times I'd been to their place. It made me wonder. Had Preston cleaned his room for me, like I'd done for him?

I'd been so engrossed in looking at everything, it wasn't until the door clicked shut that I became aware of him. We were in his bedroom, with the door shut, and alone in his house. It was like the trifecta of sin for my parents.

Wait, scratch that. I was drinking too.

I took a sip of my rum and Coke and savored just how bad I was being, and when I set my gaze on Preston, I instantly thirsted for more.

Maybe he hadn't put any effort into how he looked tonight, but it didn't matter. His brown hair was swept back and his face clean-shaven, showing off his strong jawline. It made my knees weak, and my focus jumped from the couch to the bed and back again as I wondered where I should sit.

He must have sensed what I was thinking because he motioned to the couch. "Have a seat and I'll get it."

He flipped on the light switch, and I blinked against the sudden harsh light as he strode across the room, dropping his drink off on top of the dresser before making his way to the door in the corner. I sank down onto the couch, holding my drink, and watched as he disappeared into the walk-in closet, which wasn't as neat and organized as the rest of the room.

This was more like what I'd expected. There was an overflowing laundry basket on the floor, giving me a hint that he'd hidden away his mess in an effort to impress me. Or at least not scare me off.

It made me smile.

He reappeared with a smallish box in his hands. It was as long as a shoebox but only half as wide, and it was wrapped in glossy black paper. My pulse quickened. "You got me a present?"

His expression was enigmatic. "It's educational."

He sat so close beside me on the couch that I fell into him, making my drink slosh but thankfully not spill. He took it from me and set it down on the table beside the armrest, and then he placed the box on my lap, wordlessly asking me to open it.

I hadn't a clue what it could be, so I eagerly tore at the paper.

There was a picture on the front of the box, but I didn't understand what I was looking at—

Oh, my god!

Blood rushed to my cheeks, heating my face to a million degrees. Even though we were alone, I still whispered it, like I was worried someone might hear. "You bought me a vibrator?"

His gaze slid over my face, drinking in my shocked reaction, and he couldn't have looked more pleased if he'd tried. "I assume you don't have one already."

I shook my head and struggled to catch my breath. Holy shit. My gaze dropped to the box and the picture of the 'massaging wand' inside. It was black and shaped sort of like a microphone, with a rounded head and a tapered bottom that was tipped in chrome.

No, of course I didn't own a vibrator.

It was like . . . contraband. Just sitting there in its box, resting on my lap, felt excitingly wrong. I didn't know what my parents would do if they found out I had one—but knew it wouldn't go over well.

I'd thought once about buying one while I was away at school, but decided it was too risky. My parents might have questions about the charge on my credit card, plus I shared a dorm room with a roommate who was always around. When would I ever get a chance to use it?

I crinkled up the wrapping paper in one hand, while using the other to examine the box for a lid. There was a broken piece of tape across it.

"I opened it already," he said, "and charged it up."

I gulped down a breath so loudly, he had to have heard it. There was only one reason he'd have done that. "You want me to use it now?"

"No." He pulled the box from my grasp, opened the top, and withdrew the sleek, sexy wand. "I want to use it on you . . . during."

During.

How had he taken such a simple word and filled it with so much fire? The vibrator on its own was plenty hot, but the idea of him using it on me while we had sex? That was incendiary.

I couldn't take my eyes off his strong hand clenched around the handle of the wand. It was so fucking sexy.

But perhaps my silence made him nervous.

"Because I want you to enjoy it," he said. "I know a lot of girls don't their first time." He sounded like he thought I needed convincing. "I thought this might help, but if you're not into it—no problem. I just want you to . . ."

He paused for so long, it drew my gaze back to him, and I wasn't prepared for the way he looked. This wasn't the cocky, selfish boy I'd had a crush on all through high school. This was a man who was trying to think outside himself and struggled with his newfound feelings.

"I just want you to be comfortable," he blurted. As if saying it as fast as possible would rid him of his awkwardness.

It was so surprisingly sweet, it made my heart ache. He had so much more experience than I did, but was it possible he was just as anxious about the sex as I was?

I put a hand on his cheek to reassure him. "I am comfortable."

"You'll tell me if that changes." He'd said it as a statement, but I heard the question buried inside it.

"Yes."

A hint of relief glanced through his eyes, and then was gone, replaced by a growing intensity that was so magnetic, I couldn't look away. What was he thinking about? Whatever it was, it was serious.

He rose from the couch and strode to the nightstand that was on the side of the bed he preferred, judging by the alarm clock and charging cord on top. The vibrator was plunked down there, and then he went to the dresser and retrieved his drink.

"Tell me how you want it," he said, turning to face me and leaning against the dresser.

This question gave me the same feeling as cutting into a steak I was sure was medium-rare, only to discover it was over-done. "What?"

"What are you hoping for?" He took a sip of his drink as he studied me. "Candles and romantic music? You said you always imagined your first time would be with me. What was it like?"

My mind went blank. "Uh . . ." I'd had fantasies of us together, but in them he was always my boyfriend, and we were in love—so what I wanted wasn't possible. "I don't know. It's kind of hard to explain." I leaned over, snatched up my cup from where he'd set it down, and drank a big gulp, stalling. "I guess I want it however you want it."

He shot me a serious look. "You are not ready for the way I want it."

I sat up straighter and did my best to sound confident. "Maybe I'd surprise you."

His laugh was soft. "You probably would, but I think we'll save that for another lesson." He ticked his head toward the cup in my hand. "Finish your drink so I can get you naked."

My breath caught.

His command set me on fire, and while I drank the last of my rum and Coke, lightning buzzed through my system. It was finally happening. The good girl was going to do something very, *very* bad, and I couldn't fucking wait.

FOURTEEN

Sydney

Preston finished his drink, straightened away from the dresser, and his gaze was locked on me as he strolled forward. Once again, he took my cup from my grasp and set it aside, and then offered a hand to help me up.

If he noticed I was shaking, he didn't say anything. The moment I was on my feet, his mouth was on mine, and everything else faded away. It was burned up in the heat of his kiss because the connection to him created an inferno inside me.

It barely registered that his fingers were at the bottom of my shirt and tugging it upward. It wasn't until cool air wafted across the bare skin of my stomach that I realized what he was doing. We had to break the kiss and part for only a moment as he dragged the fabric up over my head and dropped it to the carpet with an almost inaudible thump.

As soon as it was done, his lips captured mine again and his hands went to work on the snap of my shorts. It was stunning how quickly he moved, and yet a part inside me whined for him to move faster.

My knees were already weak, but when he unzipped my shorts and shoved them down over my hips, my legs went boneless. I melted into his arms, falling into his all-consuming kiss.

He'd seen me topless before, and he'd seen beneath my skirt when I wasn't wearing any underwear, but this . . . it felt so different. Much more real. And I wasn't even naked yet.

I wore my matching bra and panty set I'd picked out for tonight. The cotton fabric was a simple white, trimmed with lace at the edges, and sprinkled with pairs of tiny pink roses printed on the fabric. It was so girly.

And *innocent.*

Preston's kiss ended and he glanced down, letting out a choked-off sound of surprise as he stepped back. He gazed at my body packaged in the feminine lingerie like he both loved and hated it.

The set wasn't overtly provocative. No mesh, or low-cut cups, and it certainly wasn't a thong. If anything, the lingerie bordered on childish, but . . . shit. I thought it was sexy in a different kind of way.

Maybe even a little wrong or taboo.

The longer he stared at me, the closer I came to bursting into flames.

"Look at you." His voice was full of gravel. "Did you wear this for me? It's so . . ." he drew out my anticipation, "*virginal.*"

I exhaled loudly and crossed my arms over my chest, trying to hold myself together because I was coming unglued. When I was in his arms, I felt brave, but with the distance between us, it made room for my shyness to move in and take over.

"You're so hot, and you don't even know it." He wiped a hand over his mouth, like he wanted to say more, but needed to stop himself—except it came out anyway. "You're fucking gorgeous."

His compliments, paired with his intense stare, made me burn hotter, and my knees threatened to buckle. He sounded so genuine, but my mind immediately went into safety mode and refused to accept it.

He was just saying it to be nice—it couldn't be true.

I held my arms tighter across my scantily clad body, and tension pinched my shoulders together.

Whatever face I was making, it caused the lust in his eyes to dissipate. He blinked, and a new thought developed. "You want me to turn off the lights?"

Relief washed through me. I didn't know why, but it felt more private that way.

"Sure," I eked out.

He stepped forward and planted a searing kiss on my lips, and the connection to him was a drug that settled my nerves. My heart didn't beat quite as erratically.

"My bed's nice." His smile was easy. "You should give it a try."

When he left me and strolled toward the switch, I turned to face the bed and swallowed a breath. My unsteady legs carried me there, and as soon as I crawled onto the mattress, there was a soft snap, and the room plunged into near darkness.

I sat in the center of the bed and kept my gaze fixed on Preston. I'd expected him to come to me, but he didn't. He crossed the room back to the dresser. Was he picking up his drink?

No. He opened the top drawer and pulled something out. It clicked, and a blue-yellow flame leapt to life at the end of the lighter. It didn't take him long to light the three white pillar candles that rested on a gold charging plate, but I held my breath the entire time.

The flickering light cast a warm glow that wasn't just sexy . . . it was *romantic*.

But all thought ceased when he turned. He took in the sight of me on his bed and his expression changed to one of absolute hunger.

God, it sucked all the air from the room.

I couldn't move, couldn't blink, as he grabbed the bottom of his shirt and stretched it up over his head. As soon as he had it off, he balled the shirt in his hands and tossed it aside, revealing the perfect landscape of his chest. Even in the low light, I could see he was toned and tanned, and my gaze traced over every delicious inch of bare skin.

But he wasn't done.

His fingers worked the button and zipper of his shorts, and the fabric slid down his legs, exposing his gray underwear with a white waistband. There was a brand name I couldn't read in small print scrawled across it, and the second his shorts hit the ground, he moved to step out of them.

I wasn't prepared for the way he stalked toward me, wearing nothing but a pair of underwear that barely concealed anything. It was better than my fantasies and yet it made my anxiety spike.

Because this was happening and real, which meant it might not be perfect.

Oh, no. What if I was terrible? He might decide one time was enough, and I'd never get this again.

He cocked his head as he reached the end of his bed. "You're looking at me like you're dying."

My voice was feeble. "I'm nervous."

He exhaled a deep breath. "Don't be. It's going to be fun."

The bed jostled as he sank a knee on the mattress and climbed on, crawling on his hands and knees until he was lying on his side beside me. Then he reached over and trailed his fingertips down the center of my chest. His touch was just a whisper, and goosebumps lifted on my arms in response.

The way his fingers slowly glided across my skin was sensual, and my eyes hooded as he carved a path down past my bra and onto my bare stomach. I didn't know how to deal with this gentle, tender version of him. It was too much, and he made it impossible not to fall into my feelings for him.

I reminded myself again that it wasn't allowed, and like all the other times, it didn't do any good. It'd been foolish to think we could be friends with benefits and that I wouldn't want more, especially when I'd already wanted more for years.

As his fingertip drew circles on my trembling stomach, he leaned over and pressed his mouth to mine. Maybe his intent was to be sweet, to keep us on a slow and steady track, but once again, he'd underestimated the power of our kiss. I slid closer, matching his intensity, which made him escalate. Like me, he was competitive, and he fought to stay on top of the kiss.

To stay in command.

Except there was no way to control what was happening

between us.

The tenderness in him was crushed under a powerful need, and he shifted on the bed, moving so he was over me and my legs wrapped around his waist. The kiss shifted too.

It grew hotter. And *dirtier*.

I took in air in shallow bursts as his seductive mouth moved down the side of my neck and on to the edge of my bra. His hands slipped around me and beneath my back, urging me to arch so there was room between me and the mattress.

It was kind of nice when he struggled to undo the hooks at the back of my bra. It had to be awkward not being able to see what he was doing, plus there wasn't a lot of space to work with.

But then the tension in the band was gone, and his hurried hands pulled the bra down off my shoulders. The straps dragged along my arms as he tugged it all the way off and threw it over the side of the bed.

The second I was topless, it was like something inside him snapped. There was a desperate urgency he could no longer fight, and his rough hands seized my breasts. He squeezed and pushed them together, making it easier for him to run his tongue from one nipple to the other.

"*Oh,*" I gasped at the sharp sting of his playful bite, but . . . was it weird I liked the sensation? I clamped my legs tighter around him, making his hip bones dig into the insides of my thighs. I threaded my fingers through his thick hair, trying to get him to do it again, but I wasn't fast enough.

Preston was on the move, leaving a trail of hot, damp kisses down my stomach.

My chest rose and fell dramatically as he inched closer to the last scrap of fabric covering my body. I'd never been completely naked in front of him before, and I snagged my bottom lip between my teeth to hold back an anxious whimper.

He backed off the bed so he was kneeling at the end of it, and when I lifted my head to stare down at him, my heart stopped. His expression dripped with so much desire, it was indecent.

It loudly announced what he was planning to do, and promised I'd like it.

But what he didn't like was how high up I was lying on the bed, so he grasped my ankles and jerked me closer to him. I gasped as I slid across the silky comforter, stunned at the action but also by how much I enjoyed being manhandled.

I could barely catch my breath before his fingers curled at the sides of my 'virginal' panties and began to drag the fabric down.

My mouth was completely dry as he peeled my underwear down my legs. I was shrouded in the flickering candlelight and the fading sunlight at the edges of the blinds, but it was more than enough to see me.

"*Fuck.*" He stilled with the panties clenched in one hand, his gaze fixed on the junction of my thighs. Sex thickened his voice. "Did you do that for me?"

After I'd gotten his text this afternoon, I'd hurried into the shower and shaved myself *completely* bare. It had been precarious, and taken a lot longer than I'd expected, but it had also turned me on once it was done.

It felt like I was hiding a secret on my body. One

just for him.

My shy nod made him groan in approval, and his hands coasted up my legs, moving in a fast, efficient path to my sensitive, newly bare skin. And his mouth followed, inching up the inside of my thigh while gently urging me to open my trembling legs wider.

To make room for him. "You want me to taste this virgin pussy?"

I couldn't speak. All I could give him was a quick nod.

He dragged it out, teasing kisses at the spot where my leg joined my body while he adjusted his stance on his knees. It was like he was settling in and finding just the right position.

"Oh, shit," I cried, flinching.

The first hint of his tongue against my clit was an electric shock of pleasure. The second brush of it was more serious, making the sensation more acute. I balled the comforter beneath me into tight fists, needing something to hold on to.

Then his tongue began to flutter.

Every nerve ending in me lit up, sending sparks raining across my body. I bucked my hips, maybe wanting to run from the pleasure, or get him to do it again . . . I couldn't tell. I wasn't in control anymore.

A moan poured from my lips, and I promptly slapped a hand over my mouth to stifle it back. It had been too loud and sounded so erotic, it verged on embarrassing. I stared up at the ceiling, too scared to look at him with his head between my legs because who knew what kind of sound I'd make then? The sight would be scorching hot, overwhelming.

"This is what I wanted to do the other night." The hot,

velvet stroke of his tongue ceased only long enough for him to speak. "But you don't have to be good and stay quiet now."

I moaned through my fingers and squeezed my eyes shut, just as the muscle deep in my core clenched.

As he fucked me with his mouth, his hands decided to join in. One of them slid underneath my thigh and up onto my hip, while he used the other to press one thick finger deep inside me.

"Oh, my god," I gasped.

My hands abandoned the comforter so I could drive them into my hair. I bowed up off the mattress, writhing from the pleasurable stretch of my body around the finger he eased in and out of me. His incessant tongue whipped at my clit, and the more I seemed to enjoy it, the faster he fluttered and the deeper his finger went.

It was . . . incredible.

My heartrate was through the roof and my chest heaved, and I pictured what we looked like. How he was bent over the end of the bed with his head between my legs, a finger pumping fast enough it made the whole bed shake, while I writhed and moaned as a mindless, naked creature.

"Fuck," I groaned as he pushed a second finger in alongside the first. It was a lot, but it felt so good. "Fuck, fuck . . ."

He chuckled, thrilled at hearing me curse.

Tension was building inside me. It traveled up my quivering legs and down my arms, like all roads in my body led to the spot where he was feasting on me. I was so turned on, I was slick with arousal, and I could hear the slippery glide of his fingers as they sawed in and out.

Preston made the tiniest of adjustments to the angle he was using, but it had a huge impact. He was able to reach deeper and touch me in a place that made my toes curl into points.

My gasps and moans swelled.

I panted for air in quick, erratic bursts.

Every signal blared to him that my orgasm was about to happen.

"That's it," he urged. "Be a good girl and come for me."

His dirty command triggered a crash of ecstasy, and I cried out as it collided with me. Wave upon wave of bliss rocked my body, and I shuddered uncontrollably. If I wasn't out of my mind, maybe I would have worried that I'd been too loud, but I couldn't.

All I could focus on was not tearing apart.

He still had his fingers wedged inside me as it happened, and although I squirmed, he stayed with my undulating body, keeping them lodged inside. Every pulse squeezed at him, and he let out a heavy, appreciative sigh.

"Jesus Christ." His voice was hushed. "That's so fucking sexy."

His words filled me with even more satisfaction, and I flinched with an aftershock of pleasure.

Finally, after a lifetime, his fingers retreated, and the orgasm faded. It left me weak, and I collapsed into a sweaty heap on the mattress, before pushing out a long, slow breath. Holy hell. That had been intense. Easily the strongest orgasm I'd ever had.

I raised a shaky hand to brush the hair out of my face,

opened my eyes, and lifted my head to risk a glance at him.

In the candlelight, his pleased eyes seemed darker. They stared back at me as he rose to his feet and wiped a hand over his mouth, and it was unavoidable the way my gaze coursed down his body. It landed on the erection bulging through his underwear. Why would anyone want to be good around him? He had a body built for sin.

A cocky smile tilted his lips. He liked how I stared at him.

It only took him a second to jerk his underwear down, and then he was as naked as I was. His hard dick swung free before he ringed a hand around the tip and stroked down to the base. It was stunning how he stood over me, so far away, and yet I wasn't shy as his gaze caressed my nude body. My bashfulness had been burned up in the fire of my orgasm.

"You want this inside you?" He continued to slide his fist slowly across his length.

Even though I knew I could change my mind at any time, it still felt like this was it. No going back now.

My heart skipped and fluttered. "Yes."

FIFTEEN

Sydney

Preston never looked more attractive than when desire flooded his expression. But I didn't get to see the full intensity of it for long because he turned and strode to the nightstand.

The vibrator wasn't the first thing he went for, though.

A drawer was pulled open, a condom packet was retrieved, and then he scooped up the black wand. They were carried back to me at the end of the bed, and my heart crawled into my throat, closing it off.

I could barely breathe as he dropped the vibrator beside me and tore open the foil wrapper with steady hands. It was a moment I'd wanted for so long, but it had also been built up into this huge ordeal in my mind, even when I knew it shouldn't be.

People lost their virginity all the time, I told myself.

I tensed my hands into loose fists as the torn foil fluttered to the carpet and he fitted the condom over the head of his dick, then rolled it down. The sight of it made heat flash across my cheeks.

How the hell was all of that going to fit inside me?

"Don't worry." His tone was hushed and playful. "It'll fit."

I jolted, and it took me a moment to realize I hadn't asked it out loud. Preston was either a mind reader, or I'd been staring at him with trepidation.

His expression turned serious as he stepped in between my legs and leaned over, planting a hand on either side of me on the mattress. My eyes were wide and probably anxious, but his were reassuring.

He sank down so he was supported on his forearms, and I was trapped beneath him. The heat of his naked body was right there, and he tipped his head down the final few inches so he could brush his lips against mine in something too gentle to be called a kiss.

Just the contact of our skin against each other's caused a shiver to travel up my back and make my shoulders shake. It felt so nice, but it also set off the proximity warnings that always filled my mind whenever I came close to having sex.

I wouldn't heed them this time, I told myself.

My fingers curled into the hair at the back of his head, wordlessly pleading for him to kiss me for real. Like he meant it.

When he did? *God.* He was as desperate as I was.

That night in my bedroom, he'd had me climb on top of him and we'd ground our naked bodies together, so I had an idea of what it would feel like when his cock rubbed against me—but this was so different.

Every part of me was tense with anticipation, and when the head of his dick nudged forward, seeking entrance, the trembling that rattled me down to my core grew worse.

He broke the kiss and hesitation hung in his expression. I wished I could stop the tremor, but it was beyond my control, and a big part of it was just adrenaline anyway.

Not nerves.

Although—I had those.

It meant I had to convince him again. One of my hands slipped down his neck and across his chest until I had my palm squeezed between us and flat over his racing heart.

"I want you inside me," I whispered.

He exhaled loudly, and I didn't miss how it was tinged with relief. Because he wanted that, too, and it seemed like he wanted it *badly*. The muscles in his chest were hard as stone as he reached down and steadied himself, found the spot he needed to, and ever-so-slowly began to push inside.

The stretch of his two fingers earlier had been good, but this was a *lot* more.

I inhaled a sharp breath through my nose, and my hand on his chest instinctively pushed, trying to slow him down. The way he advanced, it didn't exactly hurt—that was too strong a word to use.

But the sensation caused a deep, uncomfortable ache.

Plus, it went on . . . *and on* . . .

And just when I reached the limit of what I could take, he sealed his mouth over mine to distract, and took the last crucial inch. I let out a little whimper of displeasure, and he solidified. The only thing that moved was his lips, and they roamed over mine, alternating between short kisses and deeper ones, giving my body time to accommodate.

To adjust to his possession.

Holy shit. There was another person inside me.

I was motionless on the bed, and he was bent over, covering me, both of us struggling to catch our breath.

Slowly, his kiss began to travel. It moved across my cheek so he could whisper the question by my ear, as if not to disturb me.

"You okay?"

My word was quiet. "Yeah."

I *was* okay.

It was still uncomfortable, but it wasn't that bad. I liked how his hips were pressed against me and how my legs were folded around him. We were utterly connected, and I—

"*Oh,*" I said abruptly.

The sensation of him moving, of his slow withdrawal wasn't at all what I'd expected. It was still uncomfortable, but not . . . unpleasant. He grasped one of my hips, pinning me to the bed while he continued to pull back, and then he began to ease forward again in a motion that was much too slow and deliberate to be called a thrust.

I arched beneath him, flattening my breasts to his chest. He was so warm and hard *everywhere.*

"Fuck, Sydney." His voice was pure smoke. "You feel so good."

His words caused me to clench inside and out, and—holy shit—he *felt* it. His eyes hazed with pleasure, and my physical ache diminished as my emotional one grew. There'd been a crease between his eyebrows as he focused on me, but when I sighed with contentment, the crease faded.

My first soft moan gave him enough confidence to truly move.

To push deeper.

The bed creaked beneath us as he established a measured

pace, and suddenly his hands couldn't stay still any longer. They coursed over my body, caressing my breasts, my waist, my legs. I followed his lead and let my hands wander over him too. Shit, it was so nice to be able to touch him unrestrained, exactly how I wanted.

"Do you like it?" he mumbled into my breasts while his body rocked against mine.

The sensation was wild and foreign, but... "Yeah. Do you?"

Half of a laugh bubbled out of him like I'd asked something obvious, and he playfully nipped at my breast, as if he needed to tease me for such a silly question. "Your pussy is so goddamn tight, it's going to make me come way too fast."

I pulled in a ragged breath through my parted lips.

Steam filled the room, squeezing us together and making our bodies slick with sweat. Our kisses were interrupted by moans, and I loved the way his competed with mine for who could be the loudest.

Everything was sprinting inside me when Preston found a new gear. My blood, my heart, my mind . . . they all rushed along at breakneck speed. The hurried thrust of his hips drove me into the mattress, and although it didn't feel like it was going to be good enough to bring me to orgasm, it *did* feel good.

Like, really good.

Each sharp movement from him injected me with pleasure.

Abruptly, he straightened to stand while still lodged inside me, taking away the heat of his body. He shifted to bury one knee up on the bed, and it changed the angle, allowing him to slip deeper.

His heavy eyes blinked, and pleasure twisted his handsome face, exaggerated by the shadows of the candlelight. His gaze drifted down the slope of my body to where we were joined, and he made a sound of satisfaction.

"Fuck, look at that," he ordered. "Look at how deep I am inside you."

I was shy, but, shit, I couldn't resist. I lifted my head just enough to peer down and see the way his dick disappeared inside me. It was hypnotic. Mesmerizing. And so erotic my blood boiled in my veins.

Words floated through my head, telling me what a bad girl I was. Letting a guy fuck me who wasn't even my boyfriend. It was shocking, and the darkest part of me reveled in it.

One of his hands captured my breast, and the other wrapped around my thigh, pulling my leg up so my knee was by his shoulder. I groaned with pleasure and clawed at the silky comforter, enjoying the feeling of him way more than I thought I would. Plus, I loved seeing the emotions play out over his face.

His lips were parted, and his chest rose and fell with enormous breaths as he sawed his cock back and forth, sliding deep. The force of it made my breasts sway and rock, even as I arched and contracted. Sweat built a glossy sheen across his forehead, but he didn't seem to notice.

His focus was only on me.

And it intensified when he let go of my leg and scooped up the vibrator.

His pace slowed a little with distraction as he searched for the button to turn it on, and when the soft buzz filled the silence of the room, it charged the air with electricity. I'd never used a vibrator before, so I had no idea what kind of sensation it'd bring.

Preston didn't tease me with it or waste any time. He put the head of the wand right above the place where he drove into me, and as soon as the vibrator made contact, it was shocking, instant bliss.

I flinched, and my hands latched on to his arms. "Holy fuck."

His tone was sexy and sinister. "You like that?"

I couldn't answer because the hit of acute pleasure stole my breath. Having an orgasm during sex had seemed impossible when we'd first started, but now it wasn't just possible— it seemed inevitable.

I squirmed beneath the sinful vibration, which was intense and incredible. My hands smoothed over his arms, caressed his stomach, gripped his hips. My touch was mindless, desperate.

Maybe the head of the vibrator was in his way, but he didn't seem bothered by it. His pace was unrelenting, tightening the tension in my core. I didn't know what, exactly, I needed, just that I had all this need, and that he'd be the only one who could satisfy it.

Greedy whines and moans trickled from me, and I no longer cared how they sounded. Any shame or embarrassment couldn't touch me when we were connected.

He didn't miss the change in pitch or the urgency

in my moans.

"Are you going to come again?" he asked.

I gulped down an enormous breath and nodded. The vibration against my clit was so good, it was almost hard to endure. I climbed toward orgasm, but it just kept going higher, and higher, until . . .

Pleasure detonated, and for a split second, it felt like the world had flown apart.

I cried out, and my hand went to his that gripped the wand, urgently trying to push it away. As I began to come, the sensation of the vibrator tipped on its side. Enjoyment crossed over and became sharp, hot discomfort on my overly sensitive skin.

He lifted the wand away and must have pressed a button because the buzzing cut off. It thumped onto the bed beside me, no longer needed. With it out of the way, it meant he could push as deep as he wanted, and he hit a spot inside me that probably would have made my vision blur if I'd had my eyes open.

But I didn't. The orgasm was too strong.

Everything was tingling, and I shivered uncontrollably, floating in the dreamy space while the sensations began to subside.

He groaned, and it sounded weirdly like frustration. His hands seized my waist, gripping me tightly while his tempo increased dramatically, and—oh, my god.

Was he coming?

He'd said he wasn't going to last long, and he made good on his warning. I blinked open my eyes to watch, fascinated by how his thrusts broke down, slowing erratically to a stop.

A lock of his hair had fallen forward, and the ends brushed at his eyes just before they slammed shut. His body hardened, and the muscle along his jaw flexed, showing he was clenching his teeth. But it didn't stop his moans, or trap any of the sounds of pleasure he gave while the orgasm rolled through him.

Deep between my legs, there were these rhythmic pulses, and his whole body shuddered in response.

It was so fucking hot.

Then he blew out a long, uneven breath, leaned down, and sealed his lips over mine. This kiss was intense and slow, and it was like he didn't care what it was doing to me. How he was still inside me, or how his kiss made me slip further into my feelings until I was hopelessly drowning in him.

When the sweeping kiss was over, he straightened and pulled away, shooting me an easy smile. He acted like what we'd done was incredibly satisfying and that was all. It was not earth shattering like it'd been for me.

"Be right back," he said.

I couldn't form words, so I said nothing. I simply watched him stroll to the door, pull it open, and walk through it.

As soon as he was gone, I reached down, ran a hand between my legs, and lifted my fingers to check. There wasn't any blood, and I breathed a sigh of relief. My friend Hailey had said she didn't bleed either when she'd had sex for the first time. I wasn't squeamish about blood, but this just made things . . . easier.

Preston had probably disappeared into the bathroom to

dispose of the condom, and while he was gone, I made the decision to get under his covers. I wasn't cold—far from it—but I was naked, and now that the sex was over, my shyness had returned.

Plus, the idea of being nestled in his bed that smelled like him? Yes, please.

Reality came crashing down on me as I moved gingerly up over the mattress and then slid between the soft sheets. I was sore.

Because you're not a virgin anymore.

There was no one to tell because we'd promised to keep these 'lessons' a secret. Hailey and I were friends from high school, so she knew all about my crush on Preston, which meant I absolutely could not tell her. Nor could I lie and say I'd given it up to someone she didn't know. She'd been my best friend for long enough that wouldn't fly with her.

She'd never let it go until she had a name.

Preston's naked form reappeared in the doorway, and he sauntered over to the side of the bed I'd left empty for him after grabbing the discarded vibrator and setting it on the nightstand. He was so comfortable. Confident without a stitch of clothing on, and I guessed that made sense.

He was gorgeous.

He looked at me and how I had the sheet tucked up under my arms, and that same easy smile was back. He got that I was bashful, but he wasn't, and the bed jostled as he climbed on to lie beside me.

Except he stayed above the covers.

His head hit the pillow, and he stretched his arms back,

lacing his fingers together behind his head. I was envious of his relaxed posture, but at the same time, we were in his bed, and this was not a new experience for him. Why wouldn't he feel comfortable?

"Can I ask you a question?" I'd hoped to sound casual, but it came out sounding small and needy.

He turned to look at me. *Of course,* his expression read.

I almost didn't want to know the answer, and yet I was desperate for it. "How was I?"

The carefree light in his eyes dimmed and seriousness moved in. The comforter rustled as he turned on his side and scooted close enough to put a heavy arm around me. "You couldn't tell? That was . . ."

His Adam's apple bobbed with a swallow as he searched for the right word. It looked like he found it, and his lips parted, but he abruptly thought better of it. His chin pulled back, and his guard went up. Whatever he was going to say— it made him nervous.

"You get an A-plus, good girl."

Except he wasn't thrilled with his answer, judging by the way his lips skewed to one side. Like my serious question deserved a serious answer.

He sobered and tried again. "You were really great."

I must have made a face, because his arm tightened, tugging me against him.

"I don't know why you don't believe me. You're good at everything you do. Why wouldn't you be amazing at sex your first time?"

My heart skipped. "You thought I was amazing?"

He grasped my chin between his thumb and forefinger, guiding me into his kiss. "Shh. No more talking until the lesson's over."

His mouth met mine, and it stoked the fire burning between us, only this fire wasn't sexual. Our kiss had no business being that full of passion, but neither of us did a damn thing to stop it. I sank into the mattress beneath the power of it, clutching at him and holding on for dear life.

He'd warned me these lessons were supposed to be about sex and nothing else, but what if it was already too late for that? My feelings for him were too strong, and every minute we spent together only magnified their intensity.

It was impossible to think clearly when his mouth was attached to mine, but worry was a knife, slicing through the fog and working its way in.

What was going to happen when we ran out of lessons?

SIXTEEN

Preston

I carried the two plastic grocery bags in and set them on the island in the kitchen, and Sydney followed me with the box of cooking stuff she'd packed from her house. When I'd asked her earlier this week if she'd be willing to make me dinner again, she'd agreed immediately, and presented me with a few different menu options.

I'd landed on shrimp risotto.

"You can leave it out," she said as I attempted to put things away in the fridge. "I need to devein the shrimp."

When I'd picked her up this evening, our first stop had been a grocery store. When I'd told her I was buying—since it was the least I could do—she asked me what my budget was. Shopping with her had been surprisingly fun. I liked that she was so picky when she was selecting produce, and how whenever she scrutinized a product, her eyebrows would pull together like she was doing deep work.

She looked so cute like that.

Unlike last time, this recipe did call for wine, and since I wasn't much of a wine guy, I grabbed the one she told me to and added it to our cart. It was ironic that she wasn't old enough to drink and yet she was the one giving me advice.

That thought reminded me. I needed to text Patrick

soon and see if he'd made any progress on that favor I'd asked him for.

As I set the package of raw shrimp on the counter, Sydney popped the lid on her plastic container and pulled out a roll of fabric. I was disappointed for a moment, until she began to carefully unroll it. It was the same apron she'd worn the last time she'd cooked for me, and she'd used it to cushion the set of knives she'd packed.

"I've got something for you." I grinned. "And before you ask, no, it's not my penis."

She glanced up at me with surprise. "What?"

I went to the pantry and retrieved the box I'd wrapped in the same black wrapping paper I'd used to wrap the vibrator. I had a ton of it left over that a client didn't want after the retirement party Distinguished Events had coordinated a few months ago.

Her movements slowed to a stop as she eyed the long, narrow box. Was she worried this was another vibrator to add to her collection? I'd sent her home with the other one after our last lesson.

You mean, the one where you came in less than ten minutes?

I tried to convince myself that at least she'd gotten a realistic experience of what it would be like if it was the guy's first time, too. My first time, I'd only made it a few pumps before it was over.

But I was disappointed in my performance and was looking forward to doing better tonight. After dinner, I'd take her down to my room, get her naked, and see how many unassisted orgasms I could give her.

My dick perked up, wanting me to persuade her to skip dinner and head down to my bed right now, but instead, I tossed the box down on the counter. It slid across the smooth granite, coming to a stop right in front of Sydney.

"It's not my birthday," she said.

I shrugged. "It's a 'thank you' for being my private chef tonight."

She picked up the box and judged its weight. "Your dad's home. Do I need to open this in your room?" Distrust made her eyes narrow. "Is it *educational*?"

I laughed and shook my head. "It's not."

When she'd learned my dad was home, she'd gotten mad I hadn't mentioned it while we were shopping. She could cook enough for three people if she'd known to buy more portions, but I'd told her there was no need. He was on call, so the chance of my dad having to leave before dinner was ready was extremely high.

I was honestly surprised his car was still here when we arrived at the house. He was off in his bedroom, probably sleeping or catching up on emails since Cassidy was hanging out with her friend Lilith.

Sydney slipped a finger under the tape and popped up a corner of the wrapping paper. As she tore the rest of it off, my pulse sped.

I couldn't argue this gift was an impulse buy in the traditional sense. I found myself at various times during the day thinking about her, and random shit too. Not just thoughts about how hot she was, or how sex with her was off-the-charts, but I wondered, like, what she was doing at that exact moment or how her day was going.

Most of all, I was curious if she thought about me as much as I did about her.

It wasn't a conscious decision to buy the knife roll for her. After one of our text exchanges about planning dinner tonight, she'd mentioned that she didn't have one yet. It'd been a casual, offhand comment, but suddenly I found myself on Amazon, searching for the perfect one for her.

She opened the tan box and pulled out the contents, not understanding what it was until she took it out of its plastic sleeve. The black canvas bag had two straps around it to hold it closed when rolled up, but when it was flat, there were slots inside to store a chef's tools.

Her gasp was quiet as she took it in, and her fingers traced over her name that was embroidered on the bag in between the clips for the shoulder strap.

"Oh, my god. You shouldn't have."

But the way she looked at it? It was clear she loved the gift.

I rubbed a hand on the back of my neck, trying to distract from my awkwardness. Yeah, I knew it was too much, but fuck it. I liked her reaction. And thank god it had shown up in time. Having it customized had added two days to the delivery, so I'd been relieved when it had arrived this afternoon.

"It's no big deal." I forced lightness into my tone. "If anything, it's a self-serving gift. This makes it easier for you to come over and cook again."

She drew in a breath, and for a moment, she looked like she didn't know what to say. But then she straightened and pulled on a smile. "Thank you."

I nodded and dropped my gaze to the counter, eager for her not to dwell on my statement. I'd told her this thing between us was just sex, and then like an idiot, I hadn't followed my own damn rule. Hanging out and buying her gifts . . . what the hell was I thinking?

My biggest problem was I didn't know if I wanted to have a fun date with her or take her downstairs and fuck her brains out.

You can do both.

But I shouldn't. Every lesson with her deepened my betrayal to Colin. When I was with her, I had to pretend he didn't exist. And when I was with him? I did the same thing.

It made me feel like shit, so I tried not to think about it.

Once she finished moving her knives into her new bag, I pulled the rest of the items from the plastic bags and laid them out for her. "What would you like me to do?"

She slipped her apron over her head and tied the strings behind her back. "Are you good in the kitchen?"

"No, I'm terrible. I'd say I do my best work in the bedroom." I gave her a wide grin and a wink.

She snorted and shook her head. "If you're a terrible cook, then the best thing you can do is stay out of my way."

It was so much fun to see her like this. All business. Confident. "Yes, ma'am."

I grabbed the wrapping paper and the rest of the trash, clearing it off the island so she had more room to work, and then sat on a stool at the breakfast bar and helped by telling her where to find things in the cabinets.

While she cleaned the shrimp, we talked about her job. She'd started waitressing at seventeen, and only a month later she'd been moved to the kitchen and done all the prep work.

Even though she worked her own station now, a lot of her experience came from watching the other chefs. The sous chef, Diego, had taken her under his wing and was a mentor, but the rest of the line was pirates, she said.

"How's that?" I asked.

She'd finished with the shrimp, moved on, and considered my question while she poured chicken broth into a pot. "They've got foul mouths, hot tempers, and cutthroat attitudes."

I peered at her dubiously. "And how's that for you?"

She turned on the burner, not bothering to look at me. "It's fine. Honestly, it's good for me. I had to learn to stand up for myself because no one else was going to." Her voice lost a little of its confidence. "Still working on doing that outside of the kitchen." She stepped away from the stove and glanced at me. "Cutting board?"

"The long cabinet next to the oven."

She got what she needed and set the wooden board down on the counter across from me. "It sucks being the only woman there sometimes."

She was young and beautiful, and the thought made ice slide down my spine. "Because they hit on you?"

She pulled out one of her knives and cut a shallot in half, then laid the flat side down and began to rapidly cut it into thin slices. "Most of the time, they don't mean it. They're just teasing me. But one of them, I'm pretty sure he was serious when he asked if I wanted to have a three-way with him and his girlfriend."

I had to stay perfectly still to keep my emotions in check. The idea of Sydney with anyone else, male or female, triggered an unacceptable amount of jealousy in me. I could tell myself it was just because I was competitive, but I knew that was bullshit.

I did my best to sound casual. "What'd you tell him?"

Her knife slowed. "I told him no, of course. So, then he said it could be just the two of us, then. His girlfriend didn't need to know. Which—gross."

"Right," I said.

Except my agreement came a little too quickly to sound natural, and it drew her suspicion. Her eyes sharpened on me, and I'd swear they could see right down to the mistake I'd made years ago, and the guilt I harbored over it.

"Okay." She put her knife down and gave me a hard look. "You don't think cheating is gross?"

"No, I do." I hoped she could hear how genuine I was.

"Then why is your face all weird?" Her eyes went wide. "Oh, my god. You've cheated!"

"Well, that depends on your definition of cheating."

Her jaw dropped and she looked at me like I was scum. "What the hell does that mean?"

I sighed. Why the fuck had I said that? "Look, it's not something I'm proud of, but I . . . sort of cheated on Cassidy once."

That did nothing to help the look of disgust she was shooting at me. "*Sort* of?"

Shit, I was going to have to explain. "It was at the end of our relationship, the summer right after our freshman year at Vanderbilt. I'd invited some people over, but it was last minute, so nobody showed up, except for this one girl named Stacy."

Later, I learned she'd told everyone else to stay away. She'd wanted me all to herself.

There was an uncomfortable tightness in my chest. "I'd had too many beers, so my thinking wasn't great. Stacy said she was cold and wanted to get in the hot tub."

My pause was too long, annoying her. "And?"

"And she didn't have a swimsuit."

Her posture stiffened. "Oh."

More like, *oh, shit.* I hadn't known that at the time, either. "She came out of the bathroom after changing, wrapped in a towel, and I'd just assumed her suit was strapless. Then, she took her first step into the hot tub, tossed her towel aside, and I realized what . . . was missing."

I got a flash of her naked body before she sank down into the bubbling water, and I'd stood dumbfounded at the side of the hot tub for a long time, considering my options. Which had been extra difficult because I was drunk.

"I should have left her," I said, "and gone back in the house, but I was wasted, and I was pissed at Cassidy."

Outrage burned in her eyes. "You're blaming *her* for your cheating?"

"No, no." I couldn't get the words out fast enough. "I know I fucked up. I'm not trying to make excuses, or say it wasn't one thousand percent my fault."

I couldn't even blame Stacy for it. Sure, she'd come on strong, and that was shady as fuck because she knew I was drunk, but she hadn't forced me to get in the hot tub with her.

I'd made that choice.

"I'm just trying to explain what led to my giant fuck-up." I placed my hands on the counter and leaned forward. "My whole life, I'd been the center of attention. For my mom, and then my dad, and then, for a while, Cassidy. That stopped when we got to college, and I didn't know how to deal with it."

It was embarrassing to admit, but I couldn't help myself. My friends knew about the Stacy incident, but I hadn't really talked about it with anyone before. It'd been bottled up for so long, it was almost a relief to get it out.

"So, I got in," I lifted my guilty, vulnerable gaze to Sydney. "And when Stacy started kissing me, I kissed her back." My voice lost all its power. "We probably would have done more, but my dad came home early, and he caught us. He was so pissed that it sobered me up right quick, and when I realized what the fuck I'd done, I got out and told her to go home."

"What'd he say to you?"

"My dad? Nothing, but it was the first time I'd ever seen him disappointed in me. He knew I was still with Cassidy."

She looked dubious. "But he said nothing?"

"You have to understand, my dad and I didn't have a good relationship back then. Fuck, for the first twelve years of my life, we didn't have a relationship at all. He chose medical school and his career over my mom and me."

Her expression shifted. "What changed?"

"He grew up. Grew out of being a selfish asshole." There

was no doubt I'd gotten that trait from him, but I liked to think I'd overcome it better and faster than he had. "For a long time, I thought it was too little, too late for us. My mom made me move in with him, and at first it sucked, but then I realized I had all the leverage. He was so eager to get me to like him, he'd let me do whatever the fuck I wanted. So, no. He didn't say anything."

She considered that for a quiet, heavy moment. "Does Cassidy know about it? That you and Stacy—"

"Yeah."

It looked like she wasn't sure if she should ask it. "Is that why you broke up?"

"No. She broke up with me before she found out about that." Before Sydney could ask, I offered it up. "I didn't tell her because I was ashamed, and truthfully, I was a shitty person back then. Since then, I've been trying hard not to go down the same path my dad did. To be different." I blinked against my uncomfortable feelings. "I don't know. To be *better.*"

She gave me a discerning look, like she was reevaluating everything about me. It made me uneasy, and I hadn't a clue what face I was making, but I hoped she could see my remorse.

"Cassidy was my best friend," I sucked in a breath, "and the first girl I ever loved. I don't know how I would have survived my first year with my dad without her. I'm always going to regret that I repaid her by treating her like shit."

Sydney's gaze was fixated on me, and the longer we held each other's stare, the more intense and tighter it became. When I'd seen her last year at my graduation party, I'd locked eyes with her and waited for her to look away, but tonight it was my turn to break first.

I dropped my gaze to the cutting board in front of her and the shallot she'd abandoned.

"You are different," she said finally. Her hand closed around the knife handle, readying to pick it up. "Think you'll ever cheat again?"

"No." My tone was absolute because I believed it absolutely. "Never."

She seemed pleased with my answer and resumed her work. Once she finished making the cuts, she moved on to dicing. The quick cuts of her knife were so skilled and precise, it was mesmerizing to watch.

"You said you and your dad didn't have a good relationship back then. It's good now?" She probably wasn't trying to sound skeptical, but I heard it anyway.

"It's . . . complicated," I admitted. "Living here with them is not ideal, but it's rent free, and it won't be for much longer."

"You're moving out?"

"If they get married? I think I'd have to."

She jolted. "They're getting married?"

"He hasn't said anything to me yet, but I think it's coming."

Once again, her knife slowed. "Oh, wow."

Was she thinking about what this meant? How my ex-girlfriend would become my stepmother? It was kind of fucked up.

She peered at me with eyes full of empathy and her voice was hushed. "How do you feel about that?"

"I don't know. Okay-ish? Which is weird. I feel like I

definitely shouldn't be okay with it, but they're both happy. Very much in love, and he treats her the way she deserves, so . . . I'm okay with it."

She tilted her head, and it looked like she was reevaluating me for a second time. "That's really mature of you."

Her compliment did something to me. Warmth spread through my center and a soft smile edged my lips. "Thanks."

She smiled back, and as her knife began to move, she held my gaze for an extra moment. It was like she didn't want to break the spell between us and—

"*Motherfucker*," she hissed, jerking her hand back from the cutting board.

It was stunning to hear that word come out of her mouth.

And I didn't understand what had happened until she lifted her hand to inspect it, and a line of bright red blood gushed down her finger.

SEVENTEEN

Preston

Sydney was calm, but panic poured into my stomach, making me leap up out of my seat. My feet couldn't move fast enough as I sprinted around the counter to get to her.

Blood ran in rivulets down her hand, and just as I reached her, she went on the move, hurrying to the sink. She slapped the lever up on the faucet to get the water going, and then shoved her hand under the stream, grimacing.

"Are you okay?" I asked, even when I knew the answer was no. There was so much blood, the cut had to be bad.

"Yeah," she gritted. Her finger came out from under the water, only to turn red again and steadily drip blood into the sink. "I just nicked it. I don't think I sliced anything off."

"You don't think you—" I repeated in shock.

Finally, my brain started to work.

"Where are you going?" she demanded as I tore out of the kitchen.

"Dad!" I crossed the living room and rushed toward his bedroom, yelling with that urgent pitch that could only mean something was wrong.

He'd heard it because by the time I had his door open, he was right on the other side.

"What's wrong?" His gaze swept over me, searching for

signs of trauma.

"She cut herself," I blurted, and started back for the kitchen, knowing he'd follow me.

He had no idea who 'she' would be, since I hadn't mentioned anyone was coming over, and I didn't know if he recognized her when he spotted her at the sink. Maybe that part of his mind turned off when he went into doctor mode. He hurried to join her at the sink and grasped her wrist.

"It's okay," he said. "Let me see."

She let him pull her hand out from under the water, and embarrassment coated her words. "I wasn't paying attention and the knife slipped."

He didn't respond to her statement. Instead, he focused on the wound, moving her hand around to see the cut from different angles.

"Do I need stitches?" It was clear she hoped his answer would be no.

He tore a paper towel off the roll and wrapped it around her finger, squeezing. "No."

She let out a sigh of relief, and her gaze moved from my father's hands to the pot of chicken stock on the stove that was boiling softly. "Preston, can you turn the heat down? If the broth reduces too much, it'll make the risotto salty."

Um, what?

"That's what you're concerned about right now?" I asked. Not the fact she'd nearly sliced off the end of her finger?

She glanced at me like I was the one being weird. "It's just a cut. Once the bleeding stops, I'll be fine to keep going." Her focus returned to my father. "Any chance you have a latex or nitrile glove I can use?"

He glanced over at me, perhaps to check out how I felt about this, but I had nothing.

She'd gotten hurt, and that had rattled me. Like, a *lot*.

Seeing her in pain had caused my heart to go out of rhythm and a cold sweat to break out across my skin. And the sight of her bleeding had pumped all this adrenaline into my system, and it was still there in my stomach, making me uneasy.

Her cut had upset me a hell of a lot more than it did her. Why the fuck was that? Was she stronger than I was, or . . .

Fuck.

I'd gotten all worked up because I *liked* her. Shit, I liked Sydney way more than I should.

My dad cleared the uncertainty from his throat, drawing my attention. "There are some gloves in the study."

He'd said it with the intention for me to go and get them, and it felt like I had no choice but to respect what she wanted. Wasn't it my fault for distracting her? I turned to head for the study at the front of the house, only for her voice to ring out.

"But turn down the heat on that burner first," she said.

Despite her injury, Sydney had no problem preparing the shrimp risotto, and doing it with minimal help from me. Luckily, she'd managed not to get any blood on the cutting board, and once my dad finished bandaging her finger, she'd slipped on a blue latex glove and got right back to work.

It was like the cut—which had to hurt—didn't bother her. It had barely slowed her down.

And that was so fucking impressive.

She was tough and in command when she was at the stove, and her confidence was a massive turn-on. Not that I didn't like the shy version of her during our lessons, but if this determined, self-assured Sydney came out to play while we were having sex? I'd be fucking done for.

As I predicted, right as she was finishing the dish, my father got called in. He said goodbye to us on his way out the door, then tossed me a look I couldn't read. Had he recognized Sydney and was wondering what the fuck I was doing with my best friend's sister?

If so, he didn't have any room to judge. When he'd gotten together with Cassidy, they'd kept it a secret from me for months.

But his look could have been something else. Maybe he was curious about this beautiful girl who'd taken command of our kitchen, and wondered what the fuck she was doing with me.

After the delicious dinner she'd made us, I'd been adamant that she let me handle the clean-up. She'd sat at the table, sipping on the wine that was left over from cooking, and watched me scrub pans and rinse plates.

"I'm not sure I've ever seen anything sexier," she said, "than Preston Lowe loading a dishwasher."

I laughed. "You need to get out more."

When it was done, she finished her wine and descended

the stairs into the basement with me right on her heels. She moved at a fast clip, like she couldn't wait to get in there, and, shit, neither could I.

Once she'd walked into my room, she pulled her phone from her pocket and set it on the table beside the couch, and I'd barely made it through the doorway before I was on her.

I kicked the door closed behind us and it slammed loudly, making her jump. But it wasn't enough for her to break our kiss. I had a hand up under her shirt, cupping one of her tits through her bra, and the little sound she made when I squeezed got me hard as quickly as the snap of a pair of fingers.

She lifted her arms when I grabbed the bottom of her shirt and began to tug it up, making it easier for me to strip it off her. She wasn't wearing the virginal white bra this time. It was a basic black one, but it was still sexy as hell. I jerked one of the straps down, making her tit tumble out, and I bent to capture it in my mouth.

I liked how responsive she was. Her back arched, like she wanted me to have all the access I needed.

"Such a good girl," I said.

While I fumbled with the clasp at the back of her bra, she grabbed the back of my shirt and tried to get it off me, and so it became a race to see who could get the other one topless first. Because I was so competitive, of course I won.

But it had been close.

Kissing her while her naked tits were pressed to my chest was fucking fire. My tongue dipped into her mouth, and she sighed with satisfaction, answering back with a stroke of her own.

It was a lot easier to undo her shorts than her bra.

As soon as I had the zipper dropped, I wedged my hand inside her underwear. I didn't bother pushing her shorts down, I left them open and sagging on her hips while my fingers slid down to her pussy.

A wicked smile burned across my lips when I discovered she was already wet.

Her whole body shivered when my fingers found her clit and stirred. She closed her eyes against the pleasure I was giving her, and her head lolled forward, planting her forehead against my shoulder.

I moved my fingers in tight circles, which wasn't that easy because it was a snug fit for my hand inside her shorts and panties, but I made it work. She moaned and grabbed my arm for support.

"Oh, I'm sorry," I teased. "Am I making it hard for you to stand?"

I didn't give her a chance to answer. I pushed a finger deep inside her scorching body, and the action made her gasp and lift onto her toes.

"I'm going to put my cock here, Sydney." I couldn't tell if it was my words or the finger I pulsed in and out of her that made her moan. "Right inside this tight, wet pussy. That's what you want, isn't it?"

She nodded as best she could with her forehead still resting on my shoulder.

But I wasn't going to let her get away with just that. "*Tell* me."

"Yes," she gasped.

Then she pushed down one of the sides of her shorts, making them fall to her ankles, and once again, giving me better access to her. I had a lot more freedom to work with, and I glanced down, enjoying the way my hand looked as it moved inside her underwear.

She seemed to enjoy the way my finger felt inside her, but she liked my fingertips on her clit even better, and so when I focused on that, she trembled so badly I worried she was going to buckle.

I pulled my hand away from her and didn't give any warning before scooping her up into my arms. She yelped with surprise, and she didn't get a chance to get used to my hold, because I marched the few steps to the edge of my bed and dropped her on top of it.

She stared up at me with wide eyes, and I tried to convince myself I didn't notice how good she looked on my bed with her long, dark hair puddled around her. It was easier when I focused on something else, so I leaned over, grabbed the sides of her black panties, and yanked them down her legs so fast there was the sound of thread ripping.

"Oops," I said.

Her chest heaved with her rapid breathing, but I got the sense it was excitement and not so much that she was nervous or shy.

After all, we'd done this before. But it was still so new, and last time had been a bit like a dress rehearsal. This time, the training wheels were coming off.

My gaze swept over her naked body, enjoying every inch,

every curve. "Open your legs," I said. "Show me where I'm going to put it."

A blush glanced through her expression, and for a second it seemed like she wasn't going to do it, but then her knees parted. Her legs slid quietly across the bedspread, and revealed the slit at the center of them, all pink and bare and *damp*.

"Good girl," I murmured.

I grew hotter the longer I stared at the pussy I was desperate to have, but I didn't want to get ahead of myself. She'd only had sex once, so it would be good to give her a little more prep. My mouth and two fingers had worked well last time, so—

My phone was in my pants' pocket, but when it vibrated with an incoming text message, I ignored it. Whatever it was, it could wait. I had more important things to focus on right now.

I dropped to my knees and buried my mouth in her sweet pussy.

Sydney's hand fisted the hair at the top of my head, and she bucked when I pushed two fingers in her. "*Fuck.*"

Had I done too much, too soon?

No. I'd caught her off-guard, but a deep moan seeped from her lips, and she squirmed with pleasure, so she clearly liked it. The hand in my hair tightened, twisting and pulling the strands, but I didn't mind. It was kind of hot.

Her body was an inferno, threatening to burn up my fingers as I fucked her with them. I used the tip of my tongue to caress her clit in short, rapid strokes, and the faster I went, the harder she panted.

The more her legs shook.

I turned my palm up to the ceiling and curled my fingers, searching for that same spot I'd found last time. She'd come so hard, I'd thought my fingers were going to break off inside her. It was a challenge to do while I was also going down on her, though. My chin was in the way, and I had to tilt my head to open up more room.

The cadence of her breathing changed abruptly. It went shallow and urgent.

Fuck, yeah.

She was getting close. I kept up my steady tempo with my fingers, driving at the exact place I'd been when her breathing shifted dramatically.

"Preston?" a distant voice called.

Sydney and I turned into statues. It sounded like whoever it was, they were making their way down the basement steps.

"You down here?" the voice asked, and this time it was loud enough for both of us to recognize it.

Fuck, fuck, *fuck!*

I reeled around, surveying my options. Colin would be at my bedroom door any second.

Sydney was so stunned, it was hard to get her to move, and since we had to hurry, I wasn't exactly gentle as I hauled her up off the bed and dragged her toward my closet. She stumbled inside the dark space, naked and breathless, and nearly tripped when she turned to look at me.

The sound of Colin knocking on my door meant I had

to ignore her frozen expression of shock. I darted across the room, collecting her clothes that were scattered across the floor.

"Just a second," I replied in a rush as I hurled the clothes into the closet. She tried to catch them, but some hit her and fell to the floor. I filled my eyes with regret and a wordless apology as I gave her a final look before shutting the door and trapping her in.

I scooped up my t-shirt and yanked it on as I went to the door and pulled it open.

"Hey, man." I forced casualness into my voice. "What are you doing here?"

He looked puzzled. "Didn't you get my text? I just finished over at Scott and Nina's, and thought since I'm already here, we could play some Call of Duty."

Scott and Nina owned the production company that sold Colin and Madison's content, and they lived just up the street. Scott was a famous porn star, and it had blown my mind to find out he lived in the same subdivision I did.

It wasn't unheard of for Colin to drop by. He had lived here in the house once and was basically family, so he knew the keypad code to the garage, and could come and go as he pleased. But usually, he gave me a heads-up.

He did, but you were too busy going down on his sister.

Colin studied me critically as I stood in the doorway, blocking him from coming in. He noticed I was out of breath and sweaty, and he tried to peer around me and get a look at my room.

"What were you doing?"

"Nothing." My answer came too quickly, in a voice that was too tight, and this very much announced I *had* been doing something.

Abruptly, he grinned. "Oh, I get it. You were—what did you call it? 'Focusing on yourself.' Sorry for interrupting your jerk-off session."

I had no response. I didn't care if he thought I was beating off alone in my room. At least it kept his suspicion at bay. I straightened, dropping my hand from the door. It wasn't an invitation, but he took it that way, and Colin strolled into the room.

My gaze darted to the closed closet door, and back to him. "Is Madison with you?"

"No, she stayed behind to do a girls-only thing. Nina said she'd drive her home after it's done."

He dropped onto the couch, making himself comfortable, and my blood pressure climbed. All that separated him from Sydney, who was probably still buck naked, was my thin closet door. If she made the smallest sound, he'd hear.

I had to get him out of here. "So, listen, I'm actually kind of tired."

He gazed up at me like I'd just said I wanted to live with my dad and Cassidy forever. "You're what?" He scrutinized me. "How hard were you jerking off in here?"

"Hilarious," I said flatly.

He glanced over at my clock. "It's not even nine."

"Yeah, well, I didn't sleep all that great last night." This at least wasn't a lie—I'd stayed up late texting with Sydney after she got off work, and then I'd stayed up even later wondering if she was using the toy I'd bought her at the same time I was jerking off.

Colin looked disappointed, and I got that. Once we'd become business partners, hanging out and being friends had taken a back seat to everything else.

"Okay, fine. Just a few matches," he said as a compromise.

My gaze flicked to the closet door. I didn't want him to get suspicious, and this seemed like the most efficient way. Maybe I could throw a few games and get us killed right away.

Hopefully she'd understand, and not think I was abandoning her.

"Yeah." I held in the sigh I wanted to make. "One match."

EIGHTEEN

Sydney

It felt like I was stuck in the closet for hours, and Preston had completely forgotten about me. After their voices went quiet and I was sure they'd left the room, I pulled on my clothes as slowly and silently as humanly possible.

When that was done, and a lot more time had ticked by, I worked up the courage to crack open the door and peer out into the room. The door to his bedroom was shut, and I could hear simulated gunfire and explosions coming from the large TV in the main living area of the basement.

I spied my phone on the side table, but it might as well have been a mile away. I didn't know if Colin would come back into Preston's room when they finished, so I had no choice but to stay put. I pulled the closet door shut and went back to the spot I'd cleared on the floor, sitting on the carpet and leaning against the wall.

I thought about menu combinations to pass the time. I catalogued different entrees, making a list of the ones I'd like to try preparing in the future, doing everything I could to distract myself.

But as time dragged on, my irritation grew.

What happened to *just one match*? I didn't know how long they usually lasted, but this seemed too long. Didn't he remember I was trapped in here?

Finally, the sounds of the video game ceased. It was quiet for another minute, and when someone opened the door to the bedroom, I held my breath. Had Colin followed Preston in?

The closet door swung open, light poured into the space, and I rapidly blinked against it before my eyes zeroed in on Preston. At least he had the decency to look concerned.

"Shit, I'm so sorry." He offered a hand to help me to my feet.

I tried my best to keep my tone even. "Is he gone?"

"Yeah, he just left." He raked a hand through his hair as he backed up, giving me space to step out of the darkness and into the room. "Fuck. That was close."

"Yeah." There was a hint of bitterness in my mouth, flavoring my words. "What happened? Did you forget about me in here?"

"No, of course not." His expression was serious. "How could I forget about you?" He said it under his breath, annoyed. "I think about you all the damn time."

His confession made the room go off-kilter.

But when I glanced at the clock and saw it after ten p.m., irritation helped me find my footing. "Then why was I stuck in there so long?"

His shoulders sagged. "Time got away from me. I didn't want him to get suspicious, and we hadn't hung out in a while." He scratched his forehead and sighed. "I feel fucking guilty about going behind his back."

My anger subsided a bit. He'd confessed earlier tonight

he was trying to be a better person. Plus, I shared the same guilt he did. Lying to my brother was about as enjoyable as the hour I'd spent hiding in the closet.

"We could tell him," I said.

"Tell him what?" Preston's gaze turned hard. "That I fucked you when he told me to keep my hands off you?"

I bristled.

Most of the time his filthy mouth turned me on, but his statement cheapened what we'd done. What I had meant was we could tell Colin we were dating, but—then again, Preston had been clear we weren't. He was my teacher, and we were just *friends*.

Ones who texted every day, had been on multiple dates, and were exclusive. Not to mention, we'd slept together. But he wasn't my boyfriend.

He didn't want that label.

"You're his best friend," I said. "I don't get why he's so against the idea of us getting together."

He looked at me with confusion, like the answer was obvious. "Because he knows I'm not good enough for you."

My breath caught in my throat. He'd said *he knows* rather than *he thinks*, and it hurt my heart to find out Preston believed he wasn't good enough for me. Four years ago, maybe there was the slightest chance that had been true, but now? He owned up to his mistakes. He tried to put other people before himself.

He *was* becoming a better person.

I swallowed down my annoyance and lifted my chin. "Well, he doesn't get to decide who's good enough for me. I'll talk to him."

"Don't," he said quickly. He moved closer and set his hands on my hips but seemed distracted by his thoughts. "It'd be better if you let me handle it. I can . . . I don't know. Put some feelers out or something."

I fought the urge to push for more.

Colin was my brother, so I knew he'd love me no matter what. Preston, on the other hand, had so much more to lose. Since he was closer to Colin than I was, and he thought it was better coming from him, I was willing to defer to his judgement.

"When?" I asked.

His dark eyes were focused as he leaned in. "Soon."

When his mouth landed on mine, the atmosphere in the room grew thick in a heartbeat, rekindling the fire we'd had earlier. His hands slipped up under the hem of my shirt, and his fingers splayed across my bare back, slowly inching up.

His tone was pure seduction. "Where were we before he showed up?"

I let out a short laugh and grabbed his forearms, pushing them down. "We don't have time for that anymore. I need to be home soon."

It was a weeknight, which meant my parents liked to be asleep by eleven—and they wouldn't go to bed until I was home.

"You could be bad and break curfew." His mouth was hot on the side of my neck, and every kiss was a tool of persuasion, begging me to stay.

God, how I wanted to.

But I sensed I had to pick my battles with my parents, and this was one I wasn't ready to fight.

When I didn't say anything, Preston straightened and gave a knowing half-smile. "All right, good girl. I'll drive you home."

Preston parked the car in my driveway, then turned to look at me seated in the passenger side. His gaze drifted over me and my box of cooking gear I'd brought over to his place that I now had resting on my lap.

"Thank you for the knife bag," I said. I was still stunned by his gift.

He was sheepish but tried to play it off like he wasn't. "Yeah, well, thanks for dinner."

Didn't he hear how that sounded like a date? Adding to it was the way he leaned over in his seat, traced his fingertips across my jawline, and placed his lips against mine.

Whoa.

This kiss . . . this *incredible* kiss he gave me wasn't about sex, or lust, or desire.

It tasted like longing. Like he would miss me when I got out of this car and walked inside. It was slow and thorough, and everything outside of him evaporated.

When his lips left mine and he drew back, his expression was conflicted, and for a moment he looked like he was considering doing it again. I sucked in a breath, silently wishing he would, but instead he simply stared at me as if I were a puzzle he couldn't solve.

Like I'd done the first time he'd kissed me, I lifted my fingers and pressed them to my lips.

"What was that?" I whispered.

"I kissed you goodnight. It's not a big deal."

Except it felt like a big deal, and I was beginning to wonder if he didn't understand what that phrase meant.

"Goodnight," he added, and his gaze turned forward to stare out the windshield as he waited for me to head inside. He was tense and all out of sorts, and I got the feeling our kiss had unsettled him as much as our first one had.

Only this time, it made my heart race in a different way. How many more times could he kiss me like that and walk away unscathed?

"Goodnight," I answered and pushed open the car door.

My dad was sitting in the living room when I came in, and it took a single glance to know he'd been waiting up for me. His arms were folded across his chest, a displeased look was fixed on his face, and his tone was brusque. "Were you out with him?"

I feigned ignorance, shifting the box so I could tuck it under an arm. "With who?"

"Preston Lowe."

I gave him a bright smile to combat his sour mood. "Oh. Yeah."

"Well, your mother and I have discussed it, and we've decided it'd be best if you don't see him anymore."

I stood utterly still and stared at him, and the harder I

looked, the more I saw the fear hiding in his eyes. He was scared about losing control of me the same way he'd done with Colin.

My lack of response unnerved him. "Did you hear me?"

"No," I said.

"No, you didn't hear me, or no—"

"*No*," I repeated, putting all the force behind it as I would a slap in the face.

The conversation was over as far as I was concerned, and since there was nothing left to discuss, I walked into the kitchen, leaving him looking like I'd turned his world upside down. I dropped my box off and then made my way upstairs, and it wasn't until I shut the door to my bedroom that I realized why.

It was the first time I'd ever told him no.

From the moment I slipped behind the wheel of my father's Audi, nervous energy began to twist my stomach. Even though I'd gotten my dad's permission to borrow his car, I'd done it under a lie.

I drove to the movie theater on the far side of town, parked in a spot, and then waited anxiously with my phone in my hand. It was only a few minutes before his text came through, but it felt like hours.

Preston: I'm here. Are you inside already?

I lifted my gaze to the entrance of the theater and saw

him making his way toward it, so I pushed open my door and got out.

"Preston," I yelled across the rooftops of the cars separating us.

His gaze scanned the parking lot, and when it landed on me, I gave him a wave, signaling for him to come over. Confusion crossed his face. Was he wondering why I was standing beside my car and not moving for the doors? He turned and headed my direction.

"Hey." He pulled to a stop a few feet away, and I had the strange feeling he'd done it to avoid getting too close. As if to prevent me from enticing him into giving me a kiss hello. "What's going on?"

I'd been kind of cryptic when I'd texted him this morning, asked him to meet me here, and said I had a surprise. My voice was tight with nerves, even as I tried to make it sound relaxed. "Hop in."

He glanced at the movie posters and showtimes that lined the front of the theater, and even more confusion filled his face. "We're not seeing a movie?"

"No." I swallowed a breath. "I have something else planned."

His gaze zeroed in, and as he studied me, I was sure he could see all the anxiety and excitement I was trying to disguise. His confusion was overridden by intrigue. "What is it?"

"Get in, and I'll show you."

It didn't take him more than a second to consider it, and then he was moving toward the passenger side.

"Whose car is this?" he asked once we were both seated

inside. "Your dad's?"

"Yeah." I buckled my seatbelt and started the engine. "He let me borrow it when I told him I was going to the movies with my friend Hailey."

A sly smile edged his lips. "Because he wouldn't let you borrow it to see me?"

"No." I reversed out of the parking spot. "They've said I'm not allowed to see you anymore."

"Is that so?"

Even though I was watching the backup camera, I could hear his wide smile from his tone, plus the thoughts in his mind. He took my parents' demand as a challenge. A rule he was happy to break.

"And yet, here we are," he teased. "Bad girl."

I switched the car into drive and glanced at him for a moment, just long enough to show him the thrill his words caused.

Preston was quiet as we exited the parking lot, and he didn't say anything either as I rounded the side of the enormous theater, but his confusion returned when I wove around a dumpster and then on to the alley at the back of the building. The wide lane of pavement was sunbaked and had seen better days, and I dodged large potholes, cracks, and puddles of gravel as we crawled along.

"Where are we going?" he asked.

Ventilation and pipes snaked across the back of the theater, and on the other side, the alley gave way to a heavily wooded area. It looked like no one ever came back here—at least, not unless something broke and needed repair.

I tucked the car in beside the center of the building, beneath the ancient-looking fire escape stairs, which seemed to be more rust than anything else, and put the car in park.

"Do you remember Sabrina Farrell?" I turned in my seat to look at him. "She was a sophomore when you were a senior."

"Not really. Why?"

"She used to work here, and we were friends, so she told me about this place." I gestured out the windshield and drew in a preparing breath. "This is where she'd go to have sex with her boyfriend, because she wasn't allowed to have boys over to her house."

He blinked, digesting the information.

"There aren't cameras back here," I said. "At least, there weren't any a few years ago, according to her, and if my parents decide to check my location, they'll see I'm at the theater." My skin grew uncomfortably warm. "It means this is the perfect place if you wanted to," my breathing went shallow, "fuck me in the back seat of my dad's car."

He flinched, but it was in a good way.

It was like the idea was so hot, he didn't know how to handle it. His lips parted so he could drag in a deep breath, and his eyes turned molten. The intensity of it made my heart skitter and sweat blossom on the back of my neck.

His tone was patronizing because he knew it was unlikely. "What if someone comes out and sees?"

"I don't care," I whispered. "I want to be bad."

"Yeah?" When he leaned in, it somehow pushed out all the air between us. "You wouldn't care if they saw you riding my dick?"

On some level, I was aware he said things like that just to watch my reaction, but he had no idea what they really did to me. How his words filled my body with smoke. How tight he could twist the tension inside me until I considered begging for release.

I shook my head, but that caused him to quirk an eyebrow in displeasure.

His order came in a low voice. "Say it."

I bit down on my bottom lip and then powered through. "I don't care if they see me riding your dick."

"Hmm. I'm not sure I believe you." His expression was a mixture of victory and pride. "Let's see if that's true."

NINTEEN

Preston

Was it fucked up that I was, like, *proud* of Sydney? When she'd asked me to meet her at the movie theater, I'd figured we'd buy tickets, go sit in the back row of some movie neither of us cared about, and do some hand stuff while pretending to pay attention to the screen.

Maybe she'd even be willing to try something riskier and go down on me. She'd lean over the armrest and quietly suck my cock while the people several rows in front of us would be oblivious.

But this idea? It was even better.

"You're a bad girl, Sydney. Asking me to fuck you in your *daddy's* car."

Because I knew what she was going for, and I was completely on board with the idea. This was a rebellion. An act of disrespect her parents had more than fucking earned.

But what I was less excited about was the cramped space of the back seat. I reached down and found the buttons for the power functions on my seat. The motor whirred quietly as I slid my chair back as far as it would go, and then I pushed open my door, letting the summer heat spill into the car. "Get out and come around to my side."

Her pretty eyes widened, and she glanced from the open

door to the back seat. "Aren't we going to get—"

"No." I pushed another button to make the seat recline. "I want you over here."

Her chest rose and fell with one hurried breath, and then she was moving. Her door was pushed open, she got out, and by the time she reached me, I was out of the car and standing beside the open door.

I flung a finger at the passenger seat that was nearly flat now. "Sit down."

Fuck, it turned me on how she did it, no hesitation, no questions asked.

Sydney climbed into the car, and although it wasn't roomy, there was enough space for me to get in too. I knelt on the floorboard, fitted myself between her parted knees, and pulled the door closed, trapping us in.

I had to hunch over a bit to keep my head from hitting the ceiling, and I put a hand on her at the base of her throat, urging her to lie back. The leather creaked beneath her as she complied, and I trailed that same hand down over the center of her body, gliding over her thin, cotton t-shirt and on to the snap of her jean shorts.

I'd just finished unbuttoning them when she turned her shoulders to the side and reached into the back seat, plucking her purse up off the floor. Her words were rushed and shy. "I got you something."

Her fingers disappeared inside her purse and then they produced something shiny. It was a foil packet, and immediately the wheels began to turn in my head. I fucking *loved* how she'd planned this all out, from the secret spot behind the theater to the way her parents wouldn't know she wasn't at the movies, and down to the condom she set beside us on the top of the center console.

An evil grin burned across my face. "When'd you buy that?"

Her eyes met mine, only to dart away. "I stopped on my way over here."

I pictured her standing in the aisle at the drugstore, staring at the different options, and imagined her face turning red. Fuck, she'd probably looked so sexy. My fingers inched down her zipper, tooth by tooth, and all the blood in my body migrated south, swelling beneath my fly. "Did you feel like a bad girl buying them?" I asked. "Did it turn you on?"

She exhaled softly. "Yes."

I made a sound of satisfaction and gripped the sides of her shorts, tugging them down. It caused her to kick off her flip flops, so she was barefoot, and she raised her knees to her chest, allowing me to work the denim over her hips. Off her shorts came, and I dropped them onto the driver's seat with a soft thump.

Her underwear was a dark green and cut low, and my dick flexed, straining against my zipper. I hadn't always liked foreplay, but I'd come a long way since high school, and now I fucking *loved* it.

Too bad there wasn't much time for it today.

Not in this hot, cramped car where my knees were uncomfortable on the scratchy floor mat, and not when she was spread out beneath me, wearing an expression that begged me to move faster.

It seemed so unlikely anyone would see us, but I glanced out the windows anyway and checked that the coast was clear. It was, so I reached a hand behind my back, grabbed a fistful of my t-shirt, and yanked it off, adding it to the pile on the driver's seat.

The car was still running, and the air conditioning was on, and even though I wasn't hot yet, I knew it was inevitable. Every lesson with her had been more scorching than the last. I grasped the headrest behind her head, leaned down, and set my mouth on hers.

Her palms were warm as they moved across my chest and glided down my arms. Since I was already supporting myself with them, I didn't have to flex my biceps to show off how toned they were. She could feel the hard muscle I'd developed after months of training at the gym, and a sense of pride expanded inside me.

As we kissed, I liked the way her hands explored. Hesitant at first, and then they grew bolder. They coasted down my back and onto my ass, before sliding around toward the front.

It was unreal how quickly she turned me on. By the time she cupped me through my shorts, I was already hard, and I pushed my hips forward, urging her to give me more pressure.

She found the outline of my dick and smoothed her palm down it, giving me a hit of pleasure that was more than enough to break the restraint I'd put on myself. I hadn't wanted to move too fast, not just because of her past, but because it was only her second time.

But that plan went out the window as she rubbed my

dick through my shorts.

I straightened onto one arm and shoved a hand under her shirt, forcing it up until her plain white bra came into view. And then I hooked a finger into one of the cups and jerked it down. Her tight nipple was a dusky pink, and as soon as it was exposed, I swooped down and closed my lips around it.

"*Oh,*" she murmured.

When I bit down, she flinched and bucked, but it was clear it was only with surprise and not pain. The grind of her hand against my cock got stronger, making me want to escalate, too. I needed her fist wrapped around me, or my fingers inside her, or my mouth on hers, or . . .

I just fucking *needed* so badly, I couldn't focus on anything. I flicked my tongue over her hardened nipple, and the smell of whatever fruity lotion or perfume she was wearing invaded my senses.

It made me fucking drunk with desire, and it wasn't until she tried to undo my shorts that I was able to bring myself back online. I straightened, nearly banging my head on the ceiling, and focused on my zipper. It took no time for me to get my shorts off, and as they dropped to a puddle around my knees, my dick fell heavy onto the front of her green panties.

There was no filter left inside me. It had been burned up by how hot she was. "Take off your shirt." I wanted it to be a request, but it came out sounding like a demand. "Show me your tits."

Her throat bobbed with a thick swallow. The seat was nearly flat, and she was lying down, which meant if anyone came outside, they wouldn't see if she got topless. Hell, they wouldn't see her at all—her body was below the windows.

They'd have to get beside the car to see in, plus she'd said she didn't care if anyone saw us.

Her decision was made. Sydney grabbed the shirt that was bunched up under her arms and peeled it up over her head. As she arched her back and wedged her hands beneath her to undo her bra, I gripped my dick and rubbed my tip over the damp crotch of her panties.

The sensation distracted her from her task. She'd gotten the bra unclasped, but her movements slowed, and her eyes hooded with pleasure, so I grabbed the center of her bra and pulled, freeing it from her arms.

She was naked except for the skimpy underwear, and she looked so fucking great. Like a wet dream against the leather of the car seat. I had to squeeze the base of my cock to get better control of myself. Her summer suntan spread across her arms and chest, but it faded away as my gaze reached her pale, teardrop-shaped breasts.

I rubbed the head of my cock against her again, teasing her clit through her whisper-thin panties, and she let out the softest, neediest little fucking moan I'd ever heard. It shot straight to my dick, making me throb and ache, and impatience got the best of me.

There should be more foreplay, a voice inside me warned. *More prep.*

But I ignored it.

I hooked a finger into the side of her underwear, pulled it out of my way, and slid my bare cock through the lips of her pussy. She was hot and slick with arousal, and the action felt so good, static played in my brain.

Like that time we'd been in her room, we were only a heartbeat away from sex. It would be easy to line us up and slip inside her raw. It'd take no effort to sink my body inside hers with absolutely nothing between us.

Every nerve ending in me tingled, begging for it, but instead I repeated the action. I put my free hand over top of my dick, pressed down, and sawed my hips back and forth, making the ridge at the head of my cock slip and slide across her clit.

We both exhaled loudly, and she shuddered beneath me, her head lolling to one side. There was a creak from the dash as she placed the balls of her feet on the flat section above the glove box. It gave me more room to spread my knees on the floorboard.

More room to maneuver.

Again and again, I brushed the sensitive underside of my tip over her swollen clit, and each stroke made her breathe harder. Her hands clamped down on my biceps and her hips swiveled erratically, like I was driving her out of her mind. Her movements seemed uncontrollable and . . . dangerous.

Sweat trickled down the side of my forehead, and I used the back of a hand to wipe it away before grasping her waist. I needed to hold on and anchor us together so she didn't move a fraction of an inch too high. She was so fucking wet, I might accidentally slide halfway inside her with one poorly timed thrust, and I couldn't let that happen.

Watching her writhe beneath me was so fucking sexy,

my tone turned wicked. "Did you want something?"

I didn't slow down either. I kept up my methodical pace, grinding our bare skin together, and she clawed at my arms. Her head tipped back, and she let loose a frustrated sigh.

"I want you to stop teasing me," she said between two enormous gasps, "and put your fucking dick inside me."

Jesus Christ.

I jolted to a stop, and an incredulous smile overtook my face. I hadn't expected that to come out of her good girl mouth, so I had to blow out a slow breath to even myself out.

"Do you have any idea," I snatched up the condom she'd brought me and tore the wrapper open, "how fucking *hot* it is to hear you talk like that?"

Her focus was glued to my hands, watching as I took out the condom and rolled it on, but meanwhile, color splashed across her cheekbones. She liked my compliment, but her shyness wasn't something she'd totally conquered yet. As she learned about sex, she was figuring out her confidence too.

And me? Well, I was happy to help.

"I love it when you say what you want," I said. I grasped the sides of her panties, and like she'd done with her shorts, as I tugged, she brought her knees to her chest, making it so I could strip her underwear off. "It turns me on." I added her last scrap of fabric to the pile. "Gets me so fucking *hard.*"

To back my statement up, I ran my sheathed dick across her pussy again, so she could feel every goddamn inch of me.

A moan drifted out of her like she'd tried to hold it back, but the sensation was too powerful to contain. Her legs parted and her feet went back to the dash, and then she settled her naked body back against the seat, as if she were getting ready.

If we saw someone coming, there was no way she could scramble back into her clothes in time, but the danger of getting caught . . .

Fuck, it only made things hotter.

I grabbed the corner of the seatback and leaned over her, making it so there was hardly any space left between our bodies, and peered down into her eyes as I began to guide myself inside her.

The blue color of her irises turned bottomless as I advanced. Her mouth fell open, and she sucked in a sharp breath, but she held my gaze and one of her hands moved to clench my bare ass.

It read to me as a signal to keep going. To push deeper.

"You're pussy is so goddamn amazing. All hot and snug, and so fucking *wet*," I mumbled mindlessly. "Are we going to leave a mess on the passenger seat of your dad's car? I bet you'd like that, wouldn't you?"

She let out a nervous sound, like the idea turned her on even though she thought it shouldn't.

I grinned. *"Bad girl."*

Down I sank, going as far as I could, while studying her for any sign she was uncomfortable. But she didn't appear to be. Her breathing was tight and shallow, and her legs surrounding my hips were quivering, but she didn't break our gaze. I got the feeling she wouldn't.

This was a challenge she was going to meet.

My dick pulsed, flexing and stretching and filling her, but I did my best not to move too fast. It was a tight fucking fit, and I wanted to give her time to adjust since I'd skipped the foreplay. As I drew back my hips, it was almost torturous because the urge to drive into her was powerfully strong.

My body wanted to thrust.

To pound, and take, and claim.

To fuck her hard enough that she'd still feel the ache of me inside her tomorrow. That way, there was a chance I'd dominate her thoughts for at least one day, the way she did to me every day.

I pressed forward, and my vision blurred from how good it felt.

Maybe I leaned down the last inch, or perhaps she rose to meet my lips—I couldn't tell. Our mouths were hungry and greedy when they pressed together. It was wild that I was kissing her, and my dick was inside her, and for the first time in my life, I wasn't sure which sensation I enjoyed more.

That was . . . scary.

I'd told myself I wasn't allowed to have feelings for her, and that was so fucking stupid. I should have known better. Sometimes, the fastest way to get me to do something was to tell me it was off limits.

TWENTY

Preston

Fuck it. I was tired of pretending this thing between Sydney and me was just sex. I already had an idea for our next *lesson*, and if she told me it sounded like a date, how the hell could I deny it?

That was what I wanted it to be.

In the past, things usually worked out for me, and it hadn't mattered much if I had to step on someone else for that to happen. But the Colin problem? It loomed large, and I didn't see a way I could get everything I wanted. Where I could be with her while staying friends with him. What if he forced me to choose?

Don't think about it.

She made that easy because her mouth was fucking addictive, and her kiss demanded all my attention. It wasn't just our lips and tongues, either. Her hands roamed over me, touching me like she couldn't get enough. As if she wanted to make sure this moment was real and happening.

The rough carpet of the floormat scrapped at my knees, but I ignored it and eased her into my slow, steady pace. The interior of the car was stiflingly hot, so when our kiss ended, we both panted in the humid air. Her skin was damp with sweat, making her stick to the leather seat, but she didn't seem to care.

When I shifted my stance on my knees and straightened, I found a different angle, and she gave a sudden moan that was soaked in pleasure.

"Yeah?" I rasped. "Does that feel good?"

"Oh, my god, yes." Abruptly, her gaze ran from mine and her expression fell.

My heart thudded and I slowed my pace. "What's wrong?"

Her focus snapped back to me, revealing her expression wasn't upset or scared—this was something . . . *else*. Something naughty and sinful. There was an electric charge in her eyes I hadn't seen before.

"I shouldn't be doing this." Her voice was hushed and affected. "I'm supposed to be a good girl."

Fuck me.

My dick jerked, and she obviously felt it because her pussy clenched on me in response. The idea of being bad turned her on and, yeah. I was into it. I moved my hips faster, thrusting harder and causing her tits to reverberate with each jolt. A dark grin lurked at the corners of my mouth.

"Oh, my god," she whined, putting her fingertips over her lips and she spoke through them. "I shouldn't have your cock inside me right now."

I exhaled loudly and slid a hand under her head, lifting her so she could see the way I disappeared inside her. "But look at how good you are at taking it."

She gasped, and she watched the slippery slide of my dick into her body from the bottom of her eyes like the sight was almost too hot to look at.

Fuck, it probably was.

I pictured what we'd look like if someone strolled up to the car and peered in. They'd see her naked, and on her back, and me kneeling between her legs, fucking her while I was bent over and trying not to bang my head on the low ceiling.

Shit, I'd bet we looked amazing.

I eased her head back down onto the seat and fumbled a palm over her breasts. She moved with me, and even though the car was a million degrees, goosebumps lifted on her arms.

I dipped down to drop short kisses on her mouth, and longer ones on the side of her neck. Her chest heaved with her labored breath, and it was punctuated with her little gasps and moans.

How the hell was each one sexier than the last?

She had a hand braced on the door and another clasped tightly on my shoulder, holding on as I built to a punishing tempo. It made the car rock, and if I kept this pace, I wasn't going to last much longer.

Her body was a vise, gripping me, and I felt it fucking everywhere. Pleasure ricocheted through me, bouncing through my limbs and gathering in my center toward the big finish.

And while I could tell she really liked what we were doing, I suspected it wasn't going to be enough to get her across the finish line before me. We needed a new position, preferably one that'd give my knees a break and my fingers access to her clit.

I ringed my fingers around the base of my dick and made sure the condom stayed in place as I pulled out of her, and it was satisfying to hear the needy, frustrated sigh she gave when I'd stopped.

"I want you on top," I demanded.

She blinked, and I could see the thought running through her mind. *How the hell are we going to accomplish that?*

Awkwardly, was the answer. She moved as close to the center as possible and turned sideways, making room for me beside the door. I got on the seat, wiggled beneath her, and when she hitched her leg up, her foot thudded loudly against the window.

Her laugh was embarrassed, but she finished the move, planting a knee on either side of my hips so she was straddling my lap. My dick was trapped between our bodies, and while the feel of it was nice, it wasn't enough. I needed to make her come, and I wanted to be inside her when it happened.

A few strands of hair were stuck to her glossy face, and as she got used to this new position, she ran a fingertip across her cheek, pushing the strands back. Her cautious gaze darted out the windows, checking to see that we were still alone, because with her on top, she wasn't hidden anymore.

But it was just us.

I had her all to myself.

My hands settled on her hips, and I shifted on the seat, adjusting her position while I nudged at her from below. "Fuck," I said. "Get that pussy on me."

She shuddered and her eyes hazed as she lowered herself onto my dick, one slow inch at a time. The pleasure was immediate for both of us, and my pulse quickened. Air tightened in my lungs, making it hard to breathe. It was like a fist had reached inside me and squeezed.

The new position was insane. I always loved cowgirl, but when it was her on top?

Goddamn.

I got to see her face twist with surprised satisfaction as she started to move. "Oh, my god," she whispered.

I groaned with enjoyment, my head thudded back against the headrest, and the muscles in my chest and arms corded. The whole experience somehow felt just as new to me as it probably did to her.

Her breasts swayed as her body undulated, and the sight of it was more erotic than I was ready for. So, I couldn't stop myself from reaching up and wrapping my hands around her tits, filling my palms with the weight of them. I had her nipples trapped in each hand between my thumb and the side of my palm, and I lifted, pushing her breasts together.

Her back arched, and as she stared down at me, I saw the sexy woman she could become if only her shyness would let her.

"Lick," I demanded.

My dirty command caused a wave of pleasure to sweep through her, and her pussy clenched. She didn't hesitate, though. Her lips parted as she lowered her chin to her chest, and she drew in a stuttering, preparing breath. Then, her pink tongue darted out so she could swipe the tip of it over her own nipple that I'd just offered to her.

All the while, her unblinking gaze was locked on mine.

"Oh, my fucking god," I groaned. "Good girl."

She loved hearing the praise, and it made her rock her hips faster.

"But I'm not a good girl," she whined in the same affected tone from before. "God, if my parents saw me right now, if they saw what we were doing . . . I'm so *bad*."

I quirked an eyebrow. "Oh, you think you're a bad girl, Sydney?"

I let go of her breasts so I could slip one hand behind her head and pull her down closer to me. Her hands landed on my chest as she ground to a halt, but that was okay. I took over. I latched my other hand on her hip and moved beneath her, thrusting upward, and matching the same tempo she'd just abandoned.

My tone came out darker and hotter than I intended. "This is what happens to *bad* girls."

I let go of her hip, reared back, and brought my hand down on her ass. The loud smack of skin hitting skin punched through the air, and it seemed to knock the breath from her.

But it was all in shock and nothing else.

My spanking hadn't been aggressive or punishing or even serious. It was sexy.

And she thought so, too, because as soon as she found some air to breathe, her eyes melted, and a moan poured out of her.

"Are you a bad girl?" I asked.

It came from her like a plea. "*Yes*."

My next spanking was just like the first. Light and play-ful, and her groan of satisfaction followed it. I pretended she needed to be scolded, as if I were annoyed with her. "You're so fucking sexy."

I dug my hand into the hair at the base of her head and

tugged her back, exposing the arch of her neck to my mouth. I sucked hard on the spot beneath her ear where her pulse was furiously beating, and drove up into her, strangling back the urge to lose control.

Everything was spiraling and racing toward a place I wasn't ready to go. If I didn't act fast, I'd come, and I'd be damned if I didn't get her to orgasm first. Last time I'd started at a disadvantage, so I didn't see using the vibrator then as cheating, but this time? My competitive nature wanted her pleasure to come from me and nothing else.

I wedged a hand between our bodies, right above where we were joined, and ground the pad of my thumb against her clit.

The muscles in her thighs tightened and her upper body flinched, giving me the impression the sensation was so powerful, it was acute. Maybe overwhelming. She dug her nails into my chest. "*Fuck.*"

"It's okay if you want to scream when you come on my cock," I encouraged. "I promise I won't tell anyone. No one has to know how hard you let me fuck you in your daddy's car."

Her eyes widened. "Oh, god."

The pitch of her moans shifted, growing more frantic and urgent, and her breathing sped up to match. *Yes,* my body chanted. My thumb stirred faster, and her desperate moans and gasps for air became so loud, I felt like I was drowning in them.

I clenched my teeth and shut my eyes for a moment, focusing on her, and tried not to think about how good she felt all wrapped around me. *Ten more seconds,* I promised my aching cock. *Hold out for ten more seconds and she'll get there.*

She only needed five.

When Sydney let out an enormous gasp, my eyes popped open, and suddenly her body began to contract and spasm. "Oh, shit. *Shit!*"

The way her orgasm seized on her was impressive. Everything shook, from her shoulders to her legs, and her eyes slammed shut. Her mouth dropped open in a silent scream, and even though there was no sound, it filled my head anyway.

I tried to watch, tried to memorize the visual of it, but the rhythmic pulses of her climax set off my own, and I was no longer the driver in my body—just a passenger along for the ride.

Scorching hot pleasure flooded through me, from my fingertips to my toes, and every one of my muscles hardened to steel. I locked up, bracing myself against the onslaught of ecstasy that consumed, and ravaged, and decimated.

Jesus fucking Christ.

It seemed to go on forever.

Wave after wave of it.

And when the orgasm finally began to recede and my muscles relaxed, I was spent. A tingling, numb bliss moved through, and I struggled to catch my breath and slow my heartrate down. God, I needed it at a tempo where it didn't seem like it was going to beat out of my chest.

Her head tipped forward, and she planted her forehead on my collarbone. It took her much longer to recover than I did, but I was content to let her stay exactly where she was, with me still lodged deep inside her. I could feel every after-shock of pleasure, every involuntary twitch she had left over from her orgasm.

The car was quiet except for her heavy breathing and the fan blowing out the life-saving air conditioning. Finally, she reluctantly peeled away from me, lifting her head and slowly blinking her dreamy eyes.

I kissed her.

Thoroughly.

And when that was done, she gingerly climbed off me. I turned on my side and flattened my ass against the door, making as much space as I could for her to lie beside me with us facing each other.

When I moved to pull the condom off, she once again reached for her purse.

"I brought a bag for you to . . ." She trailed off, either too shy to finish or too distracted watching my fingers as they knotted the condom up.

I grinned. The good girl had planned the whole thing, even down to how we'd get rid of the evidence. But as she retrieved the small plastic bag from her purse, passed it to me, and retrieved the torn wrapper from the cup holder, I got an idea.

The condom was dropped in the bag, but when she went to toss the wrapper in too, I pulled back. "How bad do you want to be?"

Confusion drew her gaze up to mine. "What?"

"You can throw that away," I motioned to the foil wrap-per and its branding that proudly announced what had been inside, "or maybe you leave it somewhere your dad will find next time he cleans his car."

Sydney's chest rose with a deep breath.

I was only half serious, and I honestly didn't expect her to even consider it, but perhaps it had sounded like a challenge to her. The thoughts in her head were loud on her face as she mulled it over and weighed the consequences.

She reached over me and placed the wrapper down in the side pocket of the passenger door, then flashed me a brilliant, proud smile.

"All right, naughty girl." I fired back a lopsided grin.

She nestled down on the seat, tucking one hand under the side of her face, and dropping the other to the tiny, empty spot of leather between us. "I guess if he gets mad enough and kicks me out, I can crash at Colin's place."

Did she realize that if she did that, it'd be impossible to keep seeing each other? Unless she stayed in the guest room at my place, like her brother had after he'd gotten kicked out.

Wait a minute. Slow the fuck down.

While dating Sydney was an idea I was starting to get on board with, living with her wasn't one. It was way too much, way too soon. But the fact I'd considered it, even just for a second, when I'd realized I might not be able to see her anymore . . . well, that told me just how much trouble I'd gotten myself into.

How strong my feelings were for her.

I set my large hand on top of hers and pretended I didn't notice the way her breath caught or how her eyes filled with excitement. She shifted the angle of her head, subtly scooting closer, and the lock of hair resting on her neck fell.

"Aw, shit," I groaned.

"What? What is it?"

I stared at the pink spot on her neck. "Looks like I, uh, gave you a hickey. Sorry."

I meant the apology, but I wasn't *that* sorry. When I'd sucked on her neck, I hadn't intended to do anything, but— fuck. I couldn't deny it looked good, and I liked the idea of leaving my mark on her.

My gaze returned to her hand pinned beneath mine.

There was a red-purple line on her skin where she'd cut her finger the other night, and the memory made tightness pinch inside my chest. This was another mark I was responsible for, but this one I wished she didn't have.

At least the cut looked like it was healing okay, and it probably wouldn't leave a scar. Eventually, both of my marks would fade away and it'd be like they'd never happened.

Was that how it'd be for us?

Yeah, I fucking hated that idea.

Her fingers tapped the leather, moving absentmindedly, and her brow furrowed.

"What are you thinking about?" I asked.

She looked like she didn't want to answer me, and her hesitant voice was hushed. "That we only have one lesson left."

"What are you talking about?" I counted them in my head and realized why my number was different from hers. "The night Colin showed up doesn't count," I explained. "We got interrupted."

"Oh." A thought occurred to her, and she clearly liked it

because a smile climbed into her eyes. "If that's true, then neither does the night in my room. We got interrupted then, too."

Huh.

She probably expected me to push back, but—no way. "You know what?" I said. "You're absolutely right."

As the date approached, Troy's launch party became Distinguished Events' primary focus. We purposefully didn't schedule anything else the final week leading up to the album's release. That way, we'd be ready to focus on any issues that arose. So far, everything was going according to plan, and I was doing all I could to make sure it stayed that way.

When Warbler requested two extra cases of hard-to-come-by champagne yesterday? Sure. Not a problem. Or the venue changing its policy and announcing VIPs had to wear wristbands instead of lanyards? I made it happen. I even pretended it was an easy switch, when in reality, it was stressful as hell.

I was sitting in Colin's living room and had just finished going over the timeline for the event with him when my phone buzzed.

> **Sydney:** I got someone to cover my shift on Thursday. Are you going to tell me what we're doing now?

Excellent.

Preston: Nope. I'll pick you up at 7.

Sydney: Really? You're not even going to give me a hint?

I sent her the emoji of an axe.

Sydney: WTF?

I chuckled, and I did it a little too loudly because it caught Colin's attention. He lowered the screen of his laptop so he could better look at me.

"Who are you texting?"

His question made the smile freeze on my face and my mind temporarily blank. "Nobody," I mumbled. "Just a friend."

Well, shit. That was the worst lie in the history of lies, and I scrambled to come up with something better. Something believable as I locked my screen and set my phone face-down on the table.

I went with the first plausible name I could come up with. "Cassidy."

Colin stared at me, and a range of emotions played out on his face. Surprise. Confusion. And finally, unease. "You're texting with your ex?"

I frowned. "Don't make it sound like that. She texted me because she had a question about the pool. The pump wasn't running."

This wasn't a total lie. Cassidy *had* sent me a message earlier today asking about this. But it was shitty what I was doing, how I was lying to him.

"Oh." He accepted my statement, his concern abandoned,

and his focus returned to his laptop. I studied my friend for one long, critical moment, and determination built inside me. This conversation was long overdue.

"Guess who I ran into the other day." I forced casualness into the words, hoping to sound natural.

He didn't take his eyes off his screen. "Who?"

"Sydney."

Well, that got his attention. His interested gaze snapped to me. "My sister? Where?"

My heart beat faster. "At the movie theater. We said hi and talked for a minute."

Actually, we fucked in your dad's car, and we talked after.

"Yeah? That's cool." He nodded but wasn't all that impressed. Our suburb was small, and running into people you knew happened all the time.

"Remember how she beat me at beer pong at our graduation party?" I asked. "When she'd never even played before?"

"Syd for the win." His expression shifted as if he were trying to hide his discomfort. "That was the motto in my family."

His tone was light, but I heard *everything* he wasn't saying buried beneath it. Sydney had always been the golden child, even before Colin entered high school. She could do no wrong, and he couldn't do a damn thing right.

But I never got the impression he resented her for that—only his parents.

"I'm not convinced she wasn't just lucky," I said.

He let out a short laugh. "If you played her again tomorrow, I'm telling you, she'd beat you. She always wins."

It was the opening I was looking for. "So, if I wanted to

ask her for a rematch some time, would that be cool?"

Colin blinked, and for a moment, he was sure I wasn't serious. But the longer my question sat with him, the more worried he became. His smile hung awkwardly. "A rematch?" he repeated, and then sobered. "You mean, like a date?"

I tossed up a hand. "No, of course not." Shit, I was over-compensating. "I mean," I sputtered, "I don't know if I'd call it that."

His eyes narrowed and his broad shoulders tensed. "Oh, yeah? What would you call it, then?"

Shit. "I just thought we could hang out or something. Me and her." I tacked it on, but it was pointless. "As friends."

He laughed again, only this one was humorless. "Yeah, no. Not a chance."

Annoyance crawled up my spine. "Why not?"

Colin's gaze was dark. "Are you seriously asking if you can date my sister?"

I should have been smarter and taken some time to consider how to respond, but my 'fuck it' attitude stormed in and said it had it covered. "What if I am?"

His expression hardened. "The answer is no. In fact, it's *hell* no."

On some level, I knew how this conversation was going to go, and yet it still hit me like a ton of bricks. I wasn't just pissed off—I was hurt. Sydney's comment from before echoed through my mind. Why was I good enough to be Colin's best friend . . . but not good enough for his sister?

Part of me already knew the answer, but I asked it anyway. "Why?"

He peered at me as if I were suddenly a stranger to him. "Because you don't date, Preston. You don't care about feelings or really want anything serious. You fuck a girl, and the next day, you're on to the next one. So, can you blame me for not wanting that for my little sister?"

I'd never had such strong, conflicting emotions at the same time. I was offended by this accusation, but I begrudgingly knew he wasn't wrong. At least, he wasn't about the last few years. I had avoided relationships and hadn't been interested in anything other than sex.

"I'm not like that anymore," I said quietly.

His face contorted. He wanted to believe me but couldn't. "Look, I love you, man, and maybe you've changed, but she's," he struggled, searching for the right descriptor, "a good girl, and you're . . ." He did me a favor by not finishing his thought. "There's no way it wouldn't end badly. She'll get hurt, and then that'll fuck things up between us."

My shoulders sagged, nearly crashing through the floor. Everything he was saying was right—I knew that. And deep down, I also knew it was too late. It was like I was driving toward the edge of a cliff, and I refused to pump the brakes or turn away. I just kept barreling straight toward it.

"Yeah." Disappointment clogged my throat, but I hoped he couldn't hear it. "You're probably right about that."

"I am. Forget about Syd," he said. "She's not your type, anyway."

I smiled to hide how hard I had my teeth clenched. He had no fucking clue how wrong he was about that.

TWENTY-ONE

Sydney

I didn't tell Preston I lasted less than twelve hours before caving. The condom wrapper that I'd tucked in the door's side pocket was hidden, and yet I felt its presence the entire drive home. It grew heavier and louder the longer I left it, and it was just after midnight when I gave up. The worry over my parents finding it was so strong, it made it impossible to sleep.

Because if they found the black foil wrapper, they'd kick me out of the house, and while I could stay with Colin and Madison, that was a *less* than ideal situation.

My brother and his girlfriend shot a lot of their scenes at their place, and I knew that because he had warned me multiple times to always text before coming over. Crashing at their apartment, even short term, would make things difficult for them, or awkward for me, or potentially both.

Plus, it'd make it ten times harder to keep up with my 'lessons' with Preston, and the last thing I wanted was for those to stop. Or for him to decide I was no longer worth the risk he was taking with his partnership with my brother and drop me.

So, I got out of my bed, snuck down to the garage, and stole back the wrapper. There were already a few bags of trash in the garbage bin, so I moved one aside and ditched the wrapper beneath it, ensuring my parents wouldn't find it before the garbage got emptied.

Even with that taken care of, the wrapper still dominated my thoughts, because it was a reminder of the scorching hot sex we'd had. I felt a low pull in my center as I got back into bed. There was an ache for him that was constant, incessant.

Shit. Was it normal to be this horny all the time? Preston had unleashed something inside me that was dark and hungry.

I couldn't use the vibrator he'd given me. Surely my parents were asleep, but the little motor inside it wasn't silent, and I was terrified of them hearing it. I'd only used it once since I'd brought it home, and that had been in the shower where the overhead fan and the water beating against the tile drowned out all other sounds.

I'd sat on the floor with my back against the cold wall, held the vibrator between my legs, and stayed as quiet as possible when the orgasm blasted through me.

> **Sydney:** I thought about you while using my educational aid in the shower.

That was the text I'd been brave enough to send him later that morning as I got ready for work.

> **Preston:** Such a good girl. Wish I could have been there.

Every time he called me that, it lit me up inside. His praise was a drug, and I was a junkie for it.

I wanted to write back that I wished he'd been there

too, but my shy fingers were impossibly sluggish, and by the time I worked up the nerve to start typing, his next message rolled through.

> **Preston:** I'd make you blow me and I'd cum inside your pretty little mouth.

A hot flash washed through me, and I gripped the phone tighter. I'd never sent sexy texts before, and suddenly my mind was running away with itself. Naughty texts were bad, but sending dirty pictures? That would be *really* bad.

My blood heated at the thought.

Yet as much as the idea had turned me on, I hadn't been able to pull the trigger on it that day. Not just because I was running behind, but because I wasn't ready. I hadn't a clue how to take a picture where I felt sexy or provocative and not hilariously awkward.

Tonight was . . . different.

Maybe because I was amped up from sneaking around and throwing away the condom wrapper, or the relief that I was safe now, but there was a confidence lingering inside me. It was wild and foreign, but exciting too.

I grabbed my phone off the nightstand and clicked on the bedside table lamp, which cast a small, warm glow around the room. Jitters fluttered in my stomach as I considered what kind of photo to take. Should I do a topless one?

Or *more*? Really go for it with full nudity?

I glanced around the room and my gaze snagged on the mirror. It made me pull in a deep breath, climb out of bed, and shed my clothes. I tried a few different poses, snapping pictures while holding my phone in front of my face, or ones where my face was out of the frame.

It wasn't that I didn't trust Preston, but the only way to protect myself from shit happening was to make sure it never existed in the digital world.

My attempts at taking a decent picture all failed. I didn't feel sexy or empowered, and the photos looked forced. As if I were trying too hard—which I was. I sighed and sat down on the side of the bed, which happened to be the same spot where Preston and I had fooled around a few weeks ago while facing the mirror.

Like I needed another memory to turn me on, or something else to intensify the ache I desperately wanted to relieve.

I remembered the feel of his hands on my body, and it caused me to slide back to my place on the bed, with my head against my pillow and my fingers between my legs. I brushed my fingertips over my clit and bit down on my lip to hold in a groan of pleasure. I wanted it to be his hand doing this, or—

Abruptly, I scooped up my phone and, without allowing myself to think about it, I took a picture. It was of me naked on the bed, shot from my chest down, with one hand between my legs and my fingers resting on my clit. I'd been leaning my hips slightly to one side and twisted my shoulders the other way, which gave me a provocative arch and made my boobs look good.

This picture? It was kind of hot.

I opened my chat with Preston and hurried to send it before I lost my nerve.

Sydney: Wish you were here.

It was after midnight, so I assumed he was asleep. I dropped my phone on the mattress beside myself and imagined him waking up tomorrow morning, sleepily looking at his phone and discovering what I'd done.

Would he be thrilled? Maybe even a little proud of how—

I jolted when the phone vibrated on the bed.

Preston: FUCK

Oh, my god. He was awake? Heat flooded my face. It was sort of like I'd passed a note to a boy I liked in middle school, only to have him read it right in front of me. Except this was on a whole new anxiety-inducing level.

I stared at the screen, waiting for the dots to show me he was typing, but there was nothing, and the longer it dragged on, the more nervous I became. What if he meant this *fuck*, as in something bad had happened?

My lungs stopped working as a horrible thought seized me.

What if he was up late playing Call of Duty with Colin right beside him? I hadn't given Preston any warning of what I was sending because I'd just assumed he'd be alone.

Three gray dots finally appeared and blinked, and anticipation made it impossible to move.

Preston: I've got something for you.

The next message was a picture, and I gasped.

I'd never been on the receiving end of a dick pic before, and up until this moment, I'd been grateful. Most of the time, dicks—at best—were funny. On their own, I didn't find them exactly attractive or all that sexy. How I felt about them had more to do with who the dick was attached to.

But seeing Preston naked, fully hard, and a fist wrapped around his cock like he was mid-stroke, was fucking erotic. It was a miracle my screen didn't melt.

Like me, he was in bed and had taken the picture from the chest down. His covers were pushed down to his knees. I stared at the picture in awe, tracing every curve of his body I could see. It was so nice to get to look at him however I wanted, for however long I wanted, without feeling shy.

The screen went dark, though, and his name flashed across the top of it.

"Hello?" I whispered.

His voice was like honey. "Good girls don't send pictures like that."

I sank down into the bed and closed my eyes. "Guess I'm not a good girl, then."

"Are you touching yourself right now?"

"Yes." I swallowed thickly, stirring my fingers over my clit. "Are you?"

"It's what I was doing when you texted me."

There was rustling in the background, and I pictured the slow, steady slide of his hand as it moved up and down his length. There hadn't been a lot of time between the exchange of our pictures, which meant he'd probably already been hard when I'd sent mine.

I was curious, and since I couldn't see him, it was easier to talk about. "Were you watching porn?"

There was a heavy breath. "No. I was thinking," he paused, "about you."

It was almost a relief to hear it. "God, me too. I was thinking about when we were in my room. When we were facing the mirror."

"When I had my fingers inside you?"

"Yes," I whispered.

"You got any of your fingers inside you right now?"

I shook my head, and then realized he couldn't see. "No. I like it better when, uh," I lowered my voice, "they're on my clit."

"Hmm. I bet you do. How come you're not using my vibrator?"

I got a strange thrill hearing him call it his. Like he still owned it even after he'd given it to me. "My parents might hear."

"It's not that loud." His laugh was sinister. "Get it and turn it on. I want to listen to you come."

His command was so sexy, I shivered with excitement, and then I reached for the bottom drawer of my nightstand.

I had no idea how to dress for my evening with Preston. He'd asked me to change my schedule because he wanted to go somewhere together on Thursday, but he wouldn't say anything more. All he'd sent me for a hint was an axe emoji, so . . . were we going to chop wood? Become lumberjacks? Was I supposed to wear flannel?

In the end, I put on white shorts, a navy-blue halter top,

and pulled my hair up into a high ponytail. Summer was in full force, and if we were doing anything outside, I wouldn't last five minutes with my hair down.

I'd just finished putting on a pair of dangling earrings when Preston texted he was in the driveway. I swiped on some lip gloss, shoved the tube of it into my purse, and headed down the stairs.

My mom was in the kitchen, and when she saw what I was wearing, she looked dismayed. "I thought you were working tonight."

"I changed my plans." I kept moving toward the door, but she followed right behind.

"Where are you going?"

"I don't know." It wasn't a lie. I grabbed the handle and pulled it open. "But don't worry. I'll be home by eleven."

She made a sound like there were too many things she wanted to say at once and they all got clogged in her throat, keeping her from saying anything. I stepped out onto the front porch, tugged the door closed behind me, and then hurried down the path to the black Dodge Charger that waited for me.

I was breathless as I got into the passenger seat because I'd walked fast, plus I was excited, and he looked so damn good. "Hi."

"Hey." He flashed a bright smile before he put the car in reverse and began to back out of the driveway. "I've got something for you."

My heart skipped and my knees pinched together. Last time he'd started a conversation with that, it had ended with me having orgasms. One hadn't been enough with the vibrator. He'd wanted to see how many I could squeeze in before he came.

Three was the answer.

"Is it in your pants?" I asked.

"No." He put the car into drive, and as he headed toward the exit of my subdivision, he pointed to the center compartment below the dashboard. There was a small envelope waiting there. "It's in there."

The plain, white envelope was invitation-sized, and when I picked it up, the much smaller card inside shifted around. I untucked the flap and pulled it out, flipping the plastic card over in my hands.

What on Earth?

"Whose license is this?" It was Felicity Gamble's, according to the information printed on the driver's license. I looked at the picture of the smiling brunette and then lifted my accusatory gaze to Preston. "And why do you have it?"

"We're just borrowing it, so I'm going to need it back at the end of the night." He kept his eyes on the road as we pulled up to a stop sign. "You and Patrick's girlfriend look close enough that you can pass for her."

My jaw dropped open at the same moment my focus returned to the driver's license in my hand, zeroing in on Felicity's date of birth. The math was quick. "She's twenty-four. I don't look twenty-four."

His tone was light and amused. "Sure you do. No one is going to care, anyway. They barely check." Abruptly, he turned serious. "But start studying, just in case the bouncer wants to be an asshole and quiz you."

As Preston drove to the highway, I started memorizing everything. Just having the borrowed license in my hand felt wrong and fucking exhilarating. None of my friends had fake IDs, and if this worked, I'd get a sneak peek at the world that was still off-limits to me for another four months.

"Hey, Felicity," he teased. "What's your address?"

I rattled it off, then double-checked that my answer was right.

"Cool." His gaze sliced my direction, and a smirk twitched on his mouth. "And what's your sign?"

I opened my mouth to answer, only to freeze. Felicity's birthday was in June, but mine was in October, and I didn't know Zodiac dates. "They're going to ask that?"

He peeled his fingers off the steering wheel to lift a hand and gesture *'maybe.'* "I've seen it before. When the girl hesitated, the bouncer knew immediately it wasn't her ID, and so he took it." His tone was serious. "Let's make sure that doesn't happen tonight."

"Felicity is okay with letting me borrow her ID?"

"Yeah. If it goes wrong, she can just say she lost it. All the risk is going to be on you." His tone was warm and persuasive. "But you've got this. It's early, so they won't care, plus a little danger doesn't bother a bad girl like you. Right?"

I swallowed a breath, so it came out sounding less confident than I wanted it to. "Nope."

The bar was on the outskirts of downtown. It was a freestanding brick building, painted in a modern black, and there was a large axe perched over the doors. The axe emoji he'd sent me the other day finally made sense.

My heart was racing at a thousand beats a minute when we reached the front door and Preston put his hand on it. He shot me a quick glance, maybe checking to see if I was ready to go through with it.

I nodded.

All the information I'd memorized pounded in my head when he pulled open the door and walked in. Usually, he'd let me go first, so I got the feeling he'd done this intentionally. Like he was the first through the door because he wanted to be a shield for me.

There was a stand just inside, and the woman who sat on a stool beside it glanced over as we came in. She smiled and sized us up instantly. "Can I see your IDs?"

I'm Felicity Gamble, I chanted repeatedly as I pulled the borrowed driver's license from my purse. Nerves made my hands clumsy, and Preston must have noticed because as soon as he had his license out, he grabbed mine and passed them both to the woman.

She looked at the first one, and her gaze flicked to him. Then she glanced at the other license, making me hold in a breath. Preston wasn't wrong—I had the same length brown hair and blue eyes as Felicity, and since the ID was a few years old, the picture was somewhat faded.

But I wasn't a spitting image of her. Our noses were different, and my chin was pointier, and—

"I made a reservation for a lane," he said.

She stopped looking at the ID, distracted by him, and then gestured to a spot behind her. "One of the guys at the booth can help you with that." She glanced at the IDs for another microsecond, nodded, and handed them back to him. "Have fun."

I slowly metered out the air in my lungs as we walked past the stand and moved deeper into the bar. The rush of excitement was intoxicating, but I did my best to play it cool.

The bar was busy but not too crowded, and the music and conversations surrounding us were interrupted by loud thuds as axes hit wooden targets. Dark wood paneling lined the walls, and stalls were partitioned off with heavy black netting, allowing multiple games to run simultaneously. The ceiling was exposed pipe and ductwork, the floors were polished concrete, and the atmosphere was pure machismo.

I was so busy watching the game in the stall closest to me, I didn't realize Preston was heading toward the bar. I hurried along to catch up. "Are we going to play?"

"Once we get some drinks." His grin was sexy. "What are you having, Felicity?"

For a half-second, I considered telling him I'd have whatever he was drinking. I wanted him to think I was cool and at ease, that I could hang with him. But then I realized he was probably going to order a beer. And more importantly, I strangely didn't feel the urge that I needed to impress him.

I liked who I was when I was around him.

And I liked who he was too.

So, I sipped on my spiked lemonade while we collected our gear and lane assignment from the booth, and then we each took a few minutes to warm up.

I'd never thrown an axe before, but it clicked right away with me, much to Preston's irritation. I understood the balance and how to throw so the blade hit the wall and not the handle.

He came close to beating me in the first game, but as my accuracy improved, his seemed to get worse, and he teetered between annoyance and embarrassment when we finished our second one. I'd won easily.

"How are you so good at this?" he huffed as he dislodged one of his axes from the wall. It had landed far below the outermost circle of the target. Like he'd been when we played beer pong, he sounded both annoyed and impressed. "We're playing again."

"Why?" I couldn't help myself. "Does losing turn you on?"

Oh, shit. The fire that burned in his eyes was seriously hot.

He put his axes down on their rest and marched over to me, trapping my waist in his hands. "I guess we'll find out after we're done here, because we're going back to my place." His gaze traced over my face, and his expression turned carnal and indecent. "And then I'm going to fuck you so hard, Sydney, you're going to be numb for *days*."

I inhaled sharply.

The lust his words injected me with left me dizzy and reeling. I imagined us in his bed, and felt him moving inside me, and my legs threatened to go boneless.

I'd wanted it to sound like I was rising to meet his challenge, but my voice was throaty with desire. "I'm ready whenever you are."

He laughed, shook his head, and turned his focus back to the game of throwing axes.

I was glad he let me buy the second round of drinks and

I only had minor pushback from him, since he'd paid for everything else, plus he'd arranged the whole evening. He clearly didn't like losing, and I suspected we weren't going to leave until he beat me once, but still—he seemed to be having a good time.

Me? This was like the perfect date, except for the tiny, little detail that it wasn't a date. It was a lesson. He'd brought me here to use a fake ID and see how good I was at being bad.

After I defeated him in the third game, I considered throwing the next one. I sensed his frustration, and I was such a people-pleaser, it was hard to take. But when I missed the target at the start of the next round, he glowered.

Preston knew *exactly* what I was doing, and he didn't like it one bit. "No pity win," he growled at me. I pressed my lips together, smashing away the smile I wanted to make. It was important to him to earn a win, and I understood. If I were in his shoes, I'd probably feel the same way.

But it meant we could be here a while, so I glanced around the noisy space and spotted the sign I was looking for above the hallway at the other end of the bar.

"I'm going to the restroom," I said. "Be right back."

I was surprised to find there was a line for the ladies' room, and while I waited at the entrance to the hall, my gaze drifted back to Preston. I caught glimpses of him through the crowd, and he seemed to be practicing while I'd stepped away. He squared his shoulders to the board, dipped the small hand axe back over his shoulder, and then flung it forward.

It landed in the wall with a satisfying *thwack*, just left of the bullseye. I smiled to myself. I'd seen him throw dozens of times now, and yet I was never prepared for just how sexy it looked. How the sleeve of his shirt wrapped around the thickness of his bicep, or the tendons in his forearm flexed.

Fuck. The crush I'd had on him in high school was nothing compared to the way I felt about him now.

Hair at my nape prickled, and a strange sensation washed down my back. There was an alert going off in my brain, trying to tell me something, and when I widened my gaze to include things outside of just Preston, I realized what it was.

There were some guys sitting at the bar who were perfectly in my line of sight, and one of them was looking at me while wearing a friendly smile.

Did . . . I know him?

He didn't look familiar, but his smile was warm, so I shot him a brief, polite smile back. Maybe he'd mistakenly thought I was looking at him when my focus had been on Preston, who was behind him. The line cleared up, so I ducked inside the tiny bathroom and didn't think anything of it until I finished.

When I came out, it looked as if the guy had been watching and waiting for me. He raised a hand and flagged me over, and it was so sure and confident, I began to second-guess myself.

Had we met before? It'd be rude to ignore him, so I strode toward the bar.

"Rachel?" he asked me.

Oh. There'd been a tension in my shoulders, and it relaxed. He thought I was someone else. "No, sorry."

He didn't miss a beat. "Oh, well. You look like a Rachel to

me." He gestured to himself. "What do you think my name is?"

Um, what?

When I didn't answer right away, he laughed. "I'll give you a hint. It's Tony."

I blinked, utterly confused. "Uh, okay."

His gaze sharpened like he was examining me for clues to my identity. "Sarah? No, wait. Kristin?" He tossed up a hand like he was giving up. "Give me a hint."

"It's Felicity," I said dryly.

"No shit, really?" His expression was dubious. "You don't look like a Felicity to me."

His comment was light and playful, but it made me uneasy because he'd hit a little too close to the mark. "Don't know what to say to that, Tony."

As I stood beside the bar, I studied him the same way he'd done to me. He looked like he was in his late twenties, and was cute enough, but there was a hint of pushiness that set my teeth on edge. I got the same vibe from him that I had gotten from Mason at that house party my freshman year, the one I'd foolishly ignored.

"What are you drinking?" he asked.

Because I was out of my element, my brain was slow and didn't understand why he was asking. "It was a spiked lemonade."

"You want another?" He turned and attempted to flag down the bartender.

"Wait—" I started.

A hand was abruptly on the small of my back and a shadow fell over me, drawing my attention up. Preston's gaze wasn't on me, it was fixed on Tony, and his smile was tight.

"Thanks, man," his tone straddled the line between being friendly and firm, "but if my girlfriend wants another drink, I'll get it for her."

TWENTY-TWO

Preston

Calling Sydney my girlfriend hadn't gone unnoticed by her. Since I was touching her, I felt the surprise rocket through her body, she didn't say a damn thing to correct me.

The guy who'd been hitting on her took one look at me, and disappointment flashed through his expression. "Oh, sorry." He peered at Sydney and barely hid his annoyance. Like he felt she'd somehow led him on. "I thought you were here on your own."

"She's not." I forced casualness into my voice, because while I didn't like it, I couldn't fault him for trying. He'd recognized how hot she was. But she was mine. "Come on, Sydney. It's your turn."

The guy was offended. "You said your name was Felicity."

It took everything in me not to smile, but it was easier when I saw the worry in her eyes at being caught in the lie.

"It is," I told him quickly. "Sydney's just my nickname for her."

I used my hand to guide her away from the bar and back to the stall with our drinks and the game we were playing.

The one where I was losing *again*.

It was hot inside the bar, and I could feel the thin sheen of sweat on my face. Throwing the axes hadn't helped, and neither did the two pints of beer I'd had, but when I'd seen Sydney get flagged over by the guy, I'd started to sweat for real.

My first thought was he knew her, but her body language quickly told me otherwise. She'd looked uncomfortable, and without a second thought, I'd come running. Part of me knew she didn't need my help shutting him down. She'd done two years of college, so of course she'd been hit on before. And while she was shy at times, she wasn't weak. Sydney didn't need me to rescue her.

But, fuck, I wanted to.

She didn't say a word when I picked up my beer and drank the last few swallows, but her intense gaze drilled into me, impatiently waiting for me to acknowledge what I'd said. It had just slipped out, and the most surprising thing to me . . . was it felt good to put it out there.

Like coming clean.

"Yeah." I set my empty glass down. "So, you're my girl-friend." I held her gaze, challenging her to look away. "It's not a big deal."

She didn't blink, but her chest rose with a deep breath as she considered it. "You're right." The smile that broke out on her face was downright victorious. "It's not."

I blinked my sleepy eyes, annoyed that I'd woken up be-cause I'd been in a deep sleep, and I could tell by the soft light coming through my bedroom window that it was way too fucking early.

I flopped over on the mattress, and my arm hit something soft and warm beneath the covers. What the hell was that? I pulled down the comforter at the same moment a fist banged on my bedroom door, and everything inside me tensed, snapping me alert.

"Preston," my dad called from behind the door. "You need to get up."

I stared at Sydney on the other side of the bed, who wore an expression of sheer panic and absolutely nothing else.

"Oh, fuck," I whispered to her.

Once we'd left Urban Axe and returned to the house, I brought my girlfriend downstairs to my room and made good on my promise. I bent her over my couch and fucked her from behind, loving the way she'd told me my dick felt huge inside her. And because the sex had been so intense and fucking amazing, we'd had to collapse on my bed afterward to rest for a few minutes.

That few minutes had lasted much longer than we'd wanted it to.

We'd slept through the night.

"Did you hear me?" My dad's tone wasn't exactly angry, but it was urgent. "Sydney's parents are in the living room."

"Oh, *fuck*," I groaned again, then lifted my voice so he'd hear. "Yeah, I'll be out in a minute."

His footsteps grew quiet as he turned and headed for the stairs.

I flung off the covers, scrambled out of bed, and was yanking on a pair of underwear before I realized she hadn't moved. Sydney was still nude and nestled down in the sheets with only her stunned face visible. She looked very much like a person going into shock.

This had to be the biggest mistake she'd ever made in her parents' eyes. One she probably couldn't recover from. She hadn't just blown her curfew—she'd spent the night with a guy. And not just any guy, but *me*. Even if we lied and said nothing happened, that we just fell asleep, they'd never buy it.

"Hey, it's going to be okay." I aimed for a soothing voice as I pulled on the same shorts from last night. "Do you need help getting dressed?"

She spoke so softly it was barely audible. "I can't."

I knew what she meant, how she didn't want to face them. "Yes, you can." I did my best to distract her from her dread. "And trust me—the conversation we're going to have with them will be a lot easier if you're not naked during it."

She looked so timid, so terrified, I couldn't stand it. A sharp ache banded across my chest.

When she'd accidentally nicked herself with her knife, she'd barely worried about it. But this? The threat of her parents cutting her out of the family was so scary, it left her immobilized.

It was because after Colin, she knew this was a cut that wouldn't heal.

I put a knee on the bed and crawled over to her, scooping her up into my arms. "It's going to be okay." It spilled from my lips. "I promise."

And before she could question how I could possibly make that promise, I claimed her mouth in a kiss that was too mind-numbing for either of us to think anymore.

It seemed to bring her back to life, though, and when it ended, she hurried into her clothes, combed a hand through her hair, and grabbed her phone.

Her face was somber as she pressed a button on the side and got no response. "My battery's dead."

The stone in my stomach grew heavier. Who knew how many times her parents had tried calling her last night? I took a deep breath and puffed up my chest, slathering on a brave face for her. We couldn't avoid it any longer. Time to get it over with.

Mr. and Mrs. Novak stood in the living room, and they looked like hell. They probably hadn't slept at all last night, and I actually felt guilty about that. Their wary gazes landed on me, and Mrs. Novak straightened sharply, visibly uncomfortable at the sight of her daughter at my side.

My dad hovered at the edge of the living room, wearing a pair of blue hospital scrubs, and I couldn't tell if he was just coming off a shift or getting ready to start one. The door to his bedroom opened, and Cassidy appeared. Her brown hair was pulled up in a haphazard ponytail, and she wore leggings, an oversized t-shirt, and zero makeup.

The commotion must have woken her, and when she saw the upset-looking Novaks and Sydney lurking next to me, her eyes went wide.

The tension in the room was so strong, no one seemed to be able to speak. Or maybe they were all just waiting for me to do it.

"I'm sorry. This is my fault," I announced. "I fell

asleep, and—"

Mr. Novak lifted a hand to tell me to shut the fuck up, and his voice dripped with disdain. "I don't care." His attention shifted to his daughter. "Your mother and I have been worried sick. You didn't tell us where you were going, and then you didn't come home last night. You couldn't be bothered to call us, and then you turned off your phone, which you know is against our rules."

She'd been silent as she lingered a half-step behind me, but now she surged forward and found her voice. "I didn't turn it off. The battery died." She lifted her chin. "I'm sorry I didn't call and that you were worried about me, but there's no need. I'm fine."

"You are not fine, young lady," her mother said. "This is so far from *fine* I barely recognize you. Let's go. We'll discuss it on the car ride home."

"I can take her home," I said.

"You stay out of this!" she snapped. "You and your family have done quite enough." Her furious gaze swung to my dad. "Undermining us at every turn with Colin. Letting her spend the night with your son. I'd ask if you have any decency, but obviously," she gestured to Cassidy, "you *don't*."

Mrs. Novak's statement was a bomb detonating. Cassidy and Sydney gasped at the same time fire exploded inside me, and it burned so hot, the only thing I could move was my hands. My fingers curled into tense fists.

My dad's reaction was similar. The muscles corded in his arms, and his face took on a dark cast that was so scary, Mrs. Novak literally took a step back. She exchanged a glance with her husband, like she was worried my dad might take a swing at her.

Thankfully, he didn't.

His hands were balled into fists so tight, his knuckles were white, but as a man used to dealing with life and death pressure, he knew how to stay calm. His voice was as icy and deliberate as his scalpel. "You're no longer welcome in my home. Leave."

She sneered. "With pleasure." Her focus turned back to her daughter. "Let's go."

Sydney was frozen in place, and her conflicted gaze bounced between me and her parents, which only angered them more. I reached out and curled my hand around hers, wanting to offer support. I didn't do it to send them over the edge, because I didn't give a fuck about them, but her dad's face turned an ugly shade of purple.

"You come home with us right now," he said, "or you don't come home at all."

All the air left her lungs in a sharp punch, and she pressed her free hand to her chest, as if she needed to protect her heart.

"Is that what you want?" Her question was soft, but as she spoke, she gathered strength. "To give me the same ulti-matum you gave Colin? Cut us off and pretend we don't exist because we couldn't live up to your perfect expectations?"

Mrs. Novak had the nerve to look at her daughter like she was being unreasonable. "We never expected you to be perfect, but what we do expect is for you—"

"I've done *everything* you ever wanted," Sydney said.

"Followed every rule, and until last night, I'd never made a mistake. That's what you demand from me. Perfection, and nothing less, because this is the *very* first time I've fallen short, and you're threatening to kick me out. No room for error and no second chance."

Her mother's mouth opened, maybe to defend herself, but nothing came out. Her brow furrowed as she searched her brain for any other time Sydney hadn't been perfect, and it looked like she was coming up emptyhanded.

"You let me think I need you," Sydney's tone was full of indignation, "but I'm realizing it's the other way around, and I'm done living my life how you want me to. So, the ultimatum is this. Either I come home with you now, and you learn to deal with that, or . . . I go stay with Colin, and you'll have driven both your kids away forever."

I was so fucking proud of her for standing up for herself. It had to be hard enough to do alone, but she'd done it this morning with an audience. Mrs. Novak's hard expression faltered as she realized she didn't have the leverage she thought she did, and I could read the thoughts running through her head clear on her face. This had been a bluff.

They'd never expected their good girl to walk away from them.

"You can make your decision on the porch," my dad quipped to the couple. "Because I'd like you to get the fuck out of our house."

Mr. and Mrs. Novak bristled at his profanity, which gave me dark satisfaction. They had a lot of balls coming in here and disrespecting my dad and Cassidy like that.

"You're a terrible father," she said.

"Are you fucking kidding?" I blurted. "He's a better parent than you'll ever be."

Every pair of eyes snapped to me in surprise, but no one looked more caught off guard than my father. Maybe he never expected me to defend him after the mistakes he'd made, but what I'd said was true.

Everyone waited on edge for her to move or say something, and Mrs. Novak's discomfort visibly grew. She chose to ignore me, and her focus went to her daughter, even though I was still holding Sydney's hand.

"I didn't sleep at all last night, so I'm not at my best right now," Mrs. Novak said, like it was a good enough substitute for an apology. "We were crazy with worry for you, and maybe we let our emotions get the better of us. It's hard to think straight." Her gaze flicked to my dad for a second before returning to her daughter. "Can we discuss this in the car?"

Sydney took a deep breath, squeezed my hand, and when I squeezed it back, she nodded.

No one spoke as the Novak family shuffled toward the front door. I followed closely behind, but stopped at the threshold, fighting the urge to stay glued to her side. Once again, I knew she didn't need rescue, but I wanted to be there for her. To help however I could.

I was no stranger to messy family drama, after all.

"I'll text you later," she said and brushed her lips against mine in something almost too short to be called a kiss, but I understood why. She was trying not to wind up her folks any more than they already were.

"You better," I teased, although I was entirely serious.

I watched them go, shut the door, and turned to face my dad and Cassidy. They both peered at me like they didn't know what to say.

"Sorry about wrecking your morning," I said. "And I'm sorry for what she said."

"That's not your fault." He scrubbed a hand over his face, making the whiskers of his short beard bristle, and his gaze turned toward his girlfriend. "Are you okay?"

"Yeah." Cassidy waved a hand like that wasn't important right now. "But I liked the part where you told them to get the fuck out of our house."

"Yeah," I said. "Me too."

She moved toward my dad and put her arms around his waist, and he instantly responded by slipping his arm around her too. It was so comfortable, so natural, and I'd seen them like this enough times it didn't feel weird to me anymore. Hell, she'd been with him longer now than she'd been with me.

She sounded dubious. "Colin's okay with you dating his sister?"

"No, not at all." I sighed and sank down onto the couch, setting my head in my hands. "He doesn't know."

"Oh," she breathed.

The silence that followed was so heavy, I struggled under it. "*You* don't have any room to judge."

"No, I don't," she said.

Her agreeing with me somehow made it worse, and I felt the urge to defend myself. "He's my best friend, but if I tell him? We're done. Our friendship's over." It was the bitter truth, and I hated it. "He made it really fucking clear she's off limits, but no. That didn't stop me. Hell, it barely slowed me down." My face twisted with displeasure. "God, I'm such a shitty friend."

She couldn't have looked more shocked if she'd tried. "Oh, my god. You *really* like her."

My dad's tone was borderline gloating. "I told you he did."

"What?" I asked.

He gave me a sad, knowing smile. "That day she cooked for you, I could tell. You haven't looked at another girl like that except for . . ." His expression hung as he tried to change course. "I haven't seen you look at someone like that in a while."

Fuck, was that true? He was talking about Cassidy, who was the only girl I'd ever loved. And he thought I was looking at Sydney the same way? That idea was terrifying.

I wasn't ready for any of that.

"You know when Colin finds out," I muttered, "he's going to throw our friendship away. Our friendship *and* our business." I crossed my arms over my chest, and I probably looked like a pouting child, but in the moment, I didn't really care. "This fucking sucks."

Cassidy extracted herself from my dad's arms and crept closer to the couch. "I know it does." Her words were quiet, but they carried enormous weight. "It's like, you know you aren't supposed to do it. That being with this person is going to hurt someone else, but you're not in control anymore. There are all these reasons you shouldn't be together, and yet—shit." She glanced at my dad. "There's nothing you can do to make yourself stop."

I'd never seen her side more painfully clear. They'd confessed they'd tried not to get involved with each other for my sake, but they'd failed miserably. The heart wanted what it wanted, and they didn't get a say in it.

"Yes," I admitted.

My dad's deep voice filled the space between us. "You've got to tell him."

"You probably don't want our advice," she said, "but he's right. He had wanted to tell you about us for months, but I wouldn't let him. I was too fucking scared. I thought if you knew, there was no way you'd forgive us, and it'd destroy your relationship with your dad." She sucked in a deep breath, and her expression filled with guarded hope. "But, Preston, look at how far we've come. It wasn't easy, but we made it work. *You* made it work, and imagine how much better it would have been if we'd told you, instead of you finding out."

"Yes, that would have been better," I said sarcastically.

The image of them fucking on the very couch I was sitting on was unfortunately seared into my brain.

Cassidy was right about us coming a long way, though, and that it hadn't been easy. But by comparison, Colin learning to deal with me dating his sister was a much smaller mountain to climb.

And it was one I was willing to try.

TWENTY-THREE

Preston

Sydney's text rolled in less than an hour after she'd left my house. I stepped out of the shower, banded a towel across my waist, and picked up my phone even though I was dripping water everywhere.

> **Sydney:** Good news. I no longer have a curfew.

> **Preston:** Really?

> **Sydney:** I think the idea of me going to stay with Colin really freaked them out.

No shit. It had done the same to me, because how the fuck was I going to see her without him knowing? I set the phone down and scrubbed my head with the towel, drying my hair.

> **Sydney:** They made a lot of concessions. But bad news. I'm not allowed to sleep over at your place, and you're not allowed over here.

"Like I'd want to go over there anyway," I grumbled to myself.

> **Preston:** Whatever. Hanging out at my place is better.

Sydney: Agreed.

As I finished drying off, my gaze snagged on my swim trunks that hung on a hook on the back of the bathroom door. I scrolled to my weather app and checked the forecast. It was supposed to be sunny and hot most of next week, and the restaurant was closed on Mondays, so she should be free.

Preston: Want me to pick you up on Monday? We can go swimming, so bring your bikini.

Sydney: I don't own a bikini.

Preston: Okay. We can skinny dip.

Sydney: LOL. I'll bring my suit. What time?

We settled on two o'clock, and she offered to make dinner after, which of course I wasn't going to turn down. The only thing that sucked about it was I'd have to wait two days to see her again.

We were both occupied with work, though. Friday and Saturday nights were her most exhausting, so our text conversation after each of her shifts was short. I was busy on Saturday, too, with a party for a client, held in an upscale club just off Broadway. It was a surprise fortieth birthday party for his wife, and the event went so well, he'd asked to extend the room reservation and the open bar all the way until close.

It had taken some negotiating with the staff, but I'd made it happen, and I'd woken up to an email on Sunday from the client, thanking me for all the extra work. The big tip he'd Venmo-ed me was awesome, too.

It was my last project before Troy's event on Friday night,

and I was glad I could focus solely on that now. I looked at my afternoon off with Sydney as the calm before the storm. A mini vacation.

"I've got something for you," I said when I picked her up.

"Of course you do." She pretended she wasn't excited, but I saw the glint in her eyes.

"It's in the back seat."

While I drove, she reached back and retrieved the present, setting the gift box wrapped in black paper on her lap. She picked at the corner, peeling up the tape, and took her time opening it like she wanted to drag out the suspense.

"Seriously?"

She looked both surprised and amused as she lifted the two pieces of fabric out of the box. The top of the bikini was navy, while the bottoms were white with navy palm fronds printed on them.

"I think you'll look hot as fuck in it, but you don't have to wear it if you don't want to." I flashed her a smile. "I told you it's cool if you want to go naked instead."

She examined the suit closer, maybe checking the size. I'd had to guess, but I felt confident I'd gotten the right one. "Wouldn't someone see?"

I'd meant it as a joke because I'd never thought she'd go for it. It was the middle of the day. But . . . "My dad and Cassidy are both at work." I shifted in my seat, trying not to get too excited about the idea of us both wet and naked. "What do you say? You want to be a bad girl?"

"Would it be my final lesson?" she teased.

I grinned. "Well, technically, we still have two left."

Her fingers trailed over the edges of the bikini in the box. "Let's start with me wearing this, and we'll see how it goes."

I could work with that. It was the best of both worlds because it'd be fun to take the bikini off her, one piece at a time.

When we got to the house, she went into my bedroom to try on her gift, and I changed into my trunks in my bathroom. I figured it'd take her a few minutes to get ready, so I grabbed drinks and towels for us and stepped outside to drop them off on the table beneath the umbrella.

Fuck, the concrete deck was hot on the soles of my bare feet. I knew I should wait for her before getting in, but the sun was so intense, I marched down the steps and waded into the water at the shallow end of the pool.

There were trees lining the fence at one end of the pool, but the shade from them wouldn't stretch over the water for at least another hour, and I only survived another minute in the heat before slipping beneath the surface. The water was cool, but it felt great.

I knelt in the shallow end, so only my head and the tops of my shoulders were above the water as I anxiously waited for her to appear. I was going to be bummed if the bikini didn't fit.

My phone was on the tile by the steps, and it abruptly chirped with a text message.

Colin: Want to get together tonight and talk launch party? I'll order pizza.

I felt both annoyance and guilt in equal parts. I'd tried to schedule a meeting with Colin earlier, but he'd gone out of town for the weekend to film something with Madison, and they'd only come back this morning.

Preston: I've got dinner plans but can swing by after.

Colin: A date? We can meet tomorrow if you want.

I slicked back my damp hair, but it didn't help my unsettled feeling.

Preston: Not a date.

I wasn't sure if I needed to elaborate, or what I'd even say, but the patio door thudded closed, pulling my attention away from my screen, and all thoughts drained from my mind.

Even though she was wearing pink heart-shaped sunglasses, the tint wasn't enough. Sydney had one hand held up to her forehead to shield her eyes from the bright sunlight. Her other arm was folded over her stomach, as if she could hide her bare skin there. Her tits looked fantastic in the blue triangles of fabric, and her bikini bottoms sat low across her hips, so her forearm was doing fuck-all to block my view of her flat, sexy stomach.

The sight of her left me speechless.

But when she spied me in the pool, she frowned. "You got in already?"

"Sorry. I got hot." I grabbed the railing and climbed the steps out of the water. "You look fucking amazing."

Her arms dropped to her sides, and she looked up at me through her sunglasses like she wasn't sure she believed me, but she wanted to. "Thank you."

Her gaze drifted down to my bare chest, tracking a water

droplet's erratic path as it crawled down my abs. She followed it all the way to my wet swim trunks that clung to my legs, and the white elastic tied at the center of my waist. The navy shorts were dotted with tiny white sharks, and since it was a pair from last summer, the cord barely kept my trunks up in place.

She gazed at them like she hoped the cord would break and my shorts would slide off. It made me peer at the thin blue straps tied behind her neck and wish the knot would come undone.

Shit. Just like that, I was scorching hot again.

We'd been staring at each other long enough without saying anything, it must have made her feel awkward.

"What?" she asked.

"I'm just checking to see if you're drooling."

She sucked in a breath and pretended not to be embarrassed, which she shouldn't be. She was welcome to ogle me anytime.

"No, sorry." Her tone turned teasing. "Would you like me to?"

I smirked. "I don't mind it when my dick is in your mouth."

She was so goddamn sexy when she got flustered. "Who talks like that?"

"I do." I chuckled. "And you love it." I padded toward her. "Come on, Sydney. Let's get you *wet*."

She issued a quiet hiss when I wrapped my damp arms around her, and she squealed in surprise as I lifted, scooping her up. My hands were on her ass, urging her to fold her legs around my hips, and as soon that was done, I carried her to the steps.

I plodded down them quickly, and when the water flooded around her waist, she squirmed and tightened her hold on me.

"It's cold," she gasped.

"Then let me distract you."

I kissed her. I'd meant for it to be sweet and playful, but the second our lips touched, things got serious. I eased us further down into the water as my tongue filled her mouth, and she let out a soft moan of approval.

Water lapped gently at our shoulders, but it did nothing to cool the fire burning inside me. When we'd started this thing, I'd thought we'd fuck a few times and get each other out of our system. But it'd done the opposite.

I only wanted her more.

We floated together, weightless in the water as she was wrapped all around me, her arms rested on my shoulders and our mouths connected. I glided us through the shallow end, going deeper until I could stand and press her back against the side of the pool.

My mouth carved a path down her neck, and as much as I'd liked causing the hickey on her, this time I was more careful. Her head tilted back, resting on the tile edge of the pool, and her breath came and went in rapid, short bursts. I had my hand on one of her tits and the other on her ass, pushing her lower body against mine while I sucked gently on the side of her neck.

"Fuck," she whispered.

My lips curled into a smile. She didn't swear that often,

so it felt like a treat whenever it happened. I loved making the good girl go bad. Corrupting her. Getting her addicted to me.

Beneath the water, I tugged the cup of her bikini to the side so I could touch her with nothing in my way. Maybe we wouldn't get completely naked, but just where it counted and I—

"Preston, can I talk to you for a minute?"

The voice was sharp and angry, and came from the other side of the pool, making my heart stop. I spun around, using my broad back to shield her from view, and stared up at the intruder.

Troy's expression was pissed, but I could tell he was hiding the worst of it from his face, probably for Sydney's benefit. He stood beside the side gate, which he'd left open when he'd come into my back yard.

Fucking hell. I couldn't believe my dumb luck.

Since my dad and Cassidy wouldn't be home, I'd thought Sydney and I would be in the clear. I knew Troy's girlfriend lived next door, but Erika was never home during the day, so I'd written her off as low risk. Plus, there was a privacy fence around her yard.

But her house was on a slope above ours, which meant she could see some of our pool and deck from her back yard.

Sydney slid out from behind me, her swimsuit back in place, and she moved into the shallow end like she wanted to put platonic space between us. As if Troy hadn't just caught us making out and this would somehow fool him.

I swam through the water to the ladder and hoisted myself up it, struggling not to look too guilty. I joined him in the shade over by the side of the house, water dripping every-where as I put my hands on my hips.

"What the hell, man?" His voice was low and angry. "You're fucking Colin's sister?"

"It's not like that."

His eyes went narrow with disbelief. "Oh. So, you're say-ing you haven't?"

Everything was uncomfortable, from the oppressive heat in the air, to the way my friend stared at me like I was a piece of shit. I rubbed my fingertips on the center of my forehead, trying to find the right words. "I'm saying it's . . . not just sex." I didn't know if she could hear our conversation, but did it matter? I was being honest. "I'm really fucking into her, okay?"

Troy stared at me like this revelation was somehow worse than me just using Sydney for sex. "Does he know?"

My shoulders slumped. "I tried talking to him, but he shut that shit down immediately."

He shifted his weight, angling his body away from me, and crossed his arms. "But, of course, you went after her anyway." He shook his head with disgust. "Jesus, Preston. You're unbelievable. Are you ever going to think about some-one other than yourself?"

Anger spiked inside me. "That's not fucking true. I know what this is going to do to our friendship. You think I wanted this? That I didn't try to fight it?"

He raised an eyebrow. "Not hard enough, apparently."

Tension twisted inside me, making me clench my jaw. "I tried, Troy. I really, *really* did. But once we got to know each other, well, then it was too late. Plus, just look at her. She's fucking gorgeous, man." My tone filled with determination. "She likes me, and I like her. Why is it so bad that we want to be together?"

He opened his mouth to say something, only to reconsider his answer. "Is that what you are? Together?"

"Yes."

It gave me hope he knew I was being genuine when his anger subsided a degree. "For how long?"

I'd only put a label on our relationship last week, but I went with the truth. "Since the end of May. But, shit, Troy. I'd been fighting it almost a year before it happened."

He blinked, dropped his arms in surprise, and stared at me like I was suddenly a new person. And then his gaze moved from me to my girlfriend, who sat on the steps of the pool and pretended not to hear what we were talking about.

But her gaze was fixed on the rippling surface of the water, and I could see from her unnatural posture that this was all an act. She was desperately trying not to reveal how my words affected her.

"If anyone knows what that's like," I said to him, "it's *you*."

Because my friend had been hopelessly in love with Erika for years before he'd finally landed her. Once he had, they'd had to keep their relationship a secret for months.

His focus slid back to me, and there was sad recognition in his eyes.

"I do," he said quietly.

There was a long moment where we just looked at each other, acknowledging without words how everything in our group was changing. I'd been there for each of them when they'd started their current relationship, and I'd done it without judgement. Was it too much to ask for the same in return?

"If this thing with Sydney has any chance of going somewhere, you've got to tell Colin."

"I'm way ahead of you." I'd made the decision not long after talking to Cassidy. "I'm telling him as soon as your launch party is over. Going behind his back? I feel horrible all the time. It fucking sucks, so trust me. I'm over it. And, yeah, I don't want to keep lying to him, but I *need* your event to go as smoothly as possible. I'll sit him down right after."

As Troy considered this, the only sound around us was the subtle windchimes nearby blowing in the breeze.

Finally, displeasure edged his face, along with acceptance. He didn't like the situation, but he didn't disagree with what I'd said either. He got that if I told Colin today, it had the potential to fuck things up personally and professionally for all three of us.

"Saturday?" he half-asked, half-demanded.

"Yes, Saturday. I promise."

"Okay. You tell him," his tone was resigned, but his expression was firm, "or I will."

TWENTY-FOUR

Preston

Sydney was still sitting on the steps in the water when Troy left. I'd stood motionless and watched as he walked back up the hill to Erika's house before I finally turned to face her. I was off balance as I strode toward the end of the pool, lumbered down the stairs, and sat on the bottom step beside her.

"How much of that," I asked, "did you hear?"

She looked nervous to answer. "All of it, but once you said that you're 'really fucking into' me, I think I stopped processing. It was hard to focus after that."

I turned on the step, making the water slosh around us. "I am, Sydney." I let out a breath. "I tried not to be."

"Yeah? Well, welcome to the club. But don't worry. It's not a big deal." She leaned in, gently knocking her shoulder into the center of my chest. "Are we really telling Colin about us?"

"We have to."

Her gaze worked over my face, like she was trying to memorize every detail. "I guess we do."

We hadn't talked about the future, or what happened when she returned to Vanderbilt. Hell, we hadn't even discussed if she'd decided she was going back. Maybe she'd been trying to stay in the bubble of summer like I had been.

Except I liked planning now, and when I started to look ahead, I was surprised to find I wasn't nervous. If anything, I was sort of excited about where this could lead. Vanderbilt wasn't far at all, and she wouldn't be under the watchful eye of her parents.

Her voice dropped to a hush. "Can I tell you a secret?"

Instantly, I flashed back to us more than a year ago, walking down the street toward her mother's borrowed car, where she'd confessed her high school crush on me. Shit, we'd come so far since then.

My heart beat faster. "Sure."

"I don't want to swim anymore. I want to go inside, get naked, and . . . fuck your brains out."

Holy shit. I couldn't have grinned harder if I'd tried. "Who talks like that?"

"I do." Her shy smile was seriously hot. "And you love it."

God, I did. "Let's fucking go, then."

Colin and I wore black dress shirts and black slacks for Troy's launch party. It was professional, but just casual enough we didn't look out of place, and helped people identify us as the coordinators. We were part of a larger team, since the first half of the evening was an exclusive show that was managed by Warbler.

The venue was a throwback to Troy's early days. Blanche's Honky Tonk was one of the places he would perform at before he broke out, and it was where Erika had discovered him. The main floor had a stage, and the second floor had more of a lounge vibe to it with a small bar to one side. There was another bar on the rooftop, which had great views of the city skyline, and would have made for great pictures of the event, but we talked Warbler out of it.

Blanche's elevator was ancient and small, which meant the large, heavy sound equipment for Troy's performance would have to be carried by hand up two narrow flights of stairs. That also meant there would be accessibility issues. Plus, we'd have to contend with the weather—not just the heat and humidity, but the chance of a summer thunderstorm.

The biggest issue was the Stella factor.

Erika may have found Troy, but Stella was the one who'd used her name to make him a star. The multiple Grammy-winning artist had just wrapped her latest tour and lived in Nashville, so it was on the schedule that she'd drop by.

Only Warbler and Distinguished Events knew, and the plan was she'd join Troy during his set, and possibly do a song of her own. She wanted to make sure the focus was on him, though, and if word got out that Stella was performing on a rooftop, shit could get chaotic. We had a lot more control if we kept things indoors.

When we finished our final walkthrough and staff meeting, Colin and I moved to stand at the end of the bar on the main floor. We each chugged a bottle of water because it was T-minus fifteen minutes to the doors opening. This was the last chance we'd get before we'd need to be 'on' the rest of the evening.

My attention was fixed on the stage, watching the opening act finishing their setup, when my phone buzzed with a text message.

> **Sydney:** I can't stop thinking about what it feels like when you're inside me.

Shit.

Her sexy text hit me like a sledgehammer made of lust. It'd been hours since we'd last texted. We'd both been too busy, and I pictured her now, hidden back in the stock room during a lull after the dinner rush at her restaurant. Her evening was winding down right as mine was ramping up, and I liked the idea that she'd used her first free moment to text me.

A smile spread across my face. I'd selfishly hoped a while back that I'd ruin sex with other people for her, but the truth was she'd done it to me. I began to type out my response, too distracted with my thoughts to sense the incoming danger.

Abruptly, the phone was plucked from my grasp.

My heart ground to a halt, but Colin simply laughed at my panicked expression, oblivious to the horrible dread that seized me, making me immobile.

"Seriously, bro. Who are you texting?" His tone was light as he glanced down at the phone he'd playfully stolen from me. "Maybe I should tell them you're too busy to talk right now."

"Gimme that back." It came out in such a rush, it had to be unmistakable how freaked out I was. Plus, I jammed my hand over his, covering the screen, but this action made his suspicion spike. Or maybe he'd caught a glimpse of the name across the top of the screen.

Sydney wasn't a common name around here.

Either way, he jerked the phone away, and when I stepped forward to grab it, he turned sideways and planted his free hand firmly in the center of my chest, blocking me.

"Colin," I said. "Don't."

It was too late though.

He was stronger and I couldn't move fast enough. His gaze zeroed in on the contact, and his expression went blank as he read the most recent conversation. Then his gaze lifted to mine, and everything around us disappeared.

"Sydney?" His eyes pleaded for it not to be true. "Like, *my sister*?"

I tried to move again, but his arm went stiff, and the hand planted on my chest and his dark expression turned into a threat. It warned me to stay fucking still as his gaze returned to the screen.

Staying still became impossible when his thumb swiped up, scrolling backward to read more.

Fucking shit. Do something!

"Stop," I said, but he wouldn't listen. Fury swelled inside him as he read. His knuckles on the hand grasping the phone went white and he tensed all over, from his powerful arms to the muscles running along his jaw.

Cold sweat broke out down my back and my heart lurched forward, banging along at a furious, breakneck speed. This was *really* fucking bad, but it was barreling toward a goddamn disaster we couldn't recover from.

"Stop scrolling." I couldn't get the words out fast

enough. "Shit, there are pictures in there you're not going to want to see."

That finally broke through to him. His thumb ceased and he stared unblinkingly at my phone like he'd just learned it was radioactive. Everything in him was motionless.

Was he even breathing?

The only good thing about him turning into a statue was it allowed me to finally pull the phone from his grasp. I jammed it in my pocket and swallowed the lump in my throat, trying to figure out what the hell to say.

There was no point in pretending or denying what he'd just read. The damage was done.

"I'm sorry," I said quietly. "We were going to tell you."

There was chaos in Colin's eyes as they stared back at me. Then, he finally moved. His fingers curled inward, digging into my chest as he fisted the front of my shirt.

"Yeah?" he snarled with disbelief.

I lifted my arms in surrender. I wasn't going to match his aggression. "I'm serious. We planned to, but I wanted to wait until after the event."

He used his grip to haul me forward, bringing us eye to eye. "What the fuck is wrong with you?" He sounded so disgusted, his words cut as sharp as a knife. "That's my baby sister."

My eyes went wide with guilt, allowing me to notice our surroundings, and it took everything in me to not react. He was my best friend, yet he glared at me like I was a monster he needed to destroy. Like he wanted to tear me apart.

It fucking hurt.

I'd been in physical fights before. It'd been the reason why I'd had to move in with my dad because back in high school, I'd struggled with my temper. Colin wouldn't be the first person to throw a punch at me, and I knew I could survive if that happened.

But our business couldn't.

So, even though he was all up in my face, I did my best to stay steady and controlled. "I get that you're pissed, and you deserve to be, but look around. We *cannot* get into this shit right now. Tonight is supposed to be about Troy."

He considered that for an eternity, before shoving me back with enough force I had to stumble back a half step. My gaze darted around the bar, checking to see how many people had witnessed this unprofessional moment.

Just one, thank fuck.

There was a bartender nearby who was watching us. She'd been stocking ice and had stopped mid-scoop. I plastered on a fake smile, acting like the whole thing between Colin and me had been a joke.

He noticed her too, and straightened, making a shitty attempt to convey there wasn't any tension between us. But his vacant expression and unnaturally stiff posture did fuck-all to sell the lie.

"I told you," he said under his breath, "I *fucking told you* I didn't want you getting involved with her."

I ran a hand down the front of my shirt, smoothing out the wrinkles from his grip. "You did."

That only pissed him off more. "She's too good for you."

"Agreed." I gave him the same line Sydney had given me.

"But guess what? We don't get to decide that."

He shook his head. "You're so fucking selfish, Preston."

I clenched my jaw, making my muscles ache. "Maybe I am, but this isn't the time or the place. We need to discuss it later."

As if on cue, one of the servers began her approach, and was nearly to us when the cold front radiating off us stopped her in her tracks. Her hesitant gaze darted from me to my partner, and I could see the thought running through her head. She wondered why Colin looked like he hated my guts.

I forced casualness into my demeanor. "What's up?"

"I had a question about the cake presentation. The time-line says we're bringing it up on stage after Troy's set, but the kitchen is asking for earlier, so they have time to cut and plate the servings."

My mind was jumbled from what had just happened, making me slow to switch my feelings off and focus on her question.

"We're not serving the cake," I said.

Confusion flooded her face, so I glanced at Colin. Hadn't he gone over this with them already? He simply stared at me, seething.

"We're not serving the presentation cake, I mean," I said. "There's sheet cake for the guests, and the kitchen can start plating that whenever they need to."

I knew it had been delivered along with the tiered pre-sentation cake, because we'd seen the trays less than an hour ago in the walk-in cooler.

"Oh." She looked relieved. "Sorry for the confusion. They

thought the flat cakes were extra just in case we needed them. I'll let everyone know."

"Thanks," I said.

Her gaze flitted to Colin, who still hadn't said a word or moved an inch. She must have decided she didn't have time to figure him out, because she flashed a brief smile at me, turned, and hurried back to the kitchen.

Was this how the night was going to go? "You can be pissed at me, but set it aside tonight for Troy."

His head turned slowly, and he leveled a hard gaze at me. "Unless it's business related," his tone was icy, "I don't want to hear a goddamn word from you for the rest of the night."

"Fine," I spat out.

The green room at the back of Blanche's was more like a closet than anything else. It had an old couch on one side and a desk on the other, plus a mirror with lights lining its perimeter.

Troy had only arrived a little while ago, and I knew this would be my one opportunity to get any face time with him tonight. The door was open to the tiny room, and I was surprised to find he was alone inside. I raised my hand to knock on the doorframe and announce myself, only to pause.

My friend looked . . . nervous.

In fact, he looked more nervous and sweatier than I'd ever seen him. Maybe Erika wasn't back here because he didn't want her to see him like this, or perhaps he liked to be alone as he prepared for a set. I didn't fault him for being anxious. Tonight was huge for him, and if I were in his shoes, I'd be doing my best not to throw up.

I lowered my hand and started to back out of the doorway, except my movement caught his attention.

"Hey, Preston." His expression brightened and he let out a deep breath, one that sounded a hell of a lot like relief.

"Hey. You okay? Can I get you anything?"

He gestured for me to come closer. "Get in here and distract me so I don't start freaking out."

I stepped inside and was eager to help, although I hadn't a clue what to say. He'd performed with Stella during one of her sold-out shows, which had been like fifty thousand people. Tonight, there were only two hundred and most were friends and family. Wouldn't this be a cakewalk by comparison?

But maybe that was the problem. Performing for tens of thousands of strangers was less pressure than for the people he cared about, or whose opinion held sway over his career's future.

"You're going to do awesome tonight," I said. "You want me to find Erika for you?"

"No!" He answered so quickly, and my question somehow made him look more nervous.

Oh, shit.

Had they broken up? Up until this moment, I'd liked her, and them together, but if she'd dumped him right before the biggest day of his life . . . well, I was going to have some less than neighborly words with the woman who lived next door.

Whatever face I was making, it must have asked for an explanation because Troy glanced out in the hall, then jammed a hand into his pocket. He pulled out a small black velvet bag, and my confusion evaporated as his fingers plucked a diamond ring from inside.

"No fucking way," I said.

It shouldn't have floored me like it did. They'd been together for nearly three years, and he'd been in love with her much longer than that—but still.

I was speechless.

He was going to ask her to marry him. My friend had found the person he wanted to spend the rest of his life with.

My voice went low. "When?"

Both of our gazes were locked on the large sparkling diamond that was surrounded by smaller ones on each side. "After my set. I was thinking that I'd—"

Footsteps came down the hall, growing louder as the person approached, and Troy scrambled to put the ring away. He'd just finished shoving the bag back into his pocket when Colin stepped into view.

He'd probably had the same thought about trying to catch Troy before his set, and when he discovered I'd beaten him to it, his eyes narrowed.

Troy let out a relaxed breath, but mine tightened in my chest, and it seemed to be the same for Colin. He didn't like that I was here, but that was too fucking bad. I'd gotten here first.

The room seemed too small to hold all of us and the tension he brought with him, but he didn't retreat. He angled his shoulders away from me and his focus shifted to our friend, and it was like I no longer existed.

"I wanted to stop by," he said, "and say hey before you went on tonight."

It didn't go unnoticed how frosty Colin's attitude was toward me, or how my posture was stiff.

"Thanks." Troy tilted his head. "What's going on with y'all?"

Colin's tone was bitter. "Turns out this asshole," he tossed a hand my direction, "is fucking my sister."

So much for keeping tonight about business.

He'd expected Troy to look shocked, for our friend to glare my direction and ask what the fuck was wrong with me.

Instead, Troy sighed. "I thought you were going to wait to tell him."

Shit.

"Wait." Colin went rigid. "*You knew?*"

Troy had a lot going on tonight, so it was understandable he wasn't thinking straight, and hadn't realized how this sounded until it was too late. He frowned and set his hands on his waist in an attempt not to look guilty.

"I only found out a few days ago."

Hurt cut through Colin's expression. "What the hell? I'm not surprised that fucker went behind my back, but you too?"

"Hey," I piped in, "this is my fault, not his. He didn't go behind your back. I asked him not to tell you because we need tonight to go smoothly. Shit, especially now." I pulled the door to the room closed and nodded to Troy. "You should show him what you showed me."

Troy didn't hesitate. He dug out the bag and then the ring from inside, leaving Colin just as stunned as I'd been. Seeing it a second time, it blew my mind all over again.

"Whoa." A smile curled at the edges of Colin's lips. "Really?"

"Yeah, really," Troy said. "I've been thinking about it for a while. Since most of our friends and family are here, I figured tonight is the night." He stared at the ring like it might sprout legs and run away if he took his gaze off it for a single second. "I'm pretty sure she's going to say yes, so I don't get why I'm so fucking nervous."

Was he serious?

"I do," I said. "This is huge and it's what you've wanted ever since you laid eyes on her."

A year ago, if he'd told me he was thinking about getting married, I might have been an asshole and tried to talk him out of it. I'd have told him he was too young, or how he hadn't reaped all the benefits of his fame and should be drowning in pussy.

I'd have done it because I was selfish and didn't want things to change. I'd have whined I wasn't ready to have a friend who was old enough to have a wife, or that she was going to take him away from me.

Fuck. Maybe he hadn't told me he'd bought a ring because he was worried I'd always react that way.

But, no.

I wasn't that guy anymore. He was happier than ever, and anyone with half a brain could see he belonged with Erika. It was strange and kind of nice that I was excited for him to take this step.

And I wasn't the only one, because Colin shifted on his feet. "Don't sweat it." The animosity toward me was shoved aside and warmth filled his voice. "She's going to say yes. You've got this."

"Yeah," I agreed. "I'm happy for you, bro."

"Me too," Colin added.

Troy's voice went uneven. "Thanks."

For a long moment, we said nothing, using the silence to acknowledge how much everything had changed so suddenly. By the end of the night, Colin knew Sydney and I were together, and Troy would be engaged.

He tucked the ring back in the bag and pocketed it, then turned his focus to the other man. "I know you're pissed about Preston, but I gotta tell you—"

A knock on the door was quickly followed by Erika's voice. "Troy? Are you in here?"

His Adam's apple bobbed with a heavy swallow, and he smoothed a hand over his hair. "Yeah. Come in."

The door popped open, she stuck her head in, and looked surprised to see he wasn't alone. "Oh. Hey, guys."

"Hey," we all said in unison. It was so overly enthusiastic and unnatural, I tried not to cringe. Plus, it took all my strength to keep a shit-eating grin at bay. She had no idea what he had planned, and I couldn't wait for the surprise.

She blinked in confusion, and flashed a smile at her boyfriend that read, *you're all being weird*. But then she moved past it. "You ready? You should probably get out here and start saying hello to folks."

"Right." Troy rolled his shoulders back like he was

shrugging out of a coat of nerves, and he strolled toward the door.

Colin's voice was heavy with meaning. "Good luck."

Troy nodded and followed her out into the hall.

I waited until I was sure they were safely out of earshot, before turning to Colin. "Think she'll cry?"

His tone was cold. "Don't talk to me."

Okay, then.

And that was how the rest of the evening went. Every interaction I had with him was curt. When I told him we should move the champagne up to the end of the set and do the cake presentation later, he gruffly told me he'd take care of it.

When Troy took the stage, I watched what I could of his first few songs, but then I had to head to the back to greet Stella and her people. I wasn't sure I'd even speak with her. Ardy, her manager, was handling it—I was there on hand in case they had any questions.

She came in through the service entrance, surrounded by her security team, and beamed a warm smile to Ardy as she tossed a lock of her blonde hair over her shoulder. She was pretty in a girl-next-door kind of way, and it was deceptively disarming. A lot of people wrote her off or underestimated her because of her looks, but Troy said she was razor-smart when it came to business. He'd learned so much from the country-turned-pop star.

When Stella made her entrance and appeared on stage with a microphone in hand, a buzz rippled through the crowd. Troy turned, did a double-take, and then an unstoppable grin burst on his face. He pushed his guitar to the side so he could give her a hug, and after a brief discussion, the duo turned to face their audience.

Everyone was fucking thrilled when he plucked at the guitar strings, and we recognized the opening strains of 'Power.' It had been a hit single he'd recorded with her, and it was released on her last album, helping him establish his name.

As I watched them, my gaze weaving through the hands holding up phones to record the performance, I was struck by how different things were now. When he'd first taken off, I'd struggled with jealousy.

Troy had become a celebrity, and, fuck, even Colin had too in his own way. They both had fans—although Colin's were mostly online. Growing up, I'd always needed to be the center of attention. Now I was the least recognizable one from our group of friends.

But I wasn't envious or jealous tonight.

I was just . . . happy. Troy worked hard and he deserved all the good things coming his way.

They closed out their duet to thunderous applause, and Troy uttered his thanks to Stella before she holstered her mic and exited the stage, leaving him to finish his set. His final number was fast and hard, getting people to stomp and dance along with its racing beat. He was sweating under the lights, but he looked confident and in command, and very aware he had everyone's undivided attention.

It worked out perfectly because when the final note was struck and the lights went down, it made it seem as if the servers with trays full of glasses of champagne had appeared from nowhere.

A center spotlight lit Troy while the house lights came up.

"I want to let y'all know how special this album is for me," he said as he grabbed the microphone and let his guitar hang on the strap over his shoulder. "And I need to acknowledge all the amazing folks at Warbler and Saga Music for their hard work."

The champagne began to work its way through the crowd, and he held up a hand, blocking out the harsh light as he searched the audience for one person in particular.

"I also need to recognize," his voice went uneven, "the enormous talent who, without her, this album wouldn't have been possible. Erika? Get up here."

She'd been standing in the audience to the side and a jolt of surprise went through her body. The crowd parted around her and cleared a path to the stage, but she waved a humble hand and shook her head. She didn't want this to be about her, but . . . that was too bad.

Troy's tone was teasing as he reached out to help her up. "I'm not taking no for an answer."

She laughed, stepped up, and took his offered hand. The stage wasn't much taller than knee height, and so it was easy for Troy to pull her up beside him. She blinked under the bright lights, not looking awkward, but also not entirely comfortable as she eyed her boyfriend.

"Some of you already know that this woman," he said, "wrote most of my songs on *Believe the Fire*. But what you might not know is . . . she's the love of my life."

The jolt that went through Erika was much bigger this time when he abruptly bent down on one knee and pulled the black bag from his pocket. Her expression froze with disbelief, and she didn't even blink as he produced the sparkling ring. Gasps swept through the crowd.

"Erika," his voice trembled with emotion as he peered up at her, "will you marry me?"

The room went silent, and everyone waited with breath held in their lungs, their gazes glued on her.

She wasn't near the microphone, so we couldn't hear the word she uttered, but her head bobbed in a nod, and my friend leapt to his feet so quickly, the guitar slung over his shoulder clanged against his back. She was pulled into his arms and their mouths smashed together in a kiss that was full of urgency and love.

They parted only long enough for a laugh and for him to slip the ring on her finger, and when they kissed again, the audience erupted in cheers. A pair of champagne flutes were lifted onto the stage and passed to the newly engaged couple. He carried his in one hand, and held onto Erika with his other, and made his way back to the microphone stand.

"Thank you so much for being here tonight," he said, "and celebrating the release of *Believe the Fire* with me. I hope y'all have an amazing night." He lifted his glass in a toast. "This has been the greatest day of my life."

The crowd roared their approval, and it was so loud and positive, it surged through me like energy, making an unstoppable grin fly across my lips. It also drove my gaze across the way to Colin, because I needed to know if he felt the same happiness I did for our friend.

My warm smile was reflected perfectly on his face. He

held my gaze for a long moment as we shared the excitement for Troy. It gave me hope. This obstacle with him seemed small and stupid in comparison.

Except his expression abruptly soured.

It was clear he'd momentarily forgotten about Sydney and me, but when reality came storming back, he ripped his disgusted gaze away.

It announced we had a very long way to go.

Well, shit.

TWENTY-FIVE

Sydney

I stayed up late, waiting for Preston to text me about how the event had gone. Some of the pictures were already online, including the picture of Troy Osbourne down on one knee. I rolled over onto my stomach on my bed, watching the TikTok someone had posted of the proposal.

Most of the comments were people wishing them congratulations, but occasionally someone would wail about how they'd missed their chance with him since now he was off the market. I smirked to myself, wondering if any of the comments were from the girls I'd been friends with in high school.

God, they'd had it *so* bad for him.

And then my smile widened because the guy I'd been in love with back then? He was my boyfriend now.

I'd done my best not to text him tonight. I knew he was busy and stressed, so I didn't want to bother him, but I'd cracked during my break. *One naughty text won't hurt.* I wasn't surprised I didn't get any response other than he marked my comment as 'loved.'

But it was nearing two in the morning, and I was struggling to keep my eyes open. We had a new server at the restaurant, and she hadn't figured out the point-of-sale system yet, so most of her tickets came out wrong. It caused cascading issues, and it had taken everyone on the line to stop Kevin, our head chef, from murdering the poor woman.

Preston: Colin knows.

I bolted upright and pulled the screen closer to my face to make sure I hadn't read it wrong.

Sydney: How?

There was no way Preston had told him. Not before the event tonight, and not without me. Had it been Troy? That seemed unlikely. He'd promised Preston he wouldn't.

Preston: He took my phone and saw your text.

"Oh, shit," I said into the quiet of my bedroom. I felt fucking awful. He shouldn't have found out like that, and it probably wouldn't have happened if I hadn't sent it.

Sydney: Oh, no. I'm so sorry. How'd he take it?

Preston: Not great. We couldn't talk about it, so I'm picking you up tomorrow morning and we'll go to his place.

I let out a slow breath. Well, at least there was a plan.

Sydney: What time?

Preston: He said he'd text me when he's up.

Sydney: Okay. How about you? How was the event?

Preston: It went great. Really tired, though.

I could only imagine.

Sydney: Get some sleep and I'll talk to you in the morning.

Preston: Thanks.

We needed to get our rest for our conversation with Colin tomorrow. I was nervous, but . . . a part of me was relieved.

It was *finally* out there.

Preston and I stood in front of Colin and Madison's apartment door, and I had my hands wrapped around the handles of a Pyrex dish. I'd gotten up early this morning and made a batch of lemon ricotta pancakes to sweeten up my brother during our discussion.

Except that had been hours ago and it was doubtful they'd taste as good reheated. I brought them anyway.

My heart banged in my chest at the same hurried tempo Preston used to knock on the door. Footsteps grew loud behind it, and it swung open to reveal my brother's irritated expression. He wasn't happy to see Preston, but he was supremely pissed to see I'd tagged along.

He tossed a hand into his apartment, gesturing for us to come inside, and stepped back from the doorway to make room. When Preston didn't move, it was clear he wanted me to go first, and Colin's focus went to the covered dish in my hands.

He eyed it with suspicion. "What that?"

"Lemon ricotta pancakes and maple candied bacon." I thrust the Pyrex container toward him, but he didn't take it. Instead, he glanced over at a clock.

"It's almost eleven-thirty."

I gave a plain look. "I thought we were going to talk first thing this morning."

He begrudgingly took the dish from me. "Yeah? Well, I thought this conversation was only going to be between me and Preston."

He strode toward the open kitchen and set the glass dish down with a thud, then popped the silicone lid so he could get inside. There were two neat stacks of savory pancakes, and the bacon was sprinkled around, but when he picked up a strip with his bare fingers, my hands clenched against the urge to stop him.

I'd wanted to warm the food and plate the four servings, finishing them off with butter and syrup. Instead, he took a bite, oblivious to what he was doing to my dish.

"I made enough of that to share with everyone," I commented.

My brother chewed the sweet, sticky bacon, and seemed to enjoy it. "Mads isn't here. She went to the gym."

Was he trying to be a jerk, or was this just the personality he'd developed from years of being a frat boy? He set his piece of bacon down on top of the stack, picked the first pancake up, and folded it to create a bacon taco. My blood heated as he casually began to eat, but I reminded myself to keep quiet.

I wanted this conversation to go the best it could.

"More for us, then," Preston said.

But when he moved to grab some for himself, my brother made a sound of disapproval that stopped him in his tracks. Colin looked at his friend like he was now an enemy.

The tension between the two men climbed and twisted until it was so taut, I couldn't breathe, couldn't move.

"There's a rule every guy knows," Colin's tone was absolute, "and it's that you don't fuck your friend's sister." He dropped his half-eaten pancake on the counter like he was suddenly too disgusted to eat. "I don't know what pisses me off more. That you did it anyway, or that everyone else knew about it except me." His expression was a mixture of hurt and anger. "This fucks *everything* up. I mean, you get that, right? Not just between us, but our business. Things with Troy." His gaze rolled to me. "Things with Syd."

"Yes," Preston said.

And that was *all* he said.

It wasn't followed with an apology or a defense or any elaboration. His simple acknowledgement only made Colin's anger burn hotter.

I felt itchy in my skin. It wasn't my brother's fault he looked a lot like our dad, but his disapproval chewed at me, and I couldn't sit still. I was most confident in the kitchen. So, I needed to get in there, into my domain, and regain control. I would heat the food and plate the dish the way I'd intended to present it, and then this would all go better.

Except Colin was blocking my route, and he wouldn't move when I tried to get by him. He was too focused on Preston to even notice me.

"That's it?" Colin demanded. "You're not sorry?"

"Yeah, I'm sorry." Although Preston didn't sound it at all. "I'm sorry you made a dumb rule that said I couldn't date Sydney."

It was like he'd slammed on the brakes with both feet. I threw him a look, asking what the hell was he doing, but he pressed forward despite it.

"But I'm not sorry I'm with her," he continued. "I knew it was going to fuck things up, and I wish it didn't. I tried to stay away, man."

Colin's expression soured. "Oh, did you?"

On the car ride over, Preston had asked if he could lead the conversation, and I had reluctantly agreed, but the urge to defend him was overpowering. "He did. Us hooking up was my idea."

"I don't want to hear about that." My brother winced. "He took advantage of you. And eventually he's going to hurt you because he fucking sucks at thinking about anyone else, or putting other people first. Case in point? The *one thing* I asked him not to do was go after you, and he fucking did it anyway."

Irritation swirled inside me, and I opened my mouth to speak, but Preston beat me to it.

"How the fuck can you say that?" His chest lifted with an indignant breath. "Yeah, sure. I haven't always been great in the past. I struggled, and maybe I was self-centered, but I've *always* been there for you, dude. Without question. Without judgement. Whenever you blew up your life and needed a safe place to land, who'd you turn to?"

His point was direct and sharp, and even though it was true, Colin didn't like hearing it.

His eyes narrowed. "So, that means what?" My brother's tone was shockingly dark. "Because you helped me out, I owe you my sister?"

Preston closed his eyes and sighed. "Fuck, no. I'm trying to remind you I'm not some terrible guy."

"You are when it comes to women." His focus sharpened on me. "Do you know that?"

There was something else he wanted to say, but it gave him pause, like he wasn't sure if he should go there. But then the decision was made, and his shoulders lifted with a deep breath.

"He cheated on Cassidy."

Oh, wow.

"What the *fuck*?" Preston demanded.

My brother ignored him and kept his gaze on me. He expected this to be a big revelation, and when I didn't immediately react, confusion splashed across his face. Anger simmered off Preston in waves and it felt like I was standing too close to a pot of boiling water.

I lifted a hand, signaling to him to keep cool.

"Yeah," I said quietly. "I know because he told me about it. That was a long time ago."

"Yeah? Well, it wasn't that long ago he'd fuck any girl who looked at him twice."

"Jesus Christ," Preston spat out.

Once again, my brother wasn't deterred. "He'll use you, Syd, and when he's had enough of you, he'll walk away. He'll dump you or ghost you because the only feelings he cares about are his own."

There was a tiny voice in the back of my head, whispering that I should listen to my brother. He'd known Preston a lot longer—and better—than I had, so he'd seen all the sides to his friend, not just the ones I'd seen in the few months we'd been together.

But . . . he wasn't the same boy he'd been when I'd had a crush on him. He'd grown and changed, and if Colin couldn't see that, it was because he was too busy being biased and feeling betrayed over something he had no business worrying about.

Preston and I were consenting adults.

I had no idea what kind of expression was on my face, but it compelled him to keep talking. "I'm not trying to be an asshole—"

"*Bullshit*," Preston snapped.

"—I'm trying to protect you." Colin rested a hand on the counter and leaned forward, perhaps wanting to give his statement more weight. "I know it doesn't seem like it, but I want what's best for you."

His words made everything inside me stop and go cold.

"Are you serious?" My heart was made of lead, dragging me down. "You sound *exactly* like Mom and Dad."

He reared back as if I'd slapped him, and the horrified realization made his eyes go wide. He'd suffered under their rule, so he should have known better.

"All my life," there was so much fire burning inside me, the words tasted ashy, "people keep telling me they want what's best for me. But not a single person, not one fucking person in this world, *except for Preston*, has ever asked me what I want."

The atmosphere shifted, freezing all the feelings of hurt and betrayal between the men in place.

"Is it because what I want doesn't matter?" I asked. "I don't get a say in it?"

Colin looked pained. "Come on, Syd. Of course you do."

"Yeah?" I gestured to the man standing beside me, the one who looked like he had so much he wanted to say but was doing his best to let me speak. "Well, I want him. Deal with it."

I had so much conviction, he couldn't argue with it.

Instead, his shoulders slumped with a sadness I didn't understand. "Shit. Is it too late? Are you already in love with him?"

I despised the dread in his voice, and it got me so worked up, I answered without thinking. "Yes."

The single word left my lips like a bullet.

It struck Colin before traveling on to embed itself in Preston's center. He jolted and stiffened awkwardly, making it clear how uncomfortable he was hearing I was in love with him. And his reaction? It didn't go unnoticed by my brother.

Oh, god. What had I done?

You told the truth.

I had—but I'd done it without thinking about the consequences. I hadn't built up the courage to tell Preston yet, and I had no idea if he felt the same, or if telling him I loved him was going to send him running.

I stared at the man I loved, and my heart stopped beating

because his gaze refused to meet mine. It was laser focused on my brother.

"And what about you?" Colin's tone was harsh and demanding. "You love her too?"

Shit, I couldn't breathe. Everything was tight with apprehension, and the longer Preston went without doing or saying anything, the more painful it became. My face gradually heated to a million degrees, and each second that ticked by, my embarrassment increased tenfold.

On some level, I understood that I'd stunned him speechless, but his silence created room for doubt. For the tiny voice to grow louder about listening to the warning Colin had given me.

Oh, my god. What if he was right?

What if Preston was going to use me until he'd had his fill, and then leave? In the beginning, he'd been clear the thing between us was only about sex. Maybe I'd gotten good at being a bad girl because I'd broken his only rule and fallen for him.

Preston's non-answer was answer enough for my brother. Colin's tone turned patronizing. "Yeah, I thought so."

Finally, Preston seemed to come back to life. "Just wait a minute."

"No," Colin said, "we're done."

The friction rose between them, inching toward disaster. It filled the space between the three of us like someone had closed the lid on a pressure cooker and cranked the flame beneath as high as it would go. The room was stifling and boiling, and I wanted to flee, because deep down in my bones,

I sensed what was coming.

"You need to decide what's more important to you," Colin declared. "Seven years of friendship and the business we built together—or fucking my little sister. Because guess what, Preston? You don't get to do both."

He was asking Preston to choose between us, and . . .

Oh, no. *No!*

I was going to lose.

In fact, by declaring I loved him, I'd probably made the choice even easier. I'd gotten too attached and freaked him out. He could use this as his exit and let my brother come off looking like the bad guy.

"Please don't do this," I whispered, begging Colin.

Preston's hands had hung at his sides, and now they balled into fists like he wanted to curl his fingers around this ridiculous ultimatum and rip it apart. "You're going to throw everything away just because I'm with Sydney?" His eyes were furious. "Who's the selfish one now?"

Colin wasn't fazed. "Does that mean you're picking her?"

The question derailed Preston. He sucked in a sharp breath, like he was preparing to do or say something big, but instead . . . he simply froze. As if he could avoid having to make the decision as long as he didn't move.

I knew it was impossible, that there were no winners here, but his hesitation was a knife in my stomach. I'd confessed I loved him, and yet he struggled with whether he should even choose me.

Shit, I couldn't just stand here and wait for the axe to fall.

I lurched forward, grabbed the silicone lid, and snapped

it back in place on the Pyrex dish.

"He's not picking anyone right now," I announced to everyone, including myself. "I just remembered I've got somewhere else to be." I grasped the container and pulled it into my arms, no longer caring if the pancake stacks and bacon pieces became a jumbled mess on the bottom. "I need you to drive me home, Preston."

"What?" He peered at me with dismay. Like I was trying to trap him when all I wanted to do was escape.

I couldn't bear to look at him any longer.

It would be too hard to watch the decision I was certain he'd make—the one where I'd lose—while it formed in his eyes. So, I turned and strode as fast as my feet would carry me toward the door.

I wasn't sure he'd follow me, but after a heartbeat, I heard his heavy, swift footsteps.

"We're not done talking about this," he lobbed at my brother as he went, "but you're being a real dick right now."

"Yeah? You've been a dick for years," he fired back, chasing us out and slamming the door behind us.

I hated everything in that moment. How I'd stupidly admitted I loved Preston, how he hadn't said it back, and most of all—how I'd come between him and my brother. This war brewing between them was my fault, and I only saw one terrible way to prevent it.

I didn't want to give him up. I'd only just gotten him.

It was so fucking unfair, I couldn't find any words, and if I opened my mouth, I worried I might scream. It was why I said nothing as I marched to the passenger side of his car and waited for him to unlock it.

He didn't move for a long time.

His angry glare was pinned on the apartment door like he was considering going back inside to try to talk to my brother again. Was he thinking about how none of this had gone the way we wanted it to?

I stood under the hot sun with my Pyrex container pressed to my chest and my arms wrapped around it, feeling nothing but cold dread inside my body.

Had he already made his decision?

Was this it for us?

Time was running out. Every second that crept by pushed us closer to the inevitable. To the end I desperately didn't want. I needed to make these final moments with him count, to make them last . . . but I didn't know how.

Abruptly, he turned and stalked to the driver's side, unlocked the doors, and climbed in without so much as glancing my way. When I got in and shut my door, he waited with his hands on the steering wheel and his gaze fixed forward, staring out the windshield vacantly.

My heart sunk into my stomach.

He was withdrawing from me, preparing to deliver the bad news. Sadness weighed me down, so it took a tremendous amount of effort to buckle my seat belt. Once it was done, he started the car, put it in gear, and pulled out of the parking space.

I attempted to study the dash in front of me like there was an interesting pattern in its texture, because I needed something to distract from the tense silence surrounding us.

It was so heavy, so uncomfortable, it was nearly intolerable.

Finally, he spoke, and his tone was quiet and heartbreaking. "You said you love me."

I turned away to look out the window, not wanting him to see the tears stinging in my eyes. "It's not a big deal."

It was foolish to hope he'd somehow agree, but instead he let out a long breath. The sound of it further crushed my heart. "No, that *is* a big deal, Sydney."

"You're right." I closed my eyes. "It is, because you don't feel the same way."

It took him a lifetime to respond. "I didn't say that."

"No, but then again, you didn't say anything at all."

Without looking at him, I could sense the frustration rolling off his shoulders. "Because it caught me off guard, okay? I had a plan going in there, but once you said that, I couldn't think straight."

"Right. I get it." Bitterness filled my mouth as I turned and gave him a hard look, not caring anymore if he could see how I was fighting back tears. "This is all my fault."

Annoyance edged into his expression. "Again, I didn't say that, and why does it sound like you're mad at me?"

My emotions had me reeling out of control, and I couldn't stop myself from blurting it out. "Because I love you, and . . . you didn't even have an answer when he gave you that ultimatum."

Preston shifted awkwardly in his seat, and his hands tightened on the steering wheel. Why the fuck did I keep telling him I loved him when I knew it made him uncomfortable?

"I didn't have an answer," he struggled with how to phrase it, "because it's fucking complicated. Troy's release party was supposed to be this huge milestone for Distinguished Events. We took on a major project, fucking rocked it, and proved we're ready for more. But instead of celebrating—I spent most of last night worrying that our company is going to collapse. We don't have staff. It's just me and Colin, and the business can't survive without him."

He peeled his gaze off the road to show me how serious he was.

"My whole life is wrapped up in this, so you've got to cut me some slack if I'm not instantly ready to risk it all."

He wasn't ready to risk it on me, and while it stung painfully, logically wasn't that the smart decision? I was just twenty and we'd only been together a few short months. We hadn't talked about the future or where we saw this going.

It meant he'd have to sacrifice his friendship and his dream . . . all for a gamble on a girl he wasn't even in love with.

If he even wanted to do that, how could I let him? How could I be that selfish?

I loved him, which meant I wanted what was best for him, and unfortunately that was a future that didn't include me.

He'd given me a lot of firsts. Sex. Love. And now heartbreak.

"What are we even doing, then?" I whispered. "Maybe our whole relationship has been no big deal."

He flinched. "What?"

"It's not worth destroying everything you want."

That pissed him off. "What are you talking about? I want

you, Sydney." He let out a frustrated sigh. "God, I wish you'd never sent me that text."

My breath caught. "What?"

He frowned and swung the car into my driveway. "I'm just saying, if you hadn't, we could have told him ourselves, and it would have been better. It would have gone the way I wanted it to."

My pulse quickened with hurt. "Are you serious?"

He threw the car in park, but his gaze didn't turn to meet mine. Instead, he stared straight ahead and looked consumed by his thoughts. "He shouldn't have found out like that." Irritation seemed to grow inside him until it spilled across his face. "You knew I was going to be with him all night. Did you not think about that? It was almost like you wanted us to get caught."

Was he fucking joking?

"Of course I didn't." My hurt morphed into anger. "You're blaming me for this? You didn't have to check your phone. When I sent that text, I thought you'd be too busy, and you wouldn't look at it until later."

"I'm not blaming you." Although he clearly was. "I'm just pointing out how it would have been better if we hadn't gotten caught."

Even though we were seated beside each other, the distance between us suddenly felt enormous. The handsome man I'd fallen for seemed to vanish right before my eyes. He was replaced by a boy who looked a hell of a lot like the cocky jerk I'd had a stupid crush on once.

Maybe he was upset and taking it out on me, which

wasn't fair, but I—

Wait a minute.

Was he trying to get me to break up with him, so he didn't have to choose?

I couldn't stop the bitterness inside me from crawling out. "Maybe it would have been *better* if we hadn't gotten together at all."

Hurt sliced through his expression. "You don't mean that."

"You say you want me, but you need your business and friendship with him, so let me make it easier on you." I swallowed the lump in my throat. "You know which one to choose. You know which one makes sense."

"No," he argued. "I shouldn't have to choose. I'll talk to him again, and I'll get him to—"

"It's fine," I lied. "I understand why you can't pick me."

Chaos burned in his eyes. "Just wait a minute."

"Maybe your original assessment was right." I stared at his lips because it hurt too much to look at him directly. "I'm probably too much of a good girl to be with you."

"Bullshit."

"Is it? What about all the stuff Colin said? It's better if we cut our losses now."

He raked a frustrated hand through his hair. "That shit he told you. I'm not the same guy I used to be."

"I believe you, but can't you see there's no way to win here? I think it's best if you take me out of the equation."

His eyes widened with realization. "Are you trying to break up with me?"

"No." My pulse raced, and my heart went out of rhythm

as I reached for the door handle. "I *am* breaking up with you."

Preston could have fought for us, but as he'd done in my brother's apartment, he fell silent, and it confirmed everything. Our break-up was the outcome he didn't want, but it was the one he needed.

I got out of the car and was surprised when he followed suit. He pushed his door shut with a loud thud, and all the emotions I'd been holding inside me threatened to escape.

"Where are you going?" I demanded. "You're not allowed inside."

His focus darted to the front door like he was checking to see if a no trespassing sign was stretched over it. He didn't find one, but his gaze went narrow. "Then, get back in my car so we can talk about this."

My legs were wobbly, and I knew if I didn't get into the safety of my house, I might cave. I'd let the selfish part of me take over and I'd plead with him to pick me, even though it was the wrong choice. No one wanted us together, and how long would it be before he began to resent me for that?

How long before he blamed me for ruining his life?

"No," I whispered, moving toward the front door.

He chased after me for a few steps, stopping at the base of the patio steps. "You want to break up? Fine. But we made a deal, and this isn't over until we finish it."

I put my hand on the door knob but turned to look at him over my shoulder. "What?"

He looked so pleased with himself like he'd found a loophole. "We've got one lesson left."

Everything in me tightened, squeezing against the

onslaught of pleasure his statement caused. But I had to stay strong. I pushed open the door, stepped inside, and gave him a hard, final look, pulling the door closed as I spoke. "No. I think I've had enough lessons."

TWENTY-SIX

Preston

How the fuck had this happened? In the last twenty-four hours, I'd lost my girlfriend, my best friend, and likely my company.

The old me would have solely blamed Colin for the mess, but I drove home from Sydney's house, angry at everything and everyone, including myself. The conversations with her and Colin wouldn't have spiraled out of control if I'd gotten one fucking second to think.

Everything had happened too fast.

Shit, she hadn't flinched or hesitated when her brother asked if she loved me. Her resounding *yes* had made me go weightless, only for me to drop like an anvil a second later. It all became so real in that moment. Serious feelings were involved, and . . .

I wasn't ready.

My emotions had gotten the better of me in the car. All the terrible but true things Colin had said had hurt me and so I'd lashed out, saying things I didn't mean. I'd fucking blamed her when it wasn't her fault.

No, the fault was all mine.

I went into the kitchen and tossed my keys down on the island with a little too much force, making them clatter angrily against the granite.

"Everything okay?" Cassidy asked.

She was sitting alone at the kitchen table. Her phone rested on the tabletop, and she must have been watching something while eating leftovers from a to-go container, but she pushed pause on her screen.

"No," I said. "Everything is not okay. Colin said I have to choose. Him and the business—or Sydney."

She drew in a long breath, leaned back in her chair, and crossed her arms. And then it looked like she wanted to say something, but she held it back.

I forced playfulness into my tone when I felt none of it. "Out with it."

"An ultimatum? I know how that feels."

"Yeah," I said quietly. "I know you do."

The night I'd discovered her and my dad together, I'd lost my shit, and I'd forced my dad to pick between us. I'd done it because I was sure she'd never win. If he'd chosen her, that was a bridge he'd burn so completely with me, there wouldn't have been a goddamn thing left.

It'd been unfair, but of course he'd chosen his son over her.

I'd apologized several times for the way I'd handled it, so I wasn't going to do it again now, but she had to be pleased karma had paid me a visit.

"You want to talk about it?"

When I nodded hesitantly, she lifted a foot and used it to push out the chair seated across from her in invitation.

It should have felt weird to go to her, but . . . it didn't.

Cassidy listened without comment as I dropped into the

chair and then launched into what happened. How Colin had seen the text message from Sydney and found out we were together. The harsh things he'd told her about me.

The way she hadn't flinched when she'd been asked if she loved me.

"I didn't just hesitate," I said. "I didn't even answer."

She tilted her head, and her evaluating gaze slid over me. "Do you?"

I rested my elbows on the table and put my head in my hands. "Fuck, I don't know. It seems too fast. Too . . ."

"Too, what?" She hit the nail on the head with one word. "Scary?"

It was tough to admit. "Yeah."

There wasn't any judgement in her expression. "What are you afraid of?"

"I don't know." My gaze dropped to the tabletop, tracing the woodgrain. "It sounds stupid, but what if I haven't, like, changed enough?"

Even without looking at her, I sensed the way her posture straightened and imagined her stunned demeanor. She didn't say anything, probably because she wasn't sure what she'd say.

"I didn't want her to get hurt," I confessed. "I didn't want to fuck things up."

Cassidy made a sound of disbelief, drawing my focus back to her. "Preston. Don't you realize asking that shows how much you've changed? You're worrying about her and not yourself."

"Well, it doesn't matter because she broke up with me."

"Wait, what?" She tilted her head. "She said she loved you, and then she dumped you?"

I tried not to wince. "She said she wanted to make things easier for me and take herself out of the equation."

There was a flicker of understanding in her eyes. "She's giving you up to salvage your friendship with Colin."

"But I don't want to lose her. What the fuck do I do?"

She looked at me like I'd just asked the dumbest question she'd ever heard. "You do the same thing your father did when I was on the losing side of your ultimatum. You fight for her. You convince him you should be with Sydney, and you don't give up until that happens." A knowing smile hinted at her lips. "You don't give up until you win."

Because she knew me and how much I hated to lose.

And that? It was all I needed to get control of myself.

Cassidy jammed her fork into her leftovers, took a bite, and contemplated me while as she ate. It was like she was watching the plan as it began to form in my head.

My chair legs squealed across the floor when I launched to my feet. "Thanks for your advice."

"You're welcome, but you didn't need it. I mean, you always get your way, Preston. Why would that suddenly stop now?"

Her comment wasn't meant to be mean, and it caused me to smile. "Right."

I was about to head up the stairs to my office, but a new thought stopped me in my tracks.

"Hey," I said. "Since we're cool with talking about all this relationship stuff, can I ask you something?" It was a question I wasn't sure I could handle hearing the answer until now. "Are you and my dad going to get married?"

Her fork had been halfway to her mouth, and she froze awkwardly, because this had to be one of the last things she'd expected. Her fork slowly lowered back to the container, and her eyes clouded over with sadness. "No, I don't think so."

"Why not?"

"Well, he'd have to ask me first," she lifted her shoulders in a defeated shrug, "and that's never going to happen."

I felt the strange urge to defend him. "I bet he's waiting until you're done with school."

Her laugh was empty, "No, it's not that."

"Okay?"

She stared at me like I was missing something huge. "He won't ask because while you'll tolerate us being together, we all know it can't go any further than that."

My heart slowed as I realized what she was saying, and my unfocused gaze drifted away from her. They'd never be more to each other than they were now because they thought I wouldn't allow it. Cassidy and my dad were sacrificing what they wanted—what I knew she hoped for—to spare my feelings.

With as terrible as I had treated them both, somehow they still put me first.

Shit. Could I ever be that selfless?

"You're saying you're not going to get married because of me?" I asked. "That's dumb."

She stared at me in total disbelief. "Uh . . . I agree. Are you saying," hope sparked inside her eyes, "you'd be all right with it if we did?"

I didn't need to think about it. "Yeah, I'd be okay. I'm not saying it'll be easy, and people might be shitheads to us about it, but—yeah. I told you I wasn't going to stand in the way of you two, and I fucking meant it."

I had a whole new perspective after seeing it from the other side with Sydney.

Cassidy looked around the room wildly like she didn't know what to do. But then her gaze snapped to me, and it came from her in an urgent rush. "You should tell your dad that."

"Okay, I will." I flashed her a smile, before turning back toward the stairs. "This was a good talk."

"Yes," she breathed, "it was."

Up the stairs I went, leaving her to consider all the new possibilities of her future, while I began to focus on mine.

After Troy knocked, the apartment door swung open and revealed a thoroughly annoyed Colin. He glared in my direction and clearly felt I'd ambushed him, but this was his fault. He'd been ignoring my texts all day, even the business ones, so I'd had to use our mutual friend as my 'in.'

Once I'd explained everything to Troy, he'd agreed to help. He'd asked Colin if he could stop by, and I'd tagged along without an invite.

"What the hell are you—"

That was as far as Colin got before I made my way inside his place, not caring if it was rude. We had shit to discuss.

"Last time I was here," I said, "I didn't get a chance to say any of the things I needed to, so this time you're going to be quiet and listen."

Madison was seated on the couch in the living room area, and my forceful tone drew her attention. I didn't mind if she overheard this. Maybe she'd see my side and help her boyfriend get his head out of his ass.

"I'm *sorry*," I announced, adding all the weight I could to the word. "It was wrong to keep my relationship with Sydney a secret, and how I pulled Troy into it too. I lied to you, and that was really shitty of me. I'm sorry for being a bad friend."

Colin acted like my apology was unexpected, but also that it wasn't enough to move the needle. He pointed at me and was going to say something, but I cut him off.

"I'm not fucking finished." I massaged the muscles at the back of my neck. "When you told me I wasn't allowed to date her, I tried to respect that. I really did. For more than a year, I ignored my feelings. I pretended they didn't exist, even when all they did was get stronger."

"I don't want to hear this," he groaned.

"Too bad." Troy's tone was plain. "You're going to." He nodded his *hello* to Madison, dropped down to sit on the other side of the couch from her, and gestured to me as if to say, *continue*.

"We both tried to fight it," I said. "I didn't want to like her. I didn't want to be so fucking into her . . . but it got to a place where I couldn't control it anymore." I gestured to his girlfriend and my voice turned sharp, cutting to the truth. "Tell me you don't know what that's like."

His posture had been confrontational with his hands jammed in the back pockets of his jeans, but as soon as he considered what I meant, his hands dropped out to hang at his sides.

I gave him the most determined look I possessed. "Your ultimatum is dumb, and if you want to play stupid games, then you're going to win stupid prizes." My chest lifted with a deep breath. "I pick Sydney."

Colin blinked. "What?"

Maybe he was bluffing or maybe not—I didn't care. "She knows about my past and how I wasn't always the greatest of guys. And as much as it confuses you—well, me too—she said she loves me anyway. So, you're not going to stand in the way of that."

He stared at me in utter disbelief, and when I didn't budge, he tossed a glance at Troy. It screamed *can you believe this guy*?

Troy stared back with a fixed look. He'd had to deal with similar shit with his mom when he'd started dating Erika, so it hadn't taken much to convince him to join Team Preston.

When Troy didn't back him up, Colin looked pissed. "You're willing to risk our friendship and everything on this?"

"On her? Yeah, I am." I scrubbed a hand over my face. "I get why you don't like it. You think I'm not going to treat her right or I'm not serious about it. But I promise I'm going to do my best, and doesn't this show you how fucking serious I am?"

I glanced at Troy, who nodded like he could answer for Colin. Or maybe he was simply trying to support me.

"I know it's too much to ask you to be happy for us," I said, "but please. I'm asking you not to throw our friendship away just because I fell in love with your sister."

I hadn't even realized what I'd said until Madison gasped, and Colin stumbled back a half-step.

Oh, my god.

It had tumbled from my mouth without warning, but now that it was out, my shoulders felt lighter. The twisting unease in my stomach disappeared. It was like guilt was falling off me for confessing a secret I hadn't even known I was keeping.

"You're in love with her?" For the first time since Colin had learned about Sydney and me, he didn't sound angry.

"Yes."

"I knew it," Troy gloated. "You should have heard him when I caught them together. He's got it *bad* for her." His tone was teasing. "It was almost kind of cute, but like . . . in a disgusting way."

"Thanks for that," I said dryly.

"No problem." Troy relaxed back into his seat on the couch. "Now, you two make up and move past this, and when it comes time to plan my wedding, I expect to get a big discount."

Something twisted in Colin's expression. Part of him wanted to forgive me and move forward, but another part of him struggled. "You love my sister," he stated. "I don't know how to handle that."

"You can do it," I said. "Getting used to my dad and Cassidy together was weird, but I managed." I swallowed a breath, giving him a moment to digest that before pushing forward. "I have an idea that might help, but it's going to take some work and all three of us to pull it off, though."

"He already pitched it to me," Troy said. "And I'm in."

Getting the guys on board was the first hurdle to overcome, and it would only get harder from here. I wouldn't just need Troy and Colin, but also a shit-ton of luck too.

Curiosity peaked out at the edges of Colin's expression, which was a good sign.

"What do you need me to do?" he asked.

TWENTY-SEVEN

Sydney

My parents were ecstatic when they learned I'd broken up with Preston. My mom hadn't made any attempt to hide her relief, and was so pleased, she didn't notice I was heartbroken. In fact, she barely noticed I was upset.

I went upstairs to my room, called my friend Hailey, and as the story spilled from me, so did the tears. She tried to comfort me, but I could tell she was annoyed I'd kept it a secret from her, which was fair. Since she'd never really understood my high school crush on Preston, she seemed happy my relationship with him had run its course.

I was a bit of a zombie as I got ready for my shift at the restaurant, and once I clocked in and began prepping my station, Diego noticed something was wrong. He was the sous chef, and Kevin was the head chef, but everyone knew Diego was the glue holding our line together.

He was the one to calm people down when Kevin lost his cool. He was the one to step in and help when a chef got into the weeds. And once I'd finished my spring semester and picked up more hours at the restaurant, he'd become my unofficial mentor.

Unofficial, because when I'd told him that, he'd claimed I was *his* mentor.

"What's up, *amigazo*?" he asked. "You're quiet tonight."

"I broke up with my boyfriend."

I said it quietly so the two dishwashers behind the line wouldn't hear. Those guys were a little too friendly, and they were persistent as hell about getting my number. They didn't hit on the female servers all that often, but I must have seemed like an easy target.

But it didn't matter how softly I'd whispered it to Diego because Oscar heard me.

"Aw, yeah," he exclaimed loudly, grinning ear to ear. "Fresh Meat's back on the menu."

I gave him a look that should kill him where he stood, but it didn't, and he went back to his sauces. I'd received the unfortunate nickname my first night on the line more than a year ago. None of the other chefs had cooked with a woman before, and definitely not one as young as I'd been, so several different phrases had been lobbed my direction.

Diversity Hire didn't stick, but Fresh Meat had.

Diego uttered something in Spanish to Oscar that I didn't understand, but I got the gist of it. Diego wasn't quite old enough to be my father, but he had three kids and he was as protective of me as if I were one of his own.

Oscar laughed off the other man's scolding, but whatever had been said, it was enough to get him to be quiet.

A text message made my phone vibrate in my back pocket, and since I was ahead on my prep work, I snuck a glance at the screen.

Preston: Can we talk?

It wasn't going to change anything, and all it was going to do was make me feel worse.

Sydney: I think it's better if we don't. Plus, I'm at work.

That excuse worked for Sunday night, but the following morning I received a new text.

Preston: I've got something for you.

I went back and forth on how to respond and couldn't come up with anything. The last thing I wanted was to get pulled into flirty texts that weren't allowed to go anywhere. I reminded myself he didn't love me and never would get the chance to, so I had to move on.

All talking to him would do was make me miss him more.

So, as terrible as it was, I left him on read and didn't answer.

It had to piss him off, because I didn't get any more texts from him the rest of the day. I had to convince myself multiple times that what I was doing was right, and what was best for him.

There was one person I really didn't want to talk to, and they were the one to reach out on Tuesday morning. Just after I finished breakfast, my phone buzzed.

Colin: I need to talk to you. Please answer your phone.

Because I'd sent all his calls straight to voicemail when they'd come through.

Sydney: Are you calling to apologize?

My phone rang a few seconds later.

"No," he said as soon as I answered. "Look, I know you broke up with Preston, but I need your help."

"That's freaking rich," I spat at him.

He launched right into his issue. "Distinguished Events has a VIP dinner booked for Monday night, and the chef we hired just backed out with a conflict."

I sighed. "You need me to recommend someone?"

"No. I'm calling to see if you wanted to take it."

"Take it?" My breath caught. "You want *me* to be the chef?"

He was quiet for a moment, maybe debating whether to say it. "Preston recommended you."

It felt like everything had flipped upside down, and I struggled to organize my thoughts. "Uh . . . how many people would it be?"

"I'm still waiting for the final head count, but probably around forty." When I didn't respond, it prompted him to continue. "We already have the space reserved. You'll set the menu, as long as it's within the budget for the event. And you can bring another chef with you, if you want to split your fee with them."

Whoa.

Did he have any idea how huge of an opportunity this was? I'd been in charge of a few dinner parties for my extended family, but this was a whole new level. I'd never done it professionally, and not at this scale.

Excitement flooded through me, and its surge was so strong, I couldn't stand still. I paced aimlessly in the kitchen as my thoughts raced, already coming up with ideas for the starter course.

"Do you want the job?" Colin asked.

Of course I wanted it, but my pacing came to an abrupt halt. "Are you sure you want me? I haven't done anything like this before."

They were taking a big risk with their company by hiring me, a total unknown.

He made a sound like my question amused him. "Come on, Syd. You're good at everything you do. I'm sure you'll crush it." He paused, and uncertainty stole into his voice. "Unless you don't think you can?"

"No, I can," I blurted, not wanting him to have any doubt.

We had a private room at the restaurant where I worked and there'd been plenty of times I'd helped get fifty plates to the window at once. This event wouldn't be quite the same, but I felt confident I could pull it off—especially if I convinced Diego to help me.

"Okay, great." Colin sounded relieved. "I'll put you in touch with the restaurant so you can get product ordered."

We spent the next few minutes going over the rest of the details such as budget and location, but when I asked who the VIPs were, he told me he wasn't allowed to say. He promised he'd email me the contract and dietary restrictions as soon as we were done talking, and it wasn't until we'd hung up that I realized what had happened.

Was this what Preston had meant when he said he had something for me?

I stared at the phone I was still clutching in my hand and considered texting him. But I was embarrassed I'd ignored him, especially after he'd been the one to recommend me for this amazing opportunity. When their chef had cancelled on them, was that the first time he'd thought about me?

Or were his thoughts always on me, like mine were on him? Even when I was trying to move on, trying to be good, he dominated my mind.

God, I should have asked Colin if Preston was going to be at the dinner. I figured he would be, but maybe I could stay hidden in the kitchen and avoid him altogether. I could handle executing a flawless three-course meal for forty VIPs far better than seeing the man I loved again.

It was too painful a reminder of what I'd lost.

I'd never eaten at The Treehouse restaurant before. The whole place had a farm-to-table vibe, but upscale, with elegant booths and modern fixtures. It didn't match my Italian-themed menu much, but if I did my job right, my food would be the focus and not the décor.

I'd gone over my prep list a million times in my head before meeting Diego at the front of The Treehouse. He took the two trays of tiramisu I'd prepared at home from my arms and gave me an excited smile before we turned our attention to the front door. The restaurant manager was waiting inside, and he gave us a quick tour of the kitchen and introduced us to the staff as they arrived.

I ignored the way he defaulted to Diego being the head chef. The guy spoke more to him than me, but because we only had two hours to service and a ton to do, I let it slide. I set my personalized knife bag on the prep table and tried not think about the man who'd given it to me.

For the main course, I'd gone with the dish I was the most confident in—my ravioli recipe. The bulk of the pasta would be filled with lobster, but we'd also fill some with mushrooms for the vegetarian guests. I went straight into making the dough since it would need time to rest, while Diego began cooking the lobsters because the meat needed to be cooked and cooled before we could create the filling.

Time went so fast, I joked to Diego I didn't even have time to sweat, although the kitchen was hotter than I was used to. I'd worn my nicest chef jacket—meaning my only one that didn't have any stains, but it was a thicker fabric and didn't breathe as well as my others.

We worked seamlessly as a team, prepping what seemed like endless trays of raviolis, but I wanted to make sure we had plenty of overage. And as soon as they were done and stored in the walk-in cooler, we shifted to the prosciutto, fig, and goat cheese truffles for the first course.

Fifteen minutes before we needed to start plating, I ticked the last item off my checklist. We were slightly behind, but it wasn't terrible, and honestly—with everything we'd had to do, it felt like a win. Diego and I came to a consensus on how to present the little truffles alongside the salad, and then we sampled the dish to make sure the balance was right.

"It needs something," I mused. "Lemon zest to finish?"

Diego grabbed the microplane and a lemon, and grated a few flecks of the rind onto the trio of mini truffles. We sampled again and found ourselves nodding to each other in agreement.

"Better," he said.

The door to the dining area swung open, drawing my attention, and instantly my pulse jumped. But it was only Colin, not Preston.

My brother took a few steps into the kitchen and looked around with something like awe. Did he feel like he was seeing backstage, where all the magic happened? He took in the industrial space with steel counters and pale gray tiles, and then spied me at the set of burners closest to the plating window.

His gaze slid over my white cap and jacket, and for a long moment he stared at me like I was unrecognizable.

"Yes?" I jerked back the handle of one of the sauté pans where I was simmering shallots in wine for the ravioli sauce.

His tone was cautious. "How are you?"

"Are you asking as my brother, or as the event planner?"

We were in such a weird spot right now. I was so angry with him for his ultimatum and for taking Preston away from me, but I was begrudgingly grateful for this job. Plus, he was my brother, and as shitty as he'd handled it, a small part of me understood how he was trying to protect me.

He moved closer and his voice fell to a hush. "Hey, look, Syd. I'm sorry about the way I reacted to you and Preston being together."

I stopped what I was doing to give him a hard look. "Can we do this later? I'm already behind schedule."

He lifted his hands and backed away, wordlessly

apologizing. But he'd had his focus on me, so he wasn't aware he was too close to the side table until he bumped into it.

"Fuck," he muttered under his breath.

I wasn't sure if he'd done it in pain, or because he'd knocked my knife bag off the tabletop. It fell to the floor with a loud thud, but thankfully my two best knives were beside me and not inside the bag. If anything else inside there got damaged, it wouldn't be that big of a deal.

Colin bent, picked it up, and as he returned the bag to the table, the embroidery caught his eye. "This is yours?"

It came out without thought. "Preston got it for me." I frowned and turned my attention back to my sauté pans. "Is he here?"

"Yeah. You want to talk to him?"

"No." It came out more forceful than I wanted it to. "Can you do me a favor and keep everyone except for the servers out of the kitchen? Diego and I need to focus."

His expression was strange. Why did he seem disappointed? But then he gave me a resigned nod. "Yeah. I'll let him know." He caught himself. "I'll let everyone know."

I didn't have time to think about his strange response. Diego was setting out plates on the main table so we could assemble the first course. I grabbed a pair of gloves from the dispenser and went to help him.

Dinner service was . . . fucking magic.

It was a perfectly aligned night where everything came together, and it seemed like everyone was in the zone. The waitstaff was friendly and communicative. The timing of the main dishes was flawless, including the one where I'd substituted gluten-free pasta for the guest who had that restriction. Every plate went out hot and we'd nailed the perfect al dente on the ravioli.

The three-course meal was a marathon, but it was one where we had to sprint in three long bursts. Dessert was less stressful since I'd already prepared it at home, but presentation was more important in this course, and so it took the longest. We carefully and cleanly cut the tiramisu in long, narrow rectangles to show off the layers of mascarpone and ladyfingers, garnishing each plate with a half of a strawberry and a chocolate tuile.

"That's a sexy looking plate," I said.

Diego laughed, nodding in agreement.

When the final tray left the kitchen loaded with the last of the desserts, I let out a tight breath.

The first two dishes had gone over well. The bussed plates that headed to the dishwashing station had been empty, and no dishes had been sent back for correction.

The anxiety inside me had calmed, but it lingered still as I worked to clean my station. I was emotionally and physically drained, yet desperate for feedback. Plus, I was incredibly proud of what Diego and I had accomplished. I scrubbed the washrag over the front lip of the stove where sauce had splattered—

My back had been turned, and I'd been too deep in my thoughts to hear the door swing open. So, I wasn't aware I was no longer alone until a deep voice startled me into place.

"I have something for you."

TWENTY-EIGHT

Sydney

I wasn't sure I wanted to turn and face Preston, but his statement left me with no choice. I slowly pivoted in my spot, dragging out the moment before I'd lay my gaze on him.

He didn't disappoint.

Preston wore a stone-gray button-down shirt, a black tie, and black slacks. It was the most dressed up I'd ever seen him, and everything about it was flawless. Not a single wrinkle marred his clothes nor was a hair out of place, and I wanted to groan at how good he looked, especially when I had to look like hot garbage.

My hair was pulled back in a low ponytail, but I was sure a bunch of flyaways had escaped from under my cap, creating awkward loops of hair by my ears. Whatever makeup I'd put on hours ago had been steamed off while cooking the ravioli and was now replaced with a thin layer of dried sweat. Stains and sauce splatters decorated the front of my jacket.

Why the hell did he stare at me like he didn't notice any of it?

His eyes were intense, trailing over me like I was the most beautiful girl he'd ever seen. It caused my heart to stop and breath to lock up in my lungs. The longing I'd been trying to hold back the last week flared wildly out of control, and

I had to grip the edge of the stove to make sure my unsteady legs didn't give out on me.

A voice inside my head reminded me I wasn't weak. I'd spent the last three hours being in total command of this kitchen, and I'd fucking nailed this dinner. He was here on my turf, in the place where I felt the most confidence.

He'd told me he had something for me and was waiting for my response. I lifted my chin, along with my shoulders. "What is it?"

God, his smile was dazzling and cryptic. "It's in the dining room. Follow me."

It took everything to stand my ground and shake my head. "I can't right now. I need to finish cleaning my station. Maybe when I'm done, you can—"

His face skewed. He hadn't expected any push back. Then, his expression shifted, and he shrugged, as if saying *fuck it.* "Some of the guests want to meet the chef."

"Oh." I straightened as excitement and nerves mixed in my stomach. Were they wanting to give me a compliment . . . or a critique? I folded my washrag, set it on the side table, and wiped my damp hands down the sides of my jacket, before following Preston out through the door.

The dining room was dramatically different from when I'd walked through before service. The lights were low and soft music played, but it was barely discernible over the conversations of dozens of people seated at the tables and booths. Some stopped talking and turned their curious gazes toward me, but when the tall blonde woman pushed back in her seat and stood, everyone else in the room disappeared.

"Oh, my god," I uttered.

When Colin said he couldn't tell me who the client was, I hadn't given it much thought. I'd figured it was someone who wanted their privacy. It had crossed my mind they could be a celebrity, but certainly not someone as freaking huge as Stella.

Her ruby red lips peeled back into a warm smile as she strolled toward me. "Sydney?"

Holy shit, she knew my name.

"Yes. I'm such a huge fan," I gushed before she'd even reached me. "I tried to get tickets to your Heartsick tour, but by the time I made it through the queue they were sold out."

She genuinely looked disappointed on my behalf. "Oh, I'm sorry to hear that. But it turns out I'm a huge fan of you, too."

"You are?" My brain no longer worked, and I couldn't process what she meant. "Why?"

Her laugh was bright and infectious. "Your food was delicious, and when Preston told me the chef was a young woman, I wanted to meet you."

"You ate my food?" My eyes went so wide, they had to be the same size as the dessert plates.

Beside me, Preston chuckled.

It was a stupid question, but thankfully she pretended it wasn't. "I hosted this dinner tonight for my friends and family to celebrate the end of the tour. A 'welcome home' of sorts." Her voice was like honey as she leaned closer, acting like we were old friends and not strangers. "I'm going to be here in Nashville while I'm working on my next album, which means I'm in the market for a personal chef." Her gaze shifted to Preston before returning to me. "He mentioned that was your dream job."

I went breathless. He'd talked me up to her? I worried I was going to melt, or spontaneously combust, or do both at the same time.

"Yes," I whispered.

"When I was starting out," she said, "someone gave me my first big break. Since then, I'm always trying to pay that forward. And I've discovered I love helping folks make their dreams come true." Her eyes sparkled. "How would you like to cook for me for a week and audition for the job?"

"Audition to be your personal chef?" I blinked, and finally my brain started to function again. "Yes. Absolutely yes. That would be amazing."

"Great." She turned and gestured to the woman who'd been seated beside her at the table. "That's Shanice, my assistant. If you give her your info, she'll get things started for us."

"Thank you so much." I did my best to sound chill and professional, even as I was screaming inside.

Stella nodded and flashed an easy smile. "Thank you for dinner, and for being able to do it last minute."

"Right." I was riding such an emotional high, I felt invincible. "Although, between us, I'm not sorry the other chef had to cancel."

She exchanged a confused look with Preston. "Other chef? I thought Sydney was your first choice?"

He smiled, and it was so convincing, she probably didn't see the panic in his eyes. But I knew him better, so I saw it all.

"She was," he said quickly. "I'm not sure what she's talking about."

"Oh. Okay." She accepted his attempt to brush it off. "Well, I'm glad Troy pitched this dinner to me, and thanks to y'all for helping pull it together."

I nodded, too stunned to speak and my mind went on overload as it tried to piece together this information.

Troy had pitched this to Stella.

She'd said it was last minute and that there'd been no other chef.

I waited until she'd gone back to her guests before turning toward Preston, and my voice dropped low. "Did you and Colin orchestrate this whole thing . . . for me?"

"Once again, I'm not sure what you're talking about." Except his smug smile said otherwise.

I opened my mouth to demand he explain, but instead he turned away from me and strolled back toward the kitchen. Fine. If he wanted to talk there, then we could—

There was a booth on the same wall as the kitchen door, so when I'd come out into the dining room, I hadn't noticed the couple who was seated there. I'd thought Preston had been leading me to the back, but no. It was toward my parents, who were tucked away in the booth, eating the tiramisu Diego and I had painstakingly plated just a few minutes ago.

I hurried to catch up to him and asked it under my breath. "What are they doing here?"

"Colin invited them."

He didn't wait for me to respond. He reached the edge of the table, drawing my parents' attention up, and their expressions shuttered.

"Hi," he announced. "Did you enjoy your free dinner?"

My breath caught. Colin and Preston had arranged this too, and paid for it? My parents looked so awkward, so uncomfortable, I almost felt bad for them.

Almost.

"Yes." My father's tone was begrudging. "Thank you."

"You're welcome." Preston gestured to me. "I shouldn't have to tell you how amazing your daughter is, but I'm going to anyway, because I think you need the reminder. She's smart and kind, and just look at her. She's freaking gorgeous."

Blood rushed to my face as my parents did as they'd been told. I felt anything but gorgeous right now in my chef attire, but there was so much conviction in his words, I couldn't help but believe it, just a little.

"And she's so insanely talented," Preston continued. "You might not see it, but everyone else in this room does, including Stella. Want to know how I know? She's looking for a personal chef and she just invited Sydney to audition for the job."

"What?" Surprise had my mother straightening in her seat and her gaze flew to me for confirmation. I nodded, and pride welled in my chest.

"You should be so proud of her," he said. "It might not be the dream you had for her, but it's *her* dream." He stood tall, looking confident and sure. "And Sydney's good at everything she does, so we all know she's going to get the job."

The sound of the rest of dining room had faded to nothing. It felt like it was just us; Preston and me as we faced my parents. My heart was in my throat, clogging the words I wanted to say.

But he had it covered. "I know you don't like me very much, and that's okay. I can deal. And I'm sure you don't want it, but my advice is that you don't get in her way. Just, fuck. Be excited for her, like I am."

If I'd thought they looked awkward before, the way they were now put it to shame. My dad's posture was the same as if he were sitting on a cactus. They didn't like the profanity, and they certainly didn't like being lectured by him, but . . .

Oh, my god. Rather than disregard what he'd said, it seemed like they were considering it. That they'd *heard* his words.

But now they weren't sure what to say.

My mom exchanged a look with my dad that screamed he needed to do something. He cleared his throat as his gaze connected with mine. My folks had seen me in my work clothes lots of times, either before a shift or when I'd come home after, but tonight was so different.

Maybe it was the first time they'd truly seen this side of me.

They'd gotten to witness what I was capable of and tried so hard to excel at. Was it foolish to hope they'd noticed the passion I'd put into the dishes I'd served tonight?

"If this is what you want," my father's eyes contained something that looked strangely like pride, "then your mother and I are happy for you."

"Yes." My mom pressed her lips together as she struggled to put how she was feeling into words. "This was really good,

Sydney." She found the word she'd been looking for. "It was impressive."

My heart stumbled and soared. Praise was so rare from them that I didn't exactly know how to handle it. The ground beneath me was unstable.

"Thank you." I smoothed a hand down the front of my jacket, unsure of where to go from here. "I'll, uh, let you finish your desserts. I should get back to the kitchen."

It was mostly so I could catch my breath. The last few minutes had been a blur, and I worried if I stayed in one place too long it'd suddenly stop being real. I glanced at the man beside me and jerked my head toward the door.

"Can I see you for a minute?"

He nodded and led the way. The moment the kitchen door finished swinging shut behind us, closing us off from the other guests, his handsome face lit up with an enormous grin. "Finally ready to talk to me, huh?"

"I don't understand," I said. "Why'd you do this? I could have bombed. You and Colin risked your company's reputation on this dinner." They'd risked it for me.

He waved it off like I was talking nonsense. "Please. Neither of us was worried. We knew you'd nail it."

I swallowed a breath and tried to calm my racing heart, but it was hopeless, especially the longer I was near him. He looked so happy, so sure, and I didn't get it at all. I wasn't his girlfriend anymore.

Had he done this as, like, a consolation prize? I couldn't be with him, but at least I could have an opportunity to get my dream job.

"Well, I'm glad you guys are okay." I forced the painful words out. "That what we had didn't come between you two."

He didn't respond for a long time, and the moment suspended between us as the intensity of his stare increased. It reminded me of the one he'd given me over a year ago across the shallow end of his pool. The connection between us was the same as it had been then.

Magnetic.

Unstoppable.

"Colin came around," he said, "once I told him I was in love with you."

The power of his words knocked me back, sent me spinning. "*What?*" There was no way I'd heard him right. "You . . . love me?"

His grin was wide and beautiful. "It's not a big deal."

I couldn't help the way my gaze darted around the kitchen, checking to make sure there weren't cameras and that I was still in reality. He *loved* me. Preston Lowe was in love with me.

"No," I whispered. "That's a *very* big deal."

He strode to me, closing the space between us with a few deliberate steps. His gaze slid over my face as if tracing every curve and wanting to memorize the way I looked at him right now.

His voice was deep and hypnotic. "You're right. It is." His hands clasped on my face, pulling me in. "But you love me too, so I figure we can be a big deal together. What do you say?"

There was no other answer, and it came from me in a

rush. "I say yes."

A thrill shot through his eyes, and he murmured it right before his lips captured mine in a searing, passionate kiss. "Good girl."

TWENTY-NINE

Preston

When the timer on Sydney's phone trilled, she tapped the screen to silence it and donned a pair of oven mitts. I stood back in my kitchen, out of her way, as she pulled open my oven door and removed the beef tenderloin she'd spent the last twenty minutes roasting.

I'd moved into this apartment one week ago, which meant she'd currently cooked more times in my kitchen than I had. I tried to help her with dinner as much as I could, but I sucked and mostly got in the way. We both liked it better when she was in charge of cooking, and I only played a minor role.

My girlfriend had come over an hour ago, and as she'd spread the garlic and rosemary butter compound on the beef, she'd told me about her day.

"I always forget how easy Stella is," she said, "until Drew stops by." She was talking about her client's new boyfriend. "He is the pickiest eater ever. Seriously, he won't let anything green come near his plate."

As I'd predicted, Sydney had aced her audition, and for the last six weeks she'd been Stella's personal chef. She worked four days a week and was fucking loving it, but she was also looking forward to her apprenticeship that would start after the first of the year.

She'd told me it was sort of like a culinary bootcamp. The apprenticeship would be challenging and hands-on since every week she'd work for a new chef in the Nashville area. She'd get to experience different kitchens and techniques.

As the tenderloin rested, she put a lid on the green beans she was sautéing and turned her attention to the mashed potatoes, adding another pad of butter as she stirred. But her gaze darted to the clock on my microwave and her brow furrowed.

"Should I slow this down?" She was worried about timing.

"No. I'm sure he'll be here any minute." My dad was usually only late if he was on call, and he wasn't tonight. I'd made sure of it when I'd invited him over for dinner earlier this week.

The words had barely left my mouth when there was a knock at my front door.

"Speak of the devil," I teased, strode across the living area, and pulled the door open. "Hey. Come on in."

My dad's gaze roamed over the space as he stepped inside. The place looked a lot better than the last time he'd been here. Along with Colin, he'd helped me move in, but I'd needed every day of the last week to unpack and figure out where I wanted to put my shit. The one-bedroom apartment was not as nice of a setup as I had at my dad's place, but it was my own.

I felt more like an adult than I ever had, especially since I'd invited my dad over to my apartment for dinner. He even brought a bottle of wine.

Sydney smiled when we made our way toward the kitchen, which was open to the living area.

"Hey, Sydney," Dad said. "Wow. It smells great in here."

"Thanks." She picked up a pair of scissors and began to cut the twine free from the cooked roast. "Dinner will be ready in a few minutes."

I took the bottle from him and got to work on opening it. "Do you want some, Sydney?"

When she nodded, I reached up into the top cabinet and pulled down three glass tumblers since I didn't have wine glasses yet. He watched me pour them and . . . his expression was weird.

"What?" I said. "She turns twenty-one next month." Plus, when had it ever bothered him before?

When he had arrived, I hadn't noticed it right away, but my dad was nervous. Like he'd anticipated me dropping some bad news or something. But as I set the glass of wine on the counter beside her, his face changed. Why did he look relieved?

Oh.

When I'd asked him to come over tonight, I'd said I needed him to come alone because I had something import-ant to talk about.

I handed him his glass, picked up mine, and led him into the living room so we'd be out of her earshot as much as possible. I also kept my voice low. "Were you thinking I was going to tell you she was pregnant?"

He let out a heavy breath. "It might have crossed my mind."

"Don't worry." I smiled. "I haven't made you a

granddad yet."

"That's . . . good." He rubbed the pads of fingers on the center of his forehead like he needed to massage away the crease that was forming there. "What was it you wanted to talk about?"

"Cassidy."

All the worry that had dissipated flooded right back into his expression, but I waved a hand, wordlessly telling him to calm down.

"Do you want to marry her?" I took a sip of my wine and studied his reaction. A range of emotions played out on his face. Surprise. Confusion. Guilt.

"I'm not trying torture you." I needed to approach it from a different angle. "Would you ask her to marry you if I didn't exist?"

"But you *do* exist, Preston." His tone was strong and genuine. "I'll always be ashamed of the years I treated you like you didn't."

I shifted on my feet, trying to fight the uncomfortableness his words caused. We didn't talk about it much, but I'd forgiven him for being selfish, and he knew that. I understood it was a disease we'd both recovered from.

Something we had in common.

"What I mean is," I said, "if you want to marry Cassidy, then you should do it."

He blinked, utterly shocked. These were not the words he'd expected to hear, and he was so excited by them, he didn't trust it. "You'd be okay with that?"

My gaze drifted over to Sydney, who sliced into the

tenderloin and seemed so pleased with the cook on the beef. It made the corner of my mouth quirk into a smile, seeing how happy this made her.

Shit, I was crazy about her.

Despite the obstacles, we'd made it work.

I turned my focus back to him. "Yes. I don't want to stand in the way of your happiness."

His lips parted to say something, only nothing came out. Instead, he took a sip of his wine and considered my revelation like it had changed his life.

Hadn't it?

"I wanted to tell you sooner," I commented, "but we were both so busy, and I didn't want to put it in a text."

He blinked and refocused on me, like I'd pulled him from a daydream. Warmth filled his face, along with emotion. "Thank you for telling me."

I nodded, trying not to let his emotion get to me. The moment between us only lasted for a single heartbeat because Sydney announced dinner was ready. We both puffed up our chests and pretended we were fine. That the conversation between us had been as normal as talking about the weather and not him marrying my ex.

The three of us came to the table, and of course, the dinner she'd prepared was awesome. It wasn't a 'fussy' dish requiring a lot of technique, she'd commented, but the flavor on the meat and the crust on the outside of the roast was fucking delicious.

She was only the third girl I'd introduced to my dad, and I could tell he was impressed with her. How could he not be?

He didn't stay long after dinner was over. If I'd had to guess, he was anxious to get home and either talk to Cassidy about it . . . or jump straight into planning how he was going to propose. When I'd asked Troy if it had been hard making the decision to propose to Erika, he'd laughed.

"What's the saying?" he asked me. "When you find the person you want to spend the rest of your life with—you want the rest of your life to start as soon as possible. It's cheesy as fuck, but it's true."

After my dad left, I set the last of the dishes in the sink and then put my arms around Sydney, burying my face into the crook of her neck. "Let's get naked."

"You want to do the dishes naked?" Her voice rasped because my lips ghosted kisses across the sensitive skin right below her ear.

"The dishes can fucking wait." I chuckled. "I can't." I sucked on her neck, making her shiver and melt into my arms. "I bet you can't either."

Because her sex drive rivaled my own. She was insatiable and I'd teased her that I'd created a monster. But I wasn't complaining. Sex with her wasn't like anything I'd had before. It was hotter, way more fun, and so much fucking deeper. Was it possible I fell a little further in love with her each time?

She didn't answer me with words, choosing instead to give me a fiery kiss.

"You want to know a secret?" I asked. "I'm glad I turned you down after our first kiss."

Outrage spilled across her expression. "Excuse me?"

"At the time, I said something like you couldn't handle me, but I'd been fucking wrong. If we'd hooked up then, I wouldn't have been ready." I brushed my lips against hers. "I wouldn't have been able to handle you."

She liked hearing that and gave a half-chuckle as we began to move toward my bedroom. "Are you sure you can now?"

"I got you to fall in love with me, didn't I?"

Her tone was smug. "I did that to you, too."

"You did," I admitted. I spoke in a stern voice and pointed a finger toward the floor. "I want your clothes here," then I gestured to the bed, "and you there, good girl."

She didn't move though. "What if I don't want to be a good girl tonight?" Her voice turned sultry. "What if I want to be *bad*?"

I grinned. "You need me to show you how it's done?"

"No." She was full of confidence. "I think I've gotten pretty good at being bad."

And then she spent the rest of the night proving it to me, over and over again.

* * *

THANK YOU

Thank you to my husband, Nick. This one was a way bigger challenge than we expected, and I couldn't have finished it without you. I love you so much!

Thank you to Nisha Sharma, Becca Mysoor, Angelina Lopez, and Mona Shroff for the fabulous dinner at Apollycon. You let me talk about all the problems I was having with this book, when I was struggling so much, and gave the best advice possible. I am so grateful.

Thank you to Aubrey Bondurant for being my writer bestie and giving me endless support.

Thank you to Lori Whitwam for your fantastic (as always) editing!

MORE BY NIKKI SLOANE

THE BLINDFOLD CLUB SERIES
Three Simple Rules
Three Hard Lessons
Three Little Mistakes
Three Dirty Secrets
Three Sweet Nothings
Three Guilty Pleasures

THE SORDID SERIES
Sordid
Torrid
Destroy

SPORTS ROMANCE
The Rivalry

THE NASHVILLE NEIGHBORHOOD
The Doctor
The Pool Boy
The Architect
The Frat Boy
The Good Girl

FILTHY RICH AMERICANS
The Initiation | The Obsession| The Deception
The Redemption
The Temptation

ABOUT NIKKI

USA Today bestselling author Nikki Sloane landed in graphic design after her careers as a waitress, a screenwriter, and a ballroom dance instructor fell through. Now she writes full-time and lives in Kentucky with her husband, two sons, and a pair of super destructive cats.

She is a four-time Romance Writers of America RITA® & Vivian® Finalist, a Passionate Plume & HOLT Medallion winner, a Goodreads Choice Awards semifinalist, and couldn't be any happier that people enjoy reading her sexy words.

www.NikkiSloane.com

www.twitter.com/AuthorNSloane

www.facebook.com/NikkiSloaneAuthor

www.instagram.com/nikkisloane

Printed in Great Britain
by Amazon